A Case of
DUPLICITY IN
DORSET

A Freddy Pilkington-Soames Adventure Book 4

CLARA BENSON

**MOUNT
STREET
PRESS**

MOUNT STREET PRESS

ClaraBenson.com

Cover design by Shayne Rutherford at
wickedgoodbookcovers.com

Interior Design & Typesetting by Ampersand Book Interiors
ampersandbookinteriors.com

WAREHAM FAMILY TREE
(MUCH SIMPLIFIED)

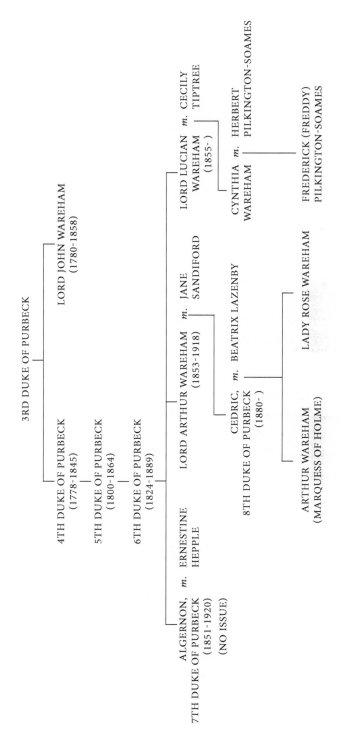

CHAPTER ONE

BEATRIX, DUCHESS OF PURBECK, put down her pen and regarded the sheet of paper in front of her doubtfully. 'But who is this professor, exactly?' she said.

'Oh, don't ask me,' said Cedric, the Duke, her husband. 'He's a Chair of something or other at some university in Scotland. Or he was, at any rate. Before he retired he produced any number of theses and dissertations that have advanced the knowledge of mankind, and for that we are supposed to thank him. Terribly clever chap, apparently.'

'But why must *we* have him?' said Bea. 'I don't like intellectuals. I don't know what to do with them. He'll use long words and make the other guests feel uncomfortable, and we'll all have to be polite and pretend we understand what he's talking about.'

'I know,' said the Duke glumly. 'I'm sorry, old girl, it's my fault. That ass Tillotson button-holed me in the lobby of the House and tricked me into it. For a terrifying minute I thought he was angling for an invitation for himself, and I was racking my brains for a way to get out of it without being rude when he suddenly changed tack and started talking about this Coddington fellow, who was simply dying to get a look at our family history, and I was so relieved we wouldn't have to put up with Tillotson and his ghastly wife that somehow I ended up inviting the other chap.'

'Well, I wish you hadn't,' said Bea. 'Still, what's done's done. We'll just have to make the best of it.'

'I dare say he'll spend most of his time in the library,' said the Duke. 'He has a craze for genealogy, it seems. Tillotson said he has a Theory about the Warehams and wants to write a book. I expect he's looking for some juicy scandals, although I don't know what he imagines he'll discover. That old story about the fifth Duke being the real father of Queen Victoria was discredited a long time ago, so I don't suppose he wants to resurrect that.'

'He's welcome to try, as long as he behaves himself,' said Bea, and dismissed the Chair temporarily from her mind. 'Now, who else have we got? By the way, Cynthia called this morning to say Herbert can't come, but she's bringing your Uncle Lucian instead.'

'Nugs? Make sure you put him at the far end of the East Wing, then,' said Cedric. 'And tell the women to lock their doors at night.'

'Don't be silly, he's not as bad as all that,' said Bea. 'And besides, he must be seventy-five at least.'

'That's never stopped him before.'

'I'll tell Freddy to keep an eye on him,' said Bea.

The Duke gave a snort.

'Hardly an improvement, is it?' he said. 'They're both as bad as each other.'

'Not at all,' said Bea. 'The Garthwaite girl is coming, so I expect Freddy will be on his best behaviour.'

'I shall believe that when I see it,' said Cedric. He was struck by a sudden thought. 'I say, she's not coming with that appalling aunt of hers, is she?'

'I'm afraid she is,' said Bea. 'Mrs. Philpott is very concerned about propriety, and won't hear of Daphne going anywhere without a chaperone, even though I told her she'd be *our* guest.'

'Lot of nonsense. We're all perfectly correct here,' said the Duke, apparently forgetting what he had just said about the proclivities of his elderly uncle.

'Naturally it's just an excuse,' went on Bea. 'I have the feeling she insisted on coming because she's set her sights on Goose for Daphne. We bumped into her on Bond Street last week, and I introduced them, and her eyes positively gleamed when she found out who he was. Then it was "Lord Holme" this, and "Lord Holme" that, and "Don't you agree, Lord Holme?" and "I look forward to seeing you at Belsingham soon, Lord Holme," until poor Goose looked quite sick, although he was polite enough, of course.'

'It's time that boy got married,' said her husband. 'Aren't there any nice girls you could invite for him? It's a pity Iris is already taken. She'd do at a pinch.'

'None that I could find at the last minute. I've given up trying to make him settle down. I expect he'll do it when he's ready.'

'It wasn't like this in my day,' said Cedric gruffly. 'I should never have dreamed of disobeying my father, but today one hears all sorts of stories about young fellows disobliging their parents and running off with chorus girls. In my day a man did what he was told and married well, for the good of the family line. There was none of this nonsense about falling in love when I was young.'

'Do you mean to say you married me purely out of duty and nothing else, dear?' said his wife. 'How very noble of you to sacrifice your feelings for the good of your family.'

'Well, obviously—I mean to say—' said the Duke hurriedly. 'It was our good luck that we happened to be fond of one another. Naturally I didn't mean to suggest—'

'Of course you didn't mean to suggest anything at all,' said the Duchess sweetly. 'Still, I think you'll find that things weren't so *very* different then.'

'Perhaps not,' admitted her husband.

'I think we'd better leave him to it. And Ro too.'

'Where *is* Ro? I thought she was meant to be helping you with the list.'

'Upstairs with Iris, I think. Mrs. Dragusha arrived about an hour ago and is probably sticking her full of pins by now. I shall go up myself when I've finished this.'

'It beats me how you women manage to spend so much on frocks,' said the Duke. 'Who else have we got?'

'Your friend Dr. Bachmann. We can give him to Mrs. Philpott. Perhaps he'll distract her from the business of capturing a husband for Daphne and give the poor girl a little peace. Then there's Ralph Uttridge, Iris's intended.'

'Hmph. I notice Iris's mother doesn't seem unduly concerned about propriety, and *she's* the widow of a bishop,' said the Duke.

'Then we still have poor Mr. Wray,' said Bea, looking at her list.

The Duke uttered a sound possibly expressive of disgust.

'Mr. Wray? I thought he'd gone. Weren't they supposed to have finished rebuilding his house by now?'

'All the bad weather has put it back, so we've got him for a few more weeks, I'm afraid,' said Bea.

'If I were a vicar and a bolt of lightning destroyed *my* house I should take the hint and retire,' her husband remarked jocularly.

'Hush! You mustn't say things like that. He'll be awfully shocked if he hears you. You know how seriously he takes everything.'

'Confound the fellow! What's the world coming to when a man can't make a joke in his own house? Well, then, is that everybody?'

'Yes,' said Bea. 'Although I wonder if we're not a little short of women.'

'Ah,' said the Duke. 'That reminds me, I meant to tell you I've invited Mrs. Fitzsimmons.'

'Oh?' said Bea. She said it casually, but her heart had begun to beat fast, and she suddenly felt cold.

'Yes. I happened to run into her the other day just as she was coming out of her house, and felt sorry for her. Rob's been dead for well over a year now, you know. It's about time Kitty started getting out more and mixing in society.'

'But she does get out. I see her name in the papers all the time,' said Bea. Kitty Fitzsimmons lived in a small side-street off Knightsbridge, and there was no reason for the Duke to have been walking past her house, but Bea forbore to comment on this.

'She's keeping a stiff upper lip,' said the Duke. 'She was dreadfully cut up about the accident, but she's determined not to let it show.'

'Well, she's doing a very good job of it,' said Bea, not quite able to keep the tartness out of her voice. Her husband heard her tone and was immediately indignant.

'Now, isn't that just like you women, to put another woman down, and a widow too! I thought better of you, Bea.'

Bea bit back the remark that had sprung to her lips.

'Does she want to come?' was all she said.

'Yes. Pathetically grateful to be invited, as a matter of fact,' said her husband with some emphasis. 'I do think you might make an effort. I don't know why you've taken such an unreasonable dislike to her. She's a splendid woman and I think she deserves a little happiness.'

There was no arguing with such wilful self-deception, and so she merely said:

'I dare say you're right. Very well, she shall have the Chrysanthemum room, and with Mrs. Dragusha that ought to be everyone.'

'Mrs. Dragusha? Have you asked her? Is she all right?'

'She appears to know how to conduct herself in polite company, if that's what you mean. Besides, she can't possibly be worse than that concert violinist we had last year. I had to look the other way when he started eating off his knife.'

'Oh, I'd forgotten about him,' said the Duke. 'Very well, then, we'll have her if you like.'

'We'll give her to Nugs. He'll be overjoyed. Now, I think that's everything. I shall just have time to speak to Mrs. Dragusha about my frock before lunch.'

'Ask her for money off her bill in return for the invitation. I saw the last one. I don't know why she charges so much money for a few scraps of satin and velvet.'

'Don't be silly, dear,' said Bea. 'There's an art to dressmaking that men will never understand, and Mrs. Dragusha is very good at what she does. Ro needs a new dress to go with the Belsingham pearls. A twenty-first birthday is a very important occasion and she'll be the centre of attention. Don't you want her to look pretty?'

Her husband grunted. He was very proud of his children, although he would never have admitted it publicly.

'Already a good-looking girl,' he said. 'Don't understand finery, but I dare say it makes her happy.' He looked down at the list his wife had been writing. 'For a private family dinner we seem to have invited a lot of strangers,' he said.

'Well, there's us, and Cynthia and Freddy and Nugs,' said Bea. 'They'll do. And at least it won't be dull, with all these others.'

'I suppose not,' said the Duke.

Chapter Two

LADY ROSE WAREHAM stood with her arms in the air and regarded herself in the full-length glass as Mrs. Dragusha, her mouth full of pins, made some minute adjustments to the side-seam of her dress.

'You see, with the cut on the bias we must be very, very careful, or there will be much unevenness in the line, and that would be a dreadful tragedy,' said Mrs. Dragusha indistinctly. 'But you are fortunate that I learned this at my mother's knee.'

Ro stood obediently as Mrs. Dragusha worked her way down to the hem. She drove the last pin home, then straightened up, regarded Ro's reflection with a practised eye, and smiled.

'See how it skims across your figure!' she said. 'Now I will sew it and you will see the difference. You young people are very lucky. For you I can use the most delicate silk charmeuse and there is no need to hide the body beneath it with panels or sequins or ruffles, for your line is perfect in itself and has no need of disguise, only enhancement. You must enjoy it while you can, for in ten, fifteen years, everything will change. You will marry and have children, and if you want to look as beautiful as you did when you were twenty, then you will have to stop eating or you will never be able to wear such a dress as this again. Look at me,' she went on. 'I eat so little, and yet still I must pull myself in with boning and many layers of stitching.'

'Well, I suppose I'll take your word for it, but you don't look as though you needed anything of the sort,' said Ro, glancing at the dressmaker.

Mrs. Dragusha received the compliment graciously. Although she was careful never to reveal her age, she might have been thirty-five or perhaps a well-preserved forty, and no-one could have denied she was a handsome woman. While not especially tall, she carried herself very straight, which gave her the illusion of height. Her hair was the palest gold, carefully waved in the latest fashion, and nobody would have dreamed of suggesting that the colour was anything but her own. Her clothes were elegant and beautifully tailored, as befitted a woman who was accustomed to dress ladies of the highest rank. Yet her smart looks and attire were deliberately understated, for she knew that in a business such as hers, to draw attention to herself and outshine her clients would not do at all. Her manner was animated but respectful—especially when in the company of the aristocracy, and this manner, combined with her undoubted ability to create beauty where none before existed, had in a very short time placed her at the very pinnacle of her business. 'Oh, it's a Dragusha, darling, you simply *must* try her out,' was a remark heard at many a ladies' luncheon or evening-party.

She had a long waiting list to which she adhered ruthlessly, and which only made her services even more in demand, and many a young woman clapped her hands together in glee on receiving the card on which was inscribed the long-awaited message that Mrs. Dragusha would be pleased to see Miss So-And-So at her premises in Conduit Street for a consultation. For the moment, her face was drawn in an expression of the utmost concentration as she stepped back and regarded Ro.

'Yes, I am glad we chose the dark and not the pale blue,' she said. 'It suits you very well, and gives depth to the hazel of your eyes.'

'Hmm,' said Ro, not displeased with the result. 'What do you think, Iris? Shall I do?'

Another girl, who had been sitting at Ro's dressing-table, rifling through her things, turned round. She had golden-brown hair and a very pretty nose covered with a delicate sprinkling of freckles which only made it prettier.

'It's gorgeous, of course,' she said. 'You *are* clever, Mrs. Dragusha.'

The dressmaker preened.

'Yes, it is true,' she said. 'Clothes, they speak to me as they do not speak to other people. I understand their language, and I bestow my talents freely upon my ladies, for it would be shameful to keep them to myself.'

Ro laughed.

'There's no false modesty about you, at any rate,' she said.

Iris had turned back to the dressing-table and was trying on a pair of Ro's earrings. She turned her head from side to side, pleased with the way they sparkled in the light.

'What a lot of jewellery you have!' she said. 'And you're so careless with it! I should never dare leave things lying around as you do.'

'Oh, most of that's not worth much,' said Ro. 'I keep the really good stuff locked away.'

'What about the pearls? Have you got them yet?'

'Not officially. Only to try on with the dress. I'm not allowed to wear them until the dinner tomorrow.'

'Where are they? May I see them?'

'In the drawer,' said Ro. She tore herself away from her reflection and went across to the bed, where she picked up a crumpled tweed skirt that she had discarded and rummaged in the pocket for her keys. She unlocked a drawer in the dressing-table and brought out a little enamelled box which was also locked. 'You see, they're perfectly safe,' she said, as she inserted another key into the lock of the box and turned it.

Iris and Mrs. Dragusha watched as Ro brought out a magnificent pearl necklace, formed of three long strings fastened with a diamond and sapphire clasp. She held them out and turned them to the light, in order to show off their iridescence to greatest advantage, and the others leaned forward and gazed at them.

'Might I—might I hold them?' said Iris hesitantly.

Ro handed them over, and Iris stepped up to the glass and held them against her breast.

'Goodness!' she said. 'They are rather marvellous, aren't they? Aren't they meant to be fantastically old and valuable?'

'They've been in the family for over a hundred years,' said Ro. 'I think they're supposed to be worth twenty thousand pounds or something ridiculous like that. Of course, there's some story behind them. One of my ancestors is meant to have slaughtered fifty Indian soldiers to get his hands on them. Quite dreadful if it's true, although I think it's probably an exaggeration. Anyway, they've been handed down through the generations, and now they're mine—or they will be this evening.'

'Put them on, do!' said Iris. 'Let's see what they look like with the dress.'

'All right,' said Ro, and took them from Iris. The clasp was open. 'Will you fasten it for me, Mrs. Dragusha?' she said. Mrs. Dragusha stepped away and shook her head. 'Oh, I forgot—you think they're bad luck, don't you?'

'It is true that they have a bad history,' conceded Mrs. Dragusha. 'I should prefer to keep away from them.'

'I don't believe in all that kind of thing,' said Ro.

Iris fastened the clasp for her, then clapped her hands together.

'You look quite spectacular, darling!' she said. 'Doesn't she?'

'Yes,' said Mrs. Dragusha. She was regarding the necklace thoughtfully. Ro turned and examined herself in the glass.

'Not bad,' she conceded. 'I have to admit, you were right about the dark blue, Mrs. Dragusha. I wasn't sure at first, but now I see why you insisted.'

'But of course,' said Mrs. Dragusha. 'That is why you pay me a lot of money and bring me all the way down here from London to do it, instead of going to some respectable old woman in the village. She will make you look like a lady, but I—I will make you look like a queen!'

Her words were characteristic, but she spoke with less than her usual ebullience. Iris glanced across at the dressmaker and saw her looking from the pearls to Ro with a frown.

'Well, I can't stand here all day gawping at myself,' said Ro. 'Help me get them off, will you?'

Once again it was Iris who stepped forward to undo the clasp of the pearl necklace.

'You had better lock them away safely,' said Mrs. Dragusha, who had not moved. 'If they are as valuable as you say, then you do not want someone to come and steal them from you.'

'Nobody will steal them,' said Ro, as she replaced the necklace in the box and locked it. 'They're kept in the safe as a rule. I've only been given them today to try them on, and they've been locked in this drawer all morning.'

'But somebody could sneak in and break the drawer open,' said Iris.

'Hardly. It would take a good while, and there are always servants and guests wandering about upstairs. I suppose someone could always sneak in through the secret passage while our backs were turned, but we'd still hear them.'

'A secret passage?' said Iris in astonishment. 'Is there really such a thing?'

'Oh, we have several,' said Ro. 'We played in them as kids, although they're a bit old hat now.'

'And there's one here in this room?'

'Behind that tapestry,' said Ro, with an indifference of manner only to be achieved by someone who has spent most of her childhood in one of England's finest stately homes.

Iris went across to where Ro had pointed. Ro's bedroom was a grand one, with a red-patterned carpet and panelled walls hung with portraits of long-forgotten members of the Wareham family which were not thought good enough to put in the gallery. Set against one wall was a four-posted bed, draped with red velvet curtains trimmed with gold braiding. On the wall to either side was a tapestry. Iris examined the one to the left, which Ro had indicated, and Mrs. Dragusha now came to join her.

'It is beautiful,' said Mrs. Dragusha, examining one part of the tapestry, which depicted a glorious array of long-tailed birds sitting in a tree.

'Dreadfully unhygienic if you ask me,' said Ro, who had been changing back into her tweed skirt. She came over and pulled the wall-hanging to one side. Underneath, the panelling was relatively bare, with only the odd carving of a fleur-de-lys here and there.

'Where is the secret passage?' said Iris.

Ro squinted at one of the carvings.

'It's one of these, but it's been so long—'

She prodded at a fleur-de-lys. Nothing happened.

'Then it must be this one next to it,' she said. She felt underneath the carving. 'Ah!'

There was the slightest of creaks, and with a little shove from Ro a door opened. It was not more than four feet high and two feet wide.

'You see how it follows the line of the panels, so you can't see it?' said Ro.

A cold draught breathed out through the newly-appeared hole in the wall. Iris poked her head in.

'It's rather narrow,' she said doubtfully.

'It's wider inside,' said Ro. 'Quite well ventilated, too. Whoever built it had fairly civilized notions, at least.'

Iris ducked through the doorway and disappeared.

'It's dark,' came her voice from a few feet away.

'Of course it's dark. Full of spiders, too, I expect.'

There came an alarmed squeak, and Iris reappeared in a hurry.

'I'll go and fetch my torch,' she said. 'I'd like to explore it properly.'

'And so you shall, my dear, only not now. Let's do it tomorrow, when the guests are here.'

Just then there was a knock at the door and the Duchess entered.

'Oh, I'd forgotten about that old secret passage,' she said, when she saw what they were doing. 'Do shut the door before a lot of dust blows in. Hallo, Mrs. Dragusha, I guessed you'd still be here. I want to speak to you about my red silk.'

The next quarter of an hour or so was taken up with matters of dress, then a bell was heard.

'Gracious, is it time for luncheon already?' said Bea. 'I feel we've hardly begun.'

'I'm famished. Odd how standing still for hours makes one hungry, isn't it?' said Ro, and started towards the door.

'Your ladyship has forgotten to put the pearls back in the drawer,' said Mrs. Dragusha.

'So I have,' said Ro with a laugh. 'After all that.'

'You are careless, darling,' said Bea. 'Perhaps you'd better bring them downstairs and have Spenlow lock them in the safe until tomorrow.'

'Perhaps I shall, just to be on the safe side,' said Ro. She picked up the enamelled box and they all left the room together and went down to luncheon.

CHAPTER THREE

MISS DAPHNE GARTHWAITE sat in the window-seat and looked out into the street below as Lavinia Philpott, her aunt and guardian, held up two frocks and glanced doubtfully from one to the other.

'I do think you might make more of an effort, darling,' said Lavinia. 'You won't make the right friends if you wear this sort of thing. Look at this. *Nobody* is wearing salmon pink this year; it's quite last season's colour. No, it won't do at all.'

'I like it,' said Daphne, without turning round. 'It suits me.'

'Oh, but how do you expect to get into the papers if you won't wear the latest fashions?'

'I don't want to get into the papers,' said Daphne.

'But you must, if you want people to pay attention. I thought you said Freddy had promised to get his mother to write about you in her column.'

'I never said that at all,' said Daphne. 'I just happened to mention that they both work for the *Clarion*, and you somehow got it into your head that they were going to put my picture in the paper. I don't know where you got that idea.'

Mrs. Philpott gave an exasperated click of the tongue.

'Really, darling, you do make things difficult. I put myself out rather a lot for you, you know. All I want is to see you well settled, as your mother would have wanted, but you're terribly obstinate at times.'

'And you're terribly obvious at times,' said Daphne. 'People can see what you're about and they don't like it.'

'What I'm about? What a dreadful expression! I'm not *about* anything. But there's no sense in being a wallflower if one wants to do well in life, as you must be aware. At least you've had the sense to find yourself a young man with connections—yes, I will say that you really have outdone yourself there. I had no idea Cynthia Pilkington-Soames was the cousin of a duke, but of course if she's Lord Lucian Wareham's daughter then it all makes sense. Now, this is a tremendous opportunity for you, so I expect you to make the most of it. I dare say there will be all kinds of important people at Belsingham this weekend, so you must do your best to shine. Try and impress the Duchess and make friends with Lady Rose. If you play your cards well you might attract the attention of young Lord Holme.'

'Oh, Goose,' said Daphne carelessly. 'He's rather good fun, but not exactly my type.'

'Goose? Is that what they call him? But why didn't you tell me you knew him?'

'Because I knew exactly what you'd say,' replied Daphne. 'I knew your eyes would gleam when you heard I'd met a marquess.'

'But he'll be the Duke of Purbeck one day. Shouldn't you like to be a duchess?'

'Good heavens, no!' said Daphne, raising her eyes in exquisite contempt. 'I should think it would be frightfully dull. One has so many duties and responsibilities that one would never have so much as a moment to oneself.'

'But Belsingham is meant to be one of the finest houses in the country. If Lord Holme took a liking to you then it could be all yours to do as you liked with.'

'But I shouldn't be able to do as I liked with it, should I? It's the sort of place where they keep a written history of every chair they've ever bought. I dare say I shouldn't even be allowed to change the wallpaper in the bedroom because Queen Elizabeth once stayed in it.'

'Don't be absurd, darling,' said Lavinia. 'Who cares about Queen Elizabeth nowadays? Why, she's been dead a hundred years or more.'

'Three hundred. And old families care about that sort of thing tremendously. I'd feel awfully out of place—and besides, I don't want to live buried in the country. I'd much prefer a smart flat in town.'

'Yes, it is easier to attract attention and get into the society columns if one spends most of one's time in London,' said Lavinia, considering. 'But who shall we get for you, then? A younger son might be better, perhaps. One with plenty of money and no responsibilities. Lord Albert Sprigg might do. Not what one might call handsome, but I dare say he's pleasant enough. His mother was American, you know. Railways, or something, I believe. He'd be a good catch.'

'Who on earth is Lord Albert Sprigg?' said Daphne. 'You don't mean that ghastly Bertie Sprigg? Why, I couldn't possibly. He's about four foot eleven, for a start.'

'I think you're exaggerating, darling. I'm certain he's at least as tall as I am. But surely that sort of thing doesn't matter?'

'It wouldn't if he were at all worth speaking to, but he's an absolute crashing bore who talks of nothing but cricket. And he's oily, too. I danced with him at the Arts Ball and he spent the whole time trying to look down the front of my dress.'

'If he's as short as you say he is, then I expect he couldn't help it,' said Lavinia. She gave a sigh. 'Well, I don't know what to suggest. I'm doing my best, but if you won't help yourself then you'll never be well settled.'

'I told you, I'm not interested in being well settled. And anyway, what's wrong with Freddy?'

'Nothing, I suppose,' said Lavinia doubtfully. 'If you could persuade him into it. But he doesn't strike me as the marrying sort. Does he have expectations?'

'I haven't the faintest,' said Daphne. 'But he's not at all stingy, I'll say that for him.'

'But that side of the family aren't exactly the thing. I've heard a few stories about Lord Lucian that it wouldn't do to repeat to you, and then of course everybody knows about Freddy's grandmother—Cecily Tiptree as was. She got fed up with Lord Lucian—not surprising, if the stories are true—and ran off with another man to the Riviera, or Italy, or somewhere like that. But you'd better not mention it. People can be very sensitive about that sort of thing.'

'Don't worry, I shan't,' said Daphne, who was already determining that by hook or by crook she would find out more about Lord Lucian and what exactly he had done to drive away his wife.

'I think you might do better than Freddy, though,' went on Mrs. Philpott. 'Iris Bagshawe obviously thought she could. You might see if you can find out from her what happened between them. A little artful questioning wouldn't go amiss, provided you don't let her see what you're getting at.'

At that Daphne turned her head away from the window for the first time.

'Is Iris Bagshawe going to be there?' she said.

'So the Duchess said,' replied Lavinia. She was examining an evening-jacket for loose sequins and so did not see the expression on the face of her niece, which had passed in an instant from boredom to irritation.

'I see,' said Daphne after a pause, and her eyes narrowed.

IN HER WELL-APPOINTED flat near Knightsbridge, Mrs. Kitty Fitzsimmons was instructing her new maid in the best methods for ensuring the very best care of Mrs. Kitty Fitzsimmons. Despite a certain tendency to pertness, the girl showed signs of having brains and a willingness to please, but according to her references, up to now she had worked only for foreign ladies, who, as far as Mrs. Fitzsimmons could judge, had somewhat eccentric ways of going about things. However, Kitty trusted that a few weeks' training would smooth off some of the rough edges, and that the two of them in time would rub along very nicely together. At present, the maid was packing for a weekend at Belsingham, as her mistress sat in a chair and gave directions.

'Now, about Friday night's dinner,' said Kitty thoughtfully. The girl regarded Mrs. Fitzsimmons appraisingly for a minute, then reached into the wardrobe and brought out a wisp of rose-coloured chiffon trimmed with cream lace and shimmering gold beads, which would undoubtedly set off Kitty's pale complexion and fair hair to perfection.

Kitty mentally gave the maid a mark of approbation.

'That *is* a favourite of mine,' she said. 'However did you guess?'

'I don't know,' said the girl. 'It just seemed obvious.'

'Well, I'd certainly wear it for any other occasion, but I think this time we'd better not. I don't want to draw the wrong sort of attention to myself at Belsingham. Better take the dark chocolate satin.'

The girl gave the briefest of grimaces, which Kitty saw.

'You don't like it?' she said. 'Why not? Is it the colour?'

'No,' said the maid, looking from the dress to Kitty. 'The colour's not bad. It's the dress.'

'But it's the latest thing,' said Kitty. 'Everyone says it suits me. Look.' She took the frock from the girl and quickly slipped into it, then turned around to display the dress to its full advantage. It was a sort of plain, fitted tunic made of satin with a very dull sheen, which looked not unlike something that might have been worn by a woman of mediaeval times. In its studied simplicity it was rather daring, and had quite evidently cost a lot of money. 'You see? Don't you think it fits me perfectly?'

'Yes,' said Valentina Sangiacomo. 'And I can't say it doesn't suit you, either, because it does. It's beautiful, and you're beautiful in it. But you oughtn't to wear it. You look like one of those martyrs from the olden days who were burnt at the stake. It's all wrong.'

'No, no,' said Kitty Fitzsimmons, with a delighted laugh at the girl's perception. 'You're quite mistaken, my dear. It's all exactly right.'

DR. BACHMANN STRAIGHTENED his tie and smoothed down his hair with a comb. He was a tall, handsome man of fifty who took care of his appearance and was not ashamed of it—although he would have disputed any suggestion that he was at all vain. He was looking forward to the weekend at Belsingham, for he had not seen his dear friend Cedric Wareham for perhaps twenty years. Cedric had in recent years become a duke following the death of his uncle, but to judge from his correspondence, which had remained as frequent and informal as ever, his changed situation had not altered him in any way for the worse. Dr. Bachmann wanted very much to see Mrs. Wareham again—the Duchess of Purbeck as she now was. Beatrix had been a pretty girl and Dr. Bachmann had rather admired her at the time, although naturally there was no question of his being able to compete with the heir presumptive to a dukedom, and so he had never so much as considered putting forward a claim. He wondered how time had treated her. And there would be other people there, too. A Professor Coddington, Cedric had said. Perhaps they could talk 'shop' and keep one another entertained. Dr. Bachmann seemed to remember he knew Professor Coddington. He had met him once or twice at academic conferences—if it was the same man—and had read some of his publications, which in Dr. Bachmann's private opinion were fit for nothing but the fire. Dr. Bachmann would never have been so ill-bred as to express this opinion out loud, but he looked forward very much to debating with Professor Coddington and demanding he justify his ideas, for Dr. Bachmann was a great upholder of academic rigour, and in his view there were far too many papers being published these days which had not been duly submitted for examination and approval by the intellectual authorities.

Here his face darkened momentarily as his mind went back to the recent past. At least here in England he could be reasonably sure that no-one knew anything of him, or would bring up that business that had caused him such misery and had very nearly cost him his career. It had all been nonsense, of course. Why, nobody could possibly have believed such a thing of him! But in the end, it had been too difficult to prove that he was in the right, and by that time his reputation had already begun to suffer, so his superiors had, with reluctance, suggested he leave the university where he had been so happy and had produced some of his best work. For some time he had struggled to find another position in a Swiss university, and at length he had been forced to leave the country, and accept an inferior position at a university in Italy. He had worked hard ever since, and he had seen to it that no further scandal had ever been attached to his name, but even though he had begun to rebuild his reputation and had achieved some modest success in his field, he was still bitter at the thought of what he had lost—and all the old feelings had returned that morning when a letter had arrived from his old university. He knew what it was, but he had not read it yet, out of fear that it might not contain the answer he was hoping for.

But he must not let this most pleasant weekend be ruined by thoughts of the past. He had much to be thankful for, and this visit to Belsingham to see his old friend promised much enjoyment. He glanced at his watch. If he left now, he would have plenty of time to buy a newspaper and other sundry requirements before his train departed. He turned to his small suitcase, which was lying open on the bed, put the unopened letter inside it and closed it with a snap, then picked it up and went out in search of a taxi.

CHAPTER FOUR

FREDDY PILKINGTON-SOAMES was very fond of his mother, but found as a rule that it was best not to spend too much time in close company with her, for she had a tendency to talk at him about subjects that either pricked his conscience, required him to put himself out, or made him feel as though he were twelve years old once again—and sometimes all three at once. Today, however, he had been forced to break his own rule, since his wretched father had, at the last minute, backed out of the visit to Belsingham for reasons that were not quite clear, and so Freddy was now in the uncomfortable position of having to drive Cynthia down to Dorset himself. To make matters worse, they had been joined by his grandfather, Lord Lucian Wareham (otherwise known as Nugs), who was seventy-five and half-deaf, and who was inclined to make off-colour jokes at inappropriate moments. Cynthia had insisted upon sitting in the front with Freddy, so Nugs had the back seat to himself, and was sitting in great state, looking out of the window and humming tunelessly. Occasionally he would interrupt his song to mutter something and then give a bark of laughter. He was easy enough to ignore; not so Cynthia, who had her son where she wanted him for the next three hours and could now say all the things to him that she had been saving up for the past month.

'I do think you might have turned up a little earlier, darling,' she was saying. 'As it is we'll only just be there in time for tea, and you know Bea hates to be kept waiting.'

'*I* wasn't late,' Freddy pointed out. '*You* weren't ready when I arrived.'

'Nonsense. I just had one or two more things to throw in, that's all. Now, listen, you will be on your best behaviour this weekend, won't you? I was sure they wouldn't invite you again after what happened last time. Of course, *we* know it was all a misunderstanding, but you oughtn't to have been wandering around at two o'clock in the morning—or if you really must go looking for food at that time of night then at least make sure you're decent first. You nearly frightened Mrs. Bates out of her wits. I understand it was all they could do to stop her giving notice.'

'A chap can't help getting a little peckish sometimes,' said Freddy grumpily. 'I didn't think anybody would be up.'

'Well, it appears half the house was up that night,' said Cynthia. 'I don't know what Alicia Chalmers was doing out of bed at the same time—and she didn't seem to know either, but she ran back to her room quickly enough when all the screaming started.'

'I expect she was peckish too,' said Freddy. There was a loud bark from the back seat, which he ignored.

Cynthia took a pause for breath and then resumed.

'Is Daphne Garthwaite really coming?' she said. 'I assume that was your fault. What on earth were you thinking?'

Freddy winced.

'I didn't invite her,' he said. 'At any rate, not exactly. It was the Philpott woman's doing. She pinned me to the wall at Lady Featherstone's tea-party and started blethering on about something or other, and somehow the conversation turned to Belsingham, and I happened to mention that we were going, and before I knew it she was thanking me within earshot of half the room for the invitation—which I'd never given, incidentally—and as soon as I tried to hush her up and say that it wasn't up to me as it's not my barn, Daphne started looking at me reproachfully and doing that thing women do where they make their lip wobble, and after that I had to jolly well get them an invitation or face the waterworks. Luckily, Bea is a sport and quite understood when I explained everything. She doesn't mind a bit, she says.'

'But *I* mind,' said Cynthia. 'If you must go running around with girls like that, then you might at least have the decency not to parade them in front of everybody.'

'She's not all that bad,' said Freddy. 'And anyway, I'm not *running around* with her, as you put it. We've been out to dinner a few times, that's all.'

'She's common,' said Cynthia. 'Oh, she hides it well enough, but I can always sense it. That aunt of hers is the limit, for a start. Her parents can't have been any sort of right-thinking people if they were prepared to let Lavinia Philpott loose on an impressionable young girl. And who *were* Daphne's parents, by the way? Her mother's dead, I know, but who was her father? Did she even *have* a father?' she said, lowering her voice.

'Of course she had a father,' said Freddy. 'He was a respectable tea-merchant who died of some putrid tropical disease while they were out in India. There's no mystery about it.'

'But why did she come back to England to foist herself onto you? You might do so much better, you know. Even if Daphne herself were unobjectionable, Lavinia Philpott is the most frightful social climber—'

'Fine-looking woman,' came a voice from the back seat. 'Plenty of soft upholstery to sink into.'

Cynthia continued, as though there had been no interruption:

'—and she has her beady eyes on a title for Daphne, I'm certain of it. You watch—I'll bet it's not you she wants, it's Goose, and she's using you to get at him. Perhaps we ought to warn him.'

'Goose can look after himself,' said Freddy. 'He knows Daphne already—and besides, she's not interested in him.'

'How can you be sure of that?'

There was a delicate silence during which Freddy steered his father's Wolseley carefully around a brewer's dray which was blocking the road. Cynthia pursed her lips and went on:

'It's *such* a pity Iris didn't want you. Now, I shouldn't have minded her a bit, but it's obvious she's got a little above herself if she thinks you're not good enough for her. I expect she wanted someone with more of a future. Ralph's terribly respectable, especially now that he's working at the Foreign Office. Someone—now, who was it?—told me he was thinking of running for Parliament one day. He's one of those types who will always make something of himself, so I shouldn't be surprised if he were to become a minister sooner or later. It's just a shame you couldn't have got yourself an important position like that. If you'd worked a little harder then you might have done just as well as he has, and then Iris might have stuck with you rather than throwing you over for him. Still, it's her loss.'

'Thank you,' said Freddy in surprise.

'Well, naturally I'm partial, but you're much better looking than he is, and you don't make one yawn with your conversation. One's jaw quite aches with trying to hold it in whenever he starts talking, I find. Does Iris know about Daphne, by the way?'

'Daphne is none of her business,' said Freddy.

'I suppose not. But aren't they friends of a sort?'

'Not exactly,' said Freddy uncomfortably. 'In fact, I should say they were rather the opposite.'

'Oh?' said Cynthia, but her mind had already flitted to another subject. 'Bea told me Kitty Fitzsimmons is coming,' she went on after a moment. 'Now, why on earth she's been invited I couldn't tell you. You know the story about her and Rob, of course. The accident was all very suspicious, and there were rumours at the time, although nothing was ever proved. She's a dangerous one, and all the more so because one can't even dislike her.'

'Dangerous? Kitty?' said Freddy, relieved the conversation had turned. 'What do you mean?'

'Well, she's terribly discreet,' said Cynthia, 'but everybody knows that no husband is safe when she's in the room.'

'Nonsense, she's a delightful woman,' said Freddy. There was an echoing grunt of agreement from the back seat.

'Of course you would say that—you're a man. And she's so terribly charming that one looks like a dreadful cat if one criticizes her, especially so soon after she lost her husband, but a woman *knows*. I shouldn't trust her an inch around your father, for example. I wonder who she's got her eye on? I have the feeling, from the tone of Bea's voice when I spoke to her, that it might be Cedric.'

'What? Cedric? I won't believe it,' said Freddy. 'He's far too stodgy to be getting up to that sort of thing.'

'Oh, but he's at that delicate age when a man is apt to lose his head,' said Cynthia. 'You remember what happened to Dickie Ratcliff, don't you? The second he turned fifty he took up Satanism and ran off to Greece with those ghastly Americans. You know the ones I mean. There was a woman with awfully silly hair—what was her name, now? I'm sure it will come to me in a minute. At any rate, the last time I heard of them they'd set up a sort of cult, and were cavorting among the temple ruins quite naked except for a few olive garlands, which can't possibly be comfortable. Far too prickly, I should think.'

'Very cool in the hot weather,' remarked Nugs. 'I'd wear nothing but a couple of fronds of greenery myself if the summers here weren't so beastly cold.'

'I can't imagine old Cedric doing anything like that,' said Freddy.

'No, but I dare say he's as susceptible to a pretty woman as any man,' said Cynthia. 'I'd warn Bea but I expect she knows perfectly well what's going on. Now, who else did she say was coming?' She fished in her little bag and brought out a letter. 'I see Mr. Wray is still there.'

'Who?' said Nugs.

'Mr. Wray,' repeated Cynthia loudly. 'He's the vicar of the parish where Bea's sister lives. His chimney was struck by lightning while he was lying in bed, and the whole roof came down. He escaped by the skin of his teeth, I understand. They're rebuilding the rectory, but in the meantime he has nowhere to live, so Jane gave him to Bea and he's been staying at Belsingham for the past few weeks. It seems his mother was a Wareham, although nothing to do with our side of the family.' She looked down at the letter again. 'And there are a couple of professors, too. I don't recognize their names. They'll probably be deadly dull.'

'It's an odd sort of mixture of people to invite to Ro's birthday dinner,' said Freddy.

'True, but the ball in London is the main thing, isn't it?' said Cynthia. 'This is just a small family party. And we shall see Ro in the Belsingham pearls at last. I hope she takes more care of them than she did of those diamonds she lost.'

'She didn't lose them,' said Freddy. 'She lent them to a friend who forgot to give them back. They were returned eventually.'

'It was most careless of her, and not the way to go on at all,' said Cynthia with a sniff. 'Cedric really ought to have a word with her about those people she runs around with in town. I'm sure most of them aren't at all the thing. There was a *most* unsuitable young man at one time, but luckily she decided he was a bore and we haven't heard about him for a while. Is that the sign for Dorchester? Look out for the turn-off. Now, you *will* remember what I said about being on your best behaviour, won't you? That goes for you too,' she said over her shoulder to Nugs. 'We'll have none of your usual nonsense, please. I won't have you setting Freddy a bad example.'

'Ha!' said Nugs. 'He's quite capable of misbehaving without any help from me, aren't you my boy? Ignore your mother. We'll have some fun this weekend, won't we?'

He and Cynthia began bickering. Freddy suppressed a sigh and directed his attention to the road ahead.

CHAPTER FIVE

IT WAS APPROACHING four o'clock when the Wolseley turned in through the grand arch at the head of the long drive that ran for two miles up to Belsingham. The place needs no introduction, of course, for who has not heard of it? So certain is it of its own fame that it complacently refuses to append anything so commonplace as a 'House' or a 'Hall' to its name—even though, given the size of the building, no-one would utter so much as a murmur of disagreement if it decided to call itself a palace. But Belsingham it was named some three hundred years ago, and Belsingham it remains to this day, the seat of the Dukes of Purbeck ever since the wealthy but untitled Member of Parliament Henry Wareham first pleased the elderly and failing Queen Bess with some minor act of courtesy and found himself unexpectedly elevated to the peerage as the first Baron Wareham—a stroke of luck which the family failed not to act upon, successively obtaining more riches and titles for themselves as the years passed, until they were finally awarded the present dukedom. Such an exalted position required a residence to match, naturally, and as time went on, first one Wareham then another added to the comfortable but modest gentleman's dwelling in which the family had lived for many years, and purchased as much of the surrounding land as possible, until the Belsingham estate became quite one of the most magnificent in the country, and the Wareham family one of the most notable families in England. Cedric, the present Duke, had never seriously expected to accede to the title, but had found himself landed with it some ten years earlier upon the death of his Uncle Algernon, the seventh Duke, who had no issue (or none that he was prepared to admit to in polite company, at any rate). Cedric duly removed to Belsingham with Beatrix and their two children Arthur and Rose, while Uncle Algernon's widow Aunt Ernestine, the Dowager Duchess, took herself off to the South of France for a rest. The present occupants were conscientious in the running of the estate, and while Bea might secretly have preferred a quiet life without the duties of a duchess, she was a practical and realistic woman who knew what was required of her, and so had settled into her situation without too many regrets.

The house itself could not be seen from the gates, but was visible only after half a mile or so of bumpy road which Cedric had been promising to have mended for the past five years at least. Even Freddy, who, as the grandson of a cadet member of the family, had been running around the place every summer for as long as he could remember, always felt his spirits lift at that first sight of the house, which came into sudden view as one rounded a tree-lined bend. The road then widened into a circular carriage drive leading to the main entrance, which was at the top of an imposing flight of steps. Freddy drew up the motor-car and handed out his mother and grandfather, just as Bea came out and hurried down the steps towards them.

'You're just in time for tea,' she said, kissing Cynthia on the cheek. 'Hallo, Nugs, I hope the journey wasn't too terribly ghastly. Do leave the car there, Freddy, and I'll get one of the men to take it round. We're in the small salon today, as the drawing-room still hasn't dried out properly after the rain got in through the broken window-pane during the last storm and ruined the carpet. It smells all damp and musty—and besides, the small salon is much pleasanter.'

She accompanied them, still talking, into the entrance-hall and thence into the room in question, which, despite its name, was a large, spacious apartment that might easily have swallowed an average-sized cottage. The ceiling was painted in shades of blue, white and pink, and framed by gilded cornicing, while the walls were hung with Old Masters collected over the years by the various Dukes. The enormous fireplace was a vision of ornately-sculpted marble, and everywhere the eye turned was some example of past money spent in abundance: here an ebony and ormolu cabinet from the time of Napoleon; there a pair of exquisitely-cast bronze nudes gazing at one another from opposite sides of a carved oak escritoire; in the corner a Chinese vase standing on a delicate brass pedestal. At the back of the room a pair of solemn footmen were attending to a table on which a smooth, white cloth was laid. China plates and cups clinked gently as the table was arranged. Freddy glanced around and saw that a number of people had already arrived and were gathered around Cedric, talking.

A young man detached himself from the company when he caught sight of them, and came to join them. This was Lord Holme, the future Duke of Purbeck, who had been christened Arthur but was commonly known as Goose.

'Hallo, old bean!' he said genially to Freddy. 'Come to stir things up again, what? Things have been deadly dull around here lately. It's about time we had some fun.'

'Nobody is to have *fun*,' said his mother firmly. 'I know exactly the sort of thing you two mean when you say that word, and I shan't allow it.'

'Rot,' said Goose. 'You laughed as much as anybody when we put Freddy in Great-Aunt Ernestine's wedding-dress and paraded him around the West field on Old Bessie. Don't tell me you don't like a joke.'

'That was quite different,' said Bea. 'There was only us then. But this is to be a formal party to present Ro with an important family heirloom, and there are several people we don't know here, so we must at least pretend to be respectable.'

'Always trying to hold the side up,' said Goose to Freddy. 'She knows it's a waste of time, but we shall let her keep her illusions for now.'

Bea shook her head and went off to see to Nugs.

'I really am glad you're here, old boy,' said Goose. 'I thought there'd only be Ralph, and you know what a frightful bore he is.'

'Mmm,' said Freddy non-committally. 'Is Iris here yet?'

'Upstairs with Ro, I think,' said Goose. 'They ought to be down by now, doing their duty and brightening the place up. Goodness knows there's nobody decent to look at here at the moment.'

'No,' said Freddy, eyeing the other guests. 'Who's the Jurassic exhibit by the table? The one who looks like an elderly greyhound?'

Goose glanced across at the man Freddy had indicated.

'That's Mr. Wray,' he said. 'His house fell down and he's got nowhere to live at the moment, so he's staying with us for a few weeks.'

'Rather tiresome for you.'

'Not particularly,' said Goose. 'He's so self-effacing that he practically blends into the wallpaper. One hardly notices he's here.'

'I see,' said Freddy. 'And what about those two over there?'

'The foreign-looking chap with the bow tie is Dr. Bachmann, Father's old pal from Oxford. The other one with the shiny head and the loud voice is one Professor Coddington. Nobody seems to know who he is—not even Father, who invited him— but according to himself he's the world's foremost authority on everything. He's here because his latest "thing" is genealogy, and apparently he has a theory about the Warehams, and wants to write a book about us, so he's wangled an invitation to come and burrow in the library.'

'What's his theory?' said Freddy.

'Haven't the foggiest,' said Goose. 'Father thinks he wants to discredit us, but then why invite him?'

'Discredit us? How?'

'Oh, there are various questions as to whether we're all quite legitimate, you know,' said Goose airily. 'Once in a while we get a letter from some crackpot who wants to claim the title, but we just ignore it. I expect this Coddington fellow thinks he's the rightful heir to the dukedom or something. Well, good luck in trying to prove it, I say. I shouldn't like to try and find anything in that tomb of a library—why, I don't think anybody's tried cataloguing it in the last hundred years or more. Mr. Wray's been digging through some of the books in there, but he seems just as confused as anybody. Ah, here they are. I see Ralph's arrived.'

Freddy looked up as Ro and Iris entered the room in company with a newcomer. Ralph Uttridge was a young man whose habitual expression was one of insufferable complacency. He was intelligent but unimaginative, and had many important connections, to whom he always said the right thing. Everything marked him out for a shining future as a diplomat or a Government minister. Freddy disliked him intensely, but would have died rather than admit it.

'Hallo, Ralph, old chap,' he said cheerfully. 'Hallo, Ro, hallo, Iris. You girls are looking splendid today. All set for next week's jollification, Ro? How many guests do you have now?'

'I'm starting to lose count,' said Ro. 'You know how these things happen—you put a name on the list, then somebody says, "Oh, but you can't invite X without Y. And if you invite Y then you'll have to invite Z too, or she'll be terribly offended and will snub you for the next twenty years." I think we're up to nearly three hundred now.'

'I'm sure the Savoy can manage,' said Freddy.

'Of course it can,' said Goose. He was unlike his sister, being shortish and fair-haired like his mother. Ro, tall with chestnut hair, bore a much closer resemblance to the Duke, but oddly enough, when the two of them stood together it was easy enough to see that they were brother and sister.

'When do we get to see the pearls?' said Freddy.

'Tonight, at dinner,' said Ro.

'You simply must see them,' said Iris to Ralph. 'Ro let me try them on and they're quite magnificent.'

'Is that so?' said Ralph. 'And I dare say you'd like something similar yourself, eh? I know a hint when I hear it. Well, we'll see.'

Iris laughingly denied having hinted at anything of the sort, while Freddy strained to the utmost not to roll his eyes.

'Ah, Freddy,' said Cedric, strolling over to join them. 'How's business at the paper?'

'A little quiet lately,' said Freddy.

'Well, glad you could come. Isn't Daphne here yet?'

'Daphne?' said Iris immediately. 'Not Daphne Garthwaite? Is she coming?'

'Yes,' said Goose.

'But why on earth?' said Iris. 'I mean,' she went on hurriedly, 'I didn't know any of you knew her.'

'Thank Freddy,' said the Duke, blithely unaware of any tension. 'He's the one who invited her.'

'I didn't—' began Freddy, but the conversation had already turned. Iris stared at him in astonishment for a moment, then turned away from him and talked determinedly to Ralph, leaving Freddy feeling somewhat foolish, although he could not have said why. He was rescued by Bea, who led him away.

'Come and speak to our Chair,' she said.

'What?'

'Professor Coddington.' She lowered her voice. 'He arrived just after lunch and I'm rather afraid he's not going to be a success. He's terribly full of himself and has already managed to put half the servants' backs up with his demands. He's spent half the afternoon contradicting everybody—including poor Mr. Wray, who's a gentle soul—and he looks as though he's spoiling for an argument with Dr. Bachmann. Go and be vacuously respectful to him and give us all a little rest.'

'Oh, so that's why I'm here, is it?' said Freddy. 'I'm to be a sort of punching-bag for guests you don't like.'

'Of course not! But nobody could possibly want to pick a fight with you, and you'll be doing me such a good turn if you'll keep an eye on him and stop him making everybody cross. If I had half your natural charm I'd do it myself, but I have a houseful of guests to entertain, which is difficult enough at the best of times. You *will* do it, won't you?'

She was looking at him affectionately, and, being as susceptible to flattery as anyone, he relented.

'All right, I'll do my best,' he said. 'Do I have to stick to him like glue?'

'Not at all. Just step in if you see him beginning to rub people up the wrong way. Now, you go on, and I'll send Samuel round with the tea.'

Freddy was duly introduced to the professor, who was delighted to have a new acquaintance upon whom to bestow the beneficence of his vast intellect.

'And so you are one of the minor Warehams, yes?' he said, once it had been explained to him where Freddy fitted into the family. 'Yes, yes, I remember now, although I gather that none of your particular branch of the family has achieved anything of note—or at least, nothing I have read about. Still, it is not every member of a noble house who is given to greatness. I dare say your mother, as a mere daughter of a younger son, did not have the beauty or the force of personality to attract a husband of high rank and thus carry on the family fame in that way.'

Freddy glanced across the room to where Cynthia, looking expensively *chic* and younger than her years, was loudly and imperturbably informing her cousin, the Duke, that he looked a fright and really ought to buy some new clothes. He was about to point out the inadvisability of the professor's repeating the remark in his mother's hearing—at least if he wished to survive the weekend—when he remembered he was supposed to be vacuously respectful, so changed the subject, and instead made some polite inquiry about the professor's academic interests. This proved to be a mistake, for it swiftly appeared that Professor Coddington liked nothing better than to hold forth at length about himself. Freddy soon learned about the professor's early genius and how it had been scandalously overlooked by first one, then another master at school; how he had gone up to university and forced his instructors—yes, *forced* them— to recognize his superiority in not one, but many disciplines; how he had published paper after paper which jealous rivals had attempted without success to discredit; and how only the worst of bad luck had prevented him from attaining the world-wide renown to which he was undeniably entitled. Freddy was trying not to yawn at a long anecdote in which the professor had, through his own deductive capabilities, detected a flagrant act of plagiarism on the part of an inferior academic and duly reported it to the authorities, when Coddington interrupted himself as Ro was passing and said:

'Ah, Lady Rose. And so tonight we will see you for the first time in the Belsingham pearls. I suppose you have heard the story behind them? It is an inglorious one of blood and despair, but it is not to be expected that a young lady such as yourself will be thinking of the sacrifices which were made in order that you might have a trinket to wear for dinner. No, indeed— you may leave those weightier thoughts to those who are older and wiser than yourself. Your task is a much easier one, for you have merely to provide decoration—and may I say you perform your responsibility admirably.'

Here he gave an absurd little bow, and Ro was forced to stop and make some reply. The professor was delighted to have another victim, and Freddy thankfully made his escape, leaving poor Ro at the mercy of the unwelcome guest.

'I say,' he said to Bea. 'I didn't realize he was quite such an excrescence. Can't you get rid of him? How did you land him in the first place?'

'Someone talked Cedric into inviting him,' said Bea. 'Still, there's nothing we can do about it now, so we shall just have to put up with him.'

Freddy looked across and saw an elegantly-dressed woman standing near the professor and Ro, listening to their conversation with her head on one side. As he watched, she introduced herself neatly into the little group, and after a decent interval Ro was able to escape.

'Whew!' she muttered as she came to join them at the tea table. 'I thought I should never get away. Mrs. Dragusha can have him for a bit. I dare say she'll know how to manage him.'

'Mrs. Dragusha? Is she the foreign-looking woman?' said Freddy. 'I think I know the name. Isn't she a seamstress or something?'

'Shh! Don't let her hear you say that! As a matter of fact, she's quite the best dressmaker in London,' said Ro. 'And terribly in demand, too. I was lucky to be able to get her. She has a waiting list of a year!'

'Or that's what she says, at any rate,' said Freddy. 'Clever of her.'

'No, but she really is worth it,' Ro assured him. 'Iris wanted her to do her wedding-dress, but she's all booked up, it seems.'

'Dear me,' said Freddy. 'I suppose she won't put herself out for anything less than a duke's daughter.'

'Yes, the title does come in useful at times,' said Ro. 'But Iris thinks I might be able to persuade Mrs. Dragusha to fit her in too. I'm to work on her this weekend.'

Cynthia just then came to claim Ro's attention, and the two ladies fell into conversation about abstruse matters of no interest to the male mind. Freddy wandered over to where Goose was talking to the foreign gentleman in the bow tie, and was duly introduced. Dr. Bachmann provided a refreshing contrast to Professor Coddington, for his manners were impeccable and he was clearly determined to be pleased with his hosts and his surroundings. He had not seen his old friend Cedric for many years, he said, and had been surprised and delighted to receive the invitation, for he had only happened to mention in passing in his letter that he was coming to England for a week or two. He had hoped perhaps to spend an evening in London with his friend, but instead the Duke had gone so far as to invite him to Belsingham for a whole weekend. He was glad to see that Cedric and Mrs. Cedric were looking as well as ever—the Duchess in particular was just as handsome as he remembered her, and he looked forward to reminiscing with her about old times. The conversation then turned to Professor Coddington, upon which Dr. Bachmann became much more circumspect. He was evidently attempting to be diplomatic, but Freddy gathered that Coddington's opinion of himself was not shared by the rest of academia, and that, far from being fêted and sought after by his fellows, the professor had been shunted from position to position, and from university to university, because nobody could stand him for more than a few months at a time.

'Kitty, darling!' came Cynthia's voice suddenly, and everybody glanced up to see that a new guest had arrived. Kitty Fitzsimmons was fair, slim and delicate—a look which on many women might have strayed towards the insipid, but which on Kitty merely drew the eye towards her extraordinary regularity of feature. Her eyes, nose and mouth all seemed to have been placed on her face with mathematical precision, at exactly the right distance from one another, and in exactly the right proportions. Her eyes were a shade of blue-green not often seen in nature, while her complexion was clear and fresh, and the envy of many a woman more than ten years younger than herself. Her pink lips curved upwards in a permanent smile, and the only lack of symmetry to be found on her face was in the single dimple which appeared and disappeared at intervals on her left cheek as she spoke. Altogether she was a delight to look at, and even though she never seemed to court attention deliberately, she had long become accustomed to hearing a room fall momentarily silent whenever she entered it. Today she was dressed elegantly but demurely in a shade of rich yellow which would have been difficult to carry off if worn by any other woman. On Kitty, however, it merely accentuated the pale gold of her hair and made her seem like a breath of summer on that chilly and blustery spring day. At Cynthia's loud greeting everyone turned, and it was strange to see how all the men appeared to stand up straighter at the sight of her. Kitty now made straight for Bea, squeezed her hand, and bestowed a genuine smile upon her.

'Hallo, Bea, darling,' she said. 'Am I late again? I'm awfully sorry, but you know I never can decide what to pack. I'm simply dreadful at making decisions. I'm not the last, am I?'

'No, we're still missing one or two,' said Bea.

'Oh, marvellous,' said Kitty. 'Then at least I shan't feel like the naughty girl at school again, as I usually do.'

Cynthia now swooped on her, and conversation, which had fallen in volume to a dull buzz, now resumed. Freddy noticed that Cedric had approached the little group consisting of Bea, Kitty and Cynthia, and was hovering around them with a particularly foolish expression upon his face. He glanced at Bea, who was looking so determinedly unsuspicious as to be perfectly obvious, and felt a pang of sympathy for her.

'Where's Daphne?' came Goose's voice at his elbow.

'Haven't the faintest,' said Freddy with a shrug.

'Good-looking girl, isn't she?'

'I suppose she is.'

'I don't know where you find all these pretty girls. The Governor's been hinting that I ought to settle down and shoulder some responsibility—but I mean to say, what's a man to do if all the girls he knows are either taken or not worth looking at? We had Agnes Rowe and her sisters here the other week—you remember them, don't you? Ghastly females to a woman. Teeth all over the place and legs thick enough to hold up a church roof. Agnes in particular has a voice that could strip the skin off one's face at twenty paces. I shouldn't have minded so much, except they were all so disapproving. They sat in a row on the sofa with their hands folded, looking down their noses and pursing up their lips every time I made so much as the slightest attempt at a cheery remark. I was relieved to find they weren't coming this weekend, I can tell you! I'm glad you thought to invite somebody decent, at any rate.'

Freddy was about to reply when Daphne herself arrived in company with Lavinia Philpott. Mrs. Philpott made straight for Bea and began to gush, quite forgetting Daphne, who scanned the room in a moment, calculated accurately which of its inhabitants were likely to snub her, and retreated to the safety of Freddy's side. Goose was overjoyed at her arrival, and was just beginning to ponder the best strategy to adopt in his campaign to win her off Freddy when they were joined by Iris, who detached a surprised Ralph abruptly from his conversation with Mr. Wray and propelled him across the room for the purpose of having an arm to cling to.

'Hallo, Daphne,' she said, smiling brightly. 'I haven't seen you in simply ages!'

Daphne clung to Freddy's arm in turn and returned the smile.

'Hallo, Iris,' she said. 'I hear you're getting married soon.'

'Yes, in six weeks,' said Iris, casting a coy glance up at her intended. 'I wanted an August wedding, but Ralph was too impatient and didn't want to wait that long. He's such a silly boy, aren't you, darling?'

'Oh, er—' said Ralph.

'I didn't know you were a friend of Ro's,' went on Iris.

'I'm not, really, although of course we've met. As a matter of fact, it was Freddy who insisted I come,' said Daphne sweetly. She gripped his arm more firmly.

'And quite right too,' said an oblivious Goose. 'The more the merrier, I say. Far too many old people here as a rule. We need more girls like you to brighten up the place.'

'And you can always trust Freddy to find them,' said Iris, more tartly than she had intended. 'There seems to be a different one each week, and I've rather lost count. I must say, I had no idea you knew each other. Where was it you met? The Excelsior Club, I expect.'

'Yes, it was, as a matter of fact,' said Daphne.

'I thought so,' said Iris. She turned to Freddy. 'Isn't that where you met those two French dancers? And the Mexican bandit's daughter? And the butcher's widow from Streatham? Or was it Clapham? I forget.'

Daphne's smile had not faltered, but Freddy was by now losing all feeling in his arm. He glared at Iris, who went on:

'Poor Freddy—he's so easily taken advantage of, especially when he's been drinking. Not that I suppose he'd been doing anything of the sort when he met you, but I shouldn't feel easy if I didn't give you a friendly warning.'

'Awfully kind of you, but it's quite unnecessary,' replied Daphne. She smiled serenely, for she felt herself the victor on the grounds: first, that possession was nine points of the law, and second, that unlike Iris, she had not lost her temper.

Goose had begun to sense an under-current, so he said to Daphne:

'I say, has anybody shown you around the house yet? It's a crumbling old pile, but we have some rather splendid daubs in the gallery and the grounds are pleasant enough.'

'Oh! That reminds me—Ro and I were going to explore the secret passage today,' said Iris.

'A secret passage!' exclaimed Daphne. 'Do you mean to say there's one here?'

'Certainly,' replied Goose. 'As a matter of fact we have several, although most of them are blocked or unusable for one reason or another. I think Iris is talking about the one between the library and Ro's room. Should you like to see it?'

'Yes please!' said Daphne. She let go of Freddy's arm and beamed at Goose in genuine excitement at the prospect. Iris had already gone to fetch Ro, and Freddy seized the opportunity to take a deep breath and flex his arm surreptitiously. He had the feeling the next few days would be awkward.

CHAPTER SIX

O N OVERHEARING THAT a secret passage was to be explored, several of the other guests expressed a lively interest in seeing it, and as a result the whole party removed to the library to watch the show. It was a dim and musty place, with a high, vaulted ceiling and a mezzanine balcony running around three sides of the room. Three large sash windows gave out on to the lawns and the countryside beyond, and since the view was a fine one, several of the guests went across to look out.

'Better not touch that one,' said Bea to Lavinia, who was struggling with the catch of one of the windows. 'It's not safe, and we're waiting for them to come and put the new weights in.'

'Oh, I do beg your pardon,' said Lavinia. 'Yes, I see you have the new weights here. I merely thought a little fresh air might dispel some of the stuffiness. But perhaps better not, if the window is dangerous. Now, Lord Holme, I'm simply dying to know where this secret passage is. You must tell us, because

I know I shall never spot the entrance myself. Is there a trap-door under the carpet?'

'Secret passages are a not uncommon feature of great houses such as this one,' announced Professor Coddington in his loud, didactic voice. 'I imagine, my dear lady, that we will find there is a secret door behind one of the bookshelves. That is how these things are usually concealed.'

'You're quite right, sir,' said Goose. He strode over to the far corner of the room, to an ordinary-looking row of shelves. 'Here.'

They all crowded around him. He beamed at everybody and indicated a large volume whose title declared it to be a book of zoological illustrations produced for the edification of children and the otherwise easily entertained. All the other books on the shelves were collections of sermons from some forty years back.

'We put this here so we'd remember where it was,' said Goose. He took the book down, reached in and felt around at the back of the shelf. 'There's a catch here, you see.'

There was a click and a creak, and something moved. Goose pushed, and a whole section of shelf swung inwards to reveal a space just big enough for a largish man to step inside. They all shuffled forward and peered in.

'Not much to see from here,' he said. 'As you can see, it runs along the back of the shelves for a way.'

'May we go in?' said Iris.

'We'll need a torch,' said Ro. 'I think there's one in that drawer.'

A torch was duly produced and handed to Goose.

'Better not all go in at once, dear,' said Bea. 'It will be a dreadful squash and nobody will be able to see a thing.'

At length it was decided that Goose, Ro, Daphne, Freddy and Iris would go first. They all crowded into the passage, Freddy bringing up the rear, and Goose switched on the torch and waved it around.

The walls of the passage were made of rough-hewn stone which felt cold to the touch. Their route ran straight for about twenty feet, then turned sharply left, then right. Here, away from the passage entrance, it was much darker, although a little light filtered through from one or two chinks in the walls.

'There are steps here,' said Goose. 'Mind you don't trip over.'

'Where are we?' said Iris.

'Somewhere behind the panelling in the hall, I think,' replied Goose.

'Yes,' came a voice behind Freddy, making him jump. It was Professor Coddington, who must have crept in behind them unnoticed. 'I have been paying close attention to the distance and the direction, and according to my calculations, we are now standing approximately parallel to the bottom of the grand staircase.'

'Are there rats here, do you think?' said Daphne nervously.

'Probably,' said Goose, and she gave a squeak.

The light from the torch bobbed above their heads as Goose began to ascend the steep stone steps, which curved around in a spiral to the left. As the torch disappeared around a bend, those at the rear were plunged into darkness. Freddy could hear the professor behind him, puffing with the effort of climbing the steps. At the top, Goose paused to allow everybody to catch up with him.

'The passage splits into two here,' he said, his face ghostly in the light of the torch. 'We want the left one.'

They all followed him along the left fork, which continued straight for another ten yards, then turned right. Just after the turn Goose stopped unexpectedly, and they all bumped into one another.

'Here we are,' he said. 'There's a door here, you see. Stand away—it opens towards us.'

The door in the panelling opened easily, having been loosened by Ro the day before, and Goose made to step through it, but Iris hung back.

'Where does the right fork go?' she said. 'May we explore that too?'

'It leads here too,' said Ro. 'But it's a longer route and a bit of a squeeze, that's all. Do you really want to see it? It's not especially interesting.'

But Iris was keen, and so Goose said, 'Come on, then,' and stepped back from the entrance to Ro's room. Instead of turning back the way they had come, however, he continued along the passage. A few yards farther on, it narrowed considerably, and the roof became lower, so they all had to duck their heads.

'Everyone all right back there?' came Goose's voice from the front. 'Don't worry, it'll get wider in a minute.'

After a few more yards the passage curved slightly, then seemed to end. Goose stopped and waited again.

'This is where the other fork comes out,' he said. 'If we turn down it we'll arrive at the top of the staircase we came up.'

They looked in the direction he indicated, and saw that here the passage turned right.

'What's that?' said Iris, who had spotted something to her left. Goose directed the torch obligingly towards it. It was a low, square doorway with a cracked wooden beam above it. 'Is it another passage?'

'That one's even narrower than this one, and leads to a dead end,' said Goose. 'I think there was a way out at one time, but it seized up. You can go and look if you want, but there's nothing much to see.'

They all peered into the opening, but the place was very cramped and uncomfortable, and so at last they moved away from it and took the right turn instead. Sure enough, this passage was wider and higher, and, after a bend or two, led back to the head of the spiral stairs.

'That's all clear enough,' said Iris. 'To get to Ro's room from the staircase you take the left fork then turn right, or the right fork then turn left.'

'Exactly,' said Goose. 'I don't know why they built it like that.'

'Perhaps the builders fell out with one another and built two rival passages,' suggested Freddy.

'Silly,' said Iris.

They returned along their original route to Ro's bedroom. Goose held the tapestry out of the way and they all stepped out. Professor Coddington began examining the panelling.

'Is it possible to lock the entrance from this side?' he said.

'I don't think so,' said Ro. 'And why should I want to, anyway?'

'For safety, of course,' he said.

'I don't see who'd want to come in,' she said. 'There's only us here most of the time.'

'We'd better go down and tell the others they can come through now,' said Daphne, and they all filed out of Ro's bedroom and back down the stairs. Freddy was the last to come out, and as he shut Ro's door he thought he caught sight of a figure flitting along the corridor, close to the wall. He frowned and looked again, but whoever it was just then whisked silently out of sight around a corner. He shrugged and followed the others down to the library. Dr. Bachmann, Ralph, Kitty Fitzsimmons and Lavinia Philpott were just preparing to enter the passage. It seemed Nugs was joining them. He made to usher Mrs. Dragusha in before him, but she retreated.

'I do not like dark spaces,' was all she said. 'I prefer to stay here, where it is light.'

'I quite understand your reticence,' said Mr. Wray. 'I have done enough scrambling about in the dark myself. I, too, shall remain here.'

'Suit yourself,' said Nugs, then glanced at Lavinia's retreating figure and, with an expression of great satisfaction, slid into the dark passage after her.

'Perhaps we ought to have warned her to take a weapon,' murmured Cedric, and was rewarded with an impatient look from his wife.

Despite Cedric's fears, the party returned a little while later safe and sound, Lavinia talking nineteen to the dozen.

'Oh, Duchess!' she cried. 'How simply thrilling to have your very own secret passage here at Belsingham! Lord Lucian was very kind, and insisted on showing me every last branch of it, even though it was very low and narrow in places. He said there was no danger of my getting lost as long as he had hold of me. And he was quite right, too! I had just a *little* squeeze to get out into Lady Rose's bedroom, but I shouldn't have missed it for the world. What intrigues and mysteries this house must have seen over the years! Illicit trysts and historical affairs of state discussed in the greatest of secrecy thanks to this secret route.'

'Jolly useful for avoiding unwanted guests, too,' murmured Cedric.

'As a matter of fact there are a few of them around the place,' said Bea. 'They're mostly forgotten about now, of course—too cold and dark to bother with.'

'I should like to see the other ones,' announced Professor Coddington. 'Perhaps someone would be good enough to show them to me.' Nobody seemed inclined to answer, and he took this as encouragement to fill the silence with his own voice. 'In my opinion, the English aristocracy has been too accustomed to abuse its privileged position in order to change the course of history without due process, thus causing harm to many innocent people, and secret passages of this kind are only one symptom of this tendency.' He addressed himself to Kitty Fitzsimmons, who had given him a politely disbelieving look. 'I see you are not convinced, madam. Evidently you consider tunnels such as this to be a harmless diversion—a few brief moments of entertainment to pass the time during a house party such as this one. But I consider them to be something more dangerous, in that they allow men of power to act in an underhanded fashion, out of the view of the common folk, when it is their duty to act in the best interests of those who serve them. Mrs. Philpott speaks of intrigues and affairs of state discussed in the greatest of secrecy—and this is precisely my objection. In my view, by its very position the aristocracy has a responsibility to use its great wealth and privilege wisely, and this means acting in a way which is beyond reproach— and, moreover, *seen* to be beyond reproach. All concealment and subterfuge ought to be avoided, or actions taken with the best of intentions may be misinterpreted, or even take a turn for the bad. However, since the common man cannot be supposed to have the intellectual capacity to discern wrongdoing, or, if he does, the means to root it out without great risk to himself, I consider it my duty as a representative of the academic world, who thus has greater resources than ordinary people to discover such misdeeds, to investigate any information which comes to my attention that might suggest that the higher members of society have been conducting themselves in an illicit manner.'

The dressing-bell had rung halfway through his speech, and most of the party had drifted out of the room by this time. Only the Duke and Duchess and Kitty were left to hear him out politely. At length he concluded his discourse to his satisfaction, then announced he would go and dress for dinner.

'Whew!' muttered Cedric to his wife as Kitty hurried out of the room. 'Can we do anything about him?'

'I don't think we can,' said Bea. 'We must put up with him, I'm afraid. I hope he doesn't insist on being shown the other secret passages. Most of them are blocked or have heavy furniture against them.'

'Oh, I don't know,' said Cedric. 'If he's so determined to think the aristocracy behave badly then perhaps we ought to try and live up to our reputation and brick him up inside one of them.'

'Silly,' said Bea, and they both went up to dress.

CHAPTER SEVEN

FREDDY WAS FEELING in need of a drink, and so he dressed quickly, with the intention of fitting in a quick one before dinner. As he arrived at the head of the stairs he bumped into Dr. Bachmann, who was distracted and not watching where he was going.

'I beg your pardon,' said Bachmann. 'I did not see you there.'

Freddy noticed that he was looking pale and upset.

'Are you quite well, sir?' he said.

'What? Oh, yes,' replied Bachmann. 'I have just remembered something, that is all—a matter of business. Yes, there is a matter of business I forgot to attend to before I left for Belsingham.'

'Was it important?'

Dr. Bachmann essayed a smile.

'A little. Still, it will have to wait now. I am sure a few more days will not matter.'

He went off, frowning. Freddy was about to continue down the stairs when he caught sight of someone coming out of a room on the West Wing corridor, and gave an exclamation.

'So it *was* you I saw earlier!' he said, as she approached. 'I thought I must have been mistaken.'

Valentina Sangiacomo curled her lip.

'What do you want? I'm in a hurry,' she said ungraciously.

Freddy regarded her with interest. She was wearing the uniform of a lady's maid, and looked fully the part, even down to the pert toss of the head.

'That's no way to talk to your betters,' he said. She threw him a look which told him clearly enough that she had her own ideas about that, and he went on, 'What are you doing here? Who brought you?'

'Mrs. Fitzsimmons,' she said.

'A lady's maid?'

'A girl has to earn a living, doesn't she?'

'I suppose so. But I can't quite see you in the part, somehow.'

'It's all right,' she said. 'She's nice enough, and I get her cast-offs. Not the really good stuff, of course. Catch them letting *us* wear sequins.'

'But does she know about your—er—character?'

'What's wrong with my character?' she said. 'It's as good as anybody else's. You're perfect yourself, are you?'

'Oh, I'm a model of virtue and rectitude,' said Freddy airily.

'Then so am I,' said Valentina, with a glare that dared him to contradict her. Since she was an expert thief who had once taught him to pick a lock, her words were evidently a matter of form. Freddy let them pass, supposing that she would hardly risk falling into her old habits now that she knew he was here at Belsingham, for suspicion was bound to fall upon her at once.

'I'm wanted downstairs or I should have more to say to you, but just you be sure and keep out of trouble,' he said.

'I will if you will,' she said, and with a knowing wink and another toss of the head she hurried off, wholly unabashed.

Freddy watched her go thoughtfully, then headed downstairs, where he found that Mrs. Dragusha and Professor Coddington had arrived before him. Mrs. Dragusha coughed when she saw him arrive, whereupon the professor turned around, spotted him, and said, 'Ah, yes, I am quite of your opinion, madam. One does not often see such fine works of art in a private home. Have you ever visited Florence? No? Then I suggest you do so as soon as you can, for in no other place will you find such an accumulation of works of artistic genius as there is to be found in that fair city. The Uffizi gallery, for example—' here he wandered off into a comparison of the relative merits of some of the lesser-known Renaissance painters according to his own expert opinion, and Freddy stopped listening. He guessed they had been talking of something else when he came in—presumably himself and Cynthia, and the inferiority of their branch of the family, given the speed with which the professor had changed the subject on Freddy's arrival. Luckily, he was freed from the necessity of joining in the conversation and attempting to sound knowledgeable about art, because just then Lavinia Philpott and Daphne arrived. Daphne was looking very fetching in pink, while Lavinia wore an astonishing creation in stiff violet silk, into which she had ruthlessly forced her not inconsiderable amplitude. Freddy hastened to help them to cocktails.

'I suppose just *one* won't matter, will it?' said Lavinia coyly, as she took the drink. 'No more, though, or it will go straight to my head, and we wouldn't want that, would we?'

'Certainly not,' said Freddy.

'It's astounding how much some people can hold,' went on Lavinia. 'In India, it was quite the done thing among *some* groups of people to drink cocktails from noon onwards. Of course, by dinner-time half of them couldn't find their way to the dining-room and the other half couldn't stand up at all. Disgraceful behaviour, I call it. I speak of the lower classes, naturally. Those of us at the higher levels of society would never have dreamt of conducting ourselves in that fashion.'

'You lived in India, did you, madam?' said Mrs. Dragusha.

'Yes indeed,' replied Lavinia. 'We spent ten years in Mahjapara, in the north. My husband was in Tea, you know. Quite six thousand acres, and all of the very highest quality Assam. My poor darling was called to a better place two years ago, and my dear sister was carried off not long after that, leaving Daphne and me all alone in the world. But India is no place for two women, and we very soon agreed that we had better return to England. And so here we are!' She gave a gay, tinkling laugh. 'As I was saying to Mrs. Fortescue-Hoggett only the other day, after so many years abroad it's so refreshing to return into the company of one's own sort. Out there, one finds oneself a kind of magnet for people one wouldn't normally mix with, and naturally one doesn't wish to give an outright snub, but sometimes one does have to be ruder than one would like. However, I'm pleased to say there's no need for that *here*.'

Cynthia had come in while Lavinia was speaking, and had heard the whole speech. Freddy saw a scornful remark hovering on his mother's lips, and attempted to forestall it by pushing a drink on her and talking loudly of something else, but she was not to be repressed.

'I told you, didn't I?' she hissed, as soon as Lavinia and Daphne had moved away. 'Six thousand acres, indeed! She said it as though her husband owned them, but I happen to know he was nothing but a shipping clerk at the Mahjapara District Tea Company, if you please. He died when a tower of tea-crates toppled onto him in the warehouse.'

Mr. Wray now entered in his usual self-effacing fashion and came to pay his compliments to Mrs. Pilkington-Soames, and so Cynthia was forced to keep the rest of her opinions to herself.

Professor Coddington was regarding Mrs. Philpott with interest.

'You lived in Mahjapara, did you?' he said. 'I know the place very well myself.'

'Oh, you do, do you?' said Lavinia.

'Yes. I have a friend there, and spent some months staying with him two years ago. I should say it was strange that we did not meet, but my friend lives up in the hills and does not mix greatly in society. However, he takes all the newspapers, so we were perfectly informed of all the goings-on in the town. If I am not much mistaken, you are the widow of Mr. Morris Philpott, yes?'

Just then Daphne gave a little cry of dismay, for Lavinia had spilt her cocktail over her.

'Dear me, how careless of me! I *am* sorry, darling,' exclaimed Lavinia, dabbing at her niece with a napkin. 'These heels are rather new and I'm not quite steady on them yet. I do hope I haven't ruined your frock. No, no, it's mostly gone on your arm, I see. Just a *little* patch of wet here on the bottom of the sleeve, and that will dry easily. How very fortunate that it was just a martini, and not one of these brightly-coloured drinks! At least it won't stain. You will forgive me, won't you? It was entirely accidental.'

Most of the spillage had gone onto the rug, and was soon cleaned up. Lavinia was furnished with another cocktail, then Kitty Fitzsimmons made her entrance on the arm of Dr. Bachmann, and all attention turned to her. Cynthia's eyes darted everywhere, registering every detail of Kitty's simple tunic, and found nothing to criticize.

'It's perfect,' she pronounced at last—just as Kitty had intended. 'On anyone else that frock would look far too plain— bland, even—but you look nothing less than an angel. Yes, quite angelic!'

'You're terribly kind,' said Kitty modestly.

Others now chimed in with their compliments, and the conversation turned to the many perfections of Kitty Fitzsimmons, who flushed slightly but seemed not at all displeased at this development. Freddy, mindful of Daphne's presence, was very careful not to stare, and turned to find Mr. Wray still standing next to him. Despite his age, the clergyman was lean and spare, with a looseness of limb that spoke of frequent healthy walks in the country. Now his brows were drawn together in a pained frown.

'Are you all right, sir?' said Freddy. Mr. Wray started slightly, as though he had only just noticed where he was.

'What? Oh, yes, I am quite well, thank you,' he replied. 'Just a mild headache. I get them sometimes—and especially so since the unfortunate incident which destroyed part of my house. I am occasionally affected by vibrations, and I believe the electrical power that was unleashed by the lightning storm may have in some way increased my sensitivity further—at least, I have certainly become more acutely aware of the disorder since it happened.'

'I say, bad luck.'

'Thank you, but it is nothing. Just a little inconvenience now and again. The worst of it is that I do not sleep at all well when it comes upon me. But it passes after a few nights, and then I am perfectly well again. I should call it my cross to bear, except that it can be useful at times. I dare say you'll think it odd, and perhaps a little disrespectful in someone of my calling, but I believe I am very susceptible to atmosphere, and have an ability to perceive things which are not discernible to most people.'

'Oh? Such as what?'

'It is difficult to explain,' said Mr. Wray. 'Let us say that among any particular company or gathering of people, I am able to sense the prevailing mood or influence even where the intention is to conceal it. It is nothing more than an impression—an intangible sensation—but it is quite unmistakable. As I said, some might think it not exactly right in a clergyman, and consider that it smacks too much of the occult, but I firmly believe it is a gift from a Higher Power, and thus to be harnessed for good. And so I have used it. On several occasions in the past I have been able to use my sense of something amiss to help restore harmony where before there was discord. I speak only of a judicious word here and there to help smooth out minor squabbles, you understand, but I have always believed that one day I should be able to use my gift to prevent a greater harm. Or at least, I *did* believe it—until today.'

'What do you mean?' said Freddy.

Mr. Wray paused before replying.

'Mr. Pilkington-Soames, have you never had a sense of your own helplessness in the face of impending disaster?' he said at last.

'Oh, all the time,' said Freddy truthfully.

'Then you will perhaps understand my situation. You will not believe me, I dare say, but I sense that a great evil has descended upon Belsingham. Something terrible is about to happen, I am almost certain of it.'

'Good Lord!' said Freddy. 'Evil, you say? Who is evil?'

'It may not be a person at all—perhaps it is just a mood or an intention, I cannot tell. But I feel a great disruption to the family lies ahead,' replied Mr. Wray. He turned to Freddy, and the look on his face was one of distress. 'Someone is in danger—and I do not know how I can prevent it!'

Chapter Eight

BEFORE FREDDY COULD question Mr. Wray further, there was a slight disturbance by the door as the Duke and Duchess entered with some ceremony. Cedric coughed, and the room fell silent.

'Ladies and gentlemen,' he said. 'My daughter, Lady Rose Wareham. In you come, then,' he finished, rather ruining the effect. All eyes were turned to the open door as Ro made her entrance in her new frock, wearing the Belsingham pearls. She was trying and not quite managing to affect an expression of boredom, for it was clear that she was as excited as anybody else about the evening; and sure enough, as everyone clapped and cheered, her face broke out into the pleased smile she had been attempting to suppress.

'You look beautiful, darling!' exclaimed Iris. 'Doesn't she, Ralph?'

Ralph duly added his compliments, as did everyone else. Mrs. Dragusha had judged quite rightly in the colour and the cut of the frock, for its clean, simple lines acted as an ideal foil to the pearls themselves, which lay in three delicate loops on Ro's breast, their sheen contrasting perfectly with the midnight blue of the satin beneath them. The dressmaker herself was clasping her hands together, smiling at the result of her efforts.

'Splendid, splendid,' said Cedric, not displeased with his daughter's reception.

'Shall we go in to dinner?' said Bea.

There was some little bustle as they all removed to the dining-room and sat in their allotted places. Ro was seated halfway down the long table, that everyone might admire her and the Belsingham pearls, and she did her best to appear gracious when she discovered that Professor Coddington was to be her right-hand neighbour. Fortunately, Freddy was on her other side to leaven the suffering, and so her birthday dinner proceeded reasonably pleasantly—at least until the professor turned away from Mr. Wray, with whom he had been conversing, and said to her:

'And so at last the pearls are yours, Lady Rose, and may I say how radiant you look in them? It is a pity—yes, it is a pity that these heirlooms always seem to have such stories of suffering behind them, but I know that your ancestors considered the deaths of forty or fifty foreigners to be a small price to pay for such a treasure.'

'Nothing to do with Ro,' said Goose cheerfully from across the table.

'Naturally,' replied Coddington. 'I hope you do not think I am apportioning blame to any of you. I spoke of the hidden sins of great families earlier, but I assure you I mean no offence to the present representatives of such houses. No, one would hope for better conduct in these modern days. In the past, for example, it was quite common for a duke or an earl to maintain a whole brood of irregular offspring in addition to his legitimate heirs. Nowadays it would be much more difficult to hide such a thing from the public eye, is that not so, Duke?'

'Oh—er—what?' said Cedric, startled.

'We know the Wareham family are not without their own skeletons in the closet, but I speak of past misdeeds, of course. You will remember my letter on the subject, no doubt.'

'Ah—certainly,' replied Cedric.

Bea was raising her eyebrows furiously at Freddy, who took the hint and was about to chime in with some fatuous remark to ease the awkwardness, when the professor went on, addressing the whole table:

'How strange Fate is! I was speaking to Lord Lucian this afternoon, who told me that the Duke nearly drowned in a river as a child. Fortunate for him that he survived the accident—but fortunate also for your branch of the family, for had he died, then the dukedom would have passed to Lord Lucian himself, and then, in due course, to Mr. Pilkington-Soames.'

Here he paused impressively, and everybody involuntarily eyed Freddy as they considered the appalling possibility.

'I say, that's not true, you know, sir,' said Goose. 'A title can't pass through the female line—or ours can't at any rate, so Cynthia rather stands in the way of Freddy's getting his hands on Belsingham.'

'Ah! That is my mistake,' said the professor, by no means disconcerted. 'How many men must have seen their ambitions thwarted by virtue of their descent through the wrong line! You know this, of course, Mr. Wray—by which I mean that you must have read of many such misfortunes during your researches here. In this case, however, perhaps Lord Holme may consider himself lucky that Lord Lucian was unable to have sons.'

Here Nugs emerged from his soup and was about to retort, but Bea caught his eye and he thought better of it. Fortunately, Cynthia was talking to Ralph and had not heard the exchange.

Coddington went on:

'Still, whatever the reason, it was not to be, and so Lady Rose is the happy woman who wears the pearls tonight.' He turned back to her and poked his head towards her as though to peer closely at the necklace. Ro hastily took off the pearls in case he took it into his head to paw at them.

'Should you like to look at them, professor?' she said.

'Thank you! I should like nothing better.' He took the pearls in his hand and held them up to the light, then squinted at them. 'I suppose these are the real ones? I know that sometimes the owners of fabulous heirlooms prefer to wear false ones and keep the real ones locked away for safety. I have also heard of cases in which real jewels have been pawned, and false ones substituted in secret. No? These are the real ones? Ah! Then they are the very pearls which were stolen from the Maharajah of Ravashnagar, who, along with his wife and his body-guard was brutally slaughtered by John Wareham in the year eighteen hundred and six. They are of national importance, and ought really to be in a museum for the enjoyment of the nation.' Here he looked around the table to make quite sure that he had the full enthralled attention of his audience. 'I am not a real expert, of course, but I have studied these things in a modest way, and it is a pity I have not my eye-glass with me, or I should examine them more closely. However, I am afraid I left it in my room.'

Ro murmured something politely, and he handed them back. Kitty Fitzsimmons, on Freddy's other side, murmured:

'That man really is the limit.'

'Isn't he, though?' Freddy replied.

'One can't even have a quiet conversation about fripperies without his interrupting with his puffed-up opinions. Only think! Iris and I were having a comfortable chat earlier about shoes, of all things, and he came and started opining about the damage high heels do to one's feet. We were just preparing to nod and agree in the hope that he'd go away, when he started dropping heavy hints to Iris about how it was as well to be fully informed of the past of the man one was to marry, as though Ralph were anything but the straightest!'

'Well, quite,' said Freddy, then added curiously, 'What did he say about him, out of interest?'

'Oh, nothing that I could understand,' said Kitty. 'At least, nothing that meant anything. I think the professor likes to give the impression that he knows things, even when he doesn't. Then he started saying horrid things about Rob, nodding and smiling all the while as though he thought I should like nothing better than to listen to his stuff.'

'I'm sorry,' said Freddy.

'Don't be,' said Kitty cheerfully. 'I'm used to that sort of thing. As a matter of fact, it was quite refreshing to hear it said out loud instead of whispered behind people's hands as I pass. Still, it's hardly good manners.'

'It certainly isn't.'

'If this were a novel,' went on Kitty, 'Professor Coddington is the sort of person who'd be found dead in the study with a knife in his back, and we'd all be suspects.'

'So he is,' said Freddy. 'And who should you have as the murderer?'

Kitty's single dimple appeared as she looked thoughtfully around the table.

'It's usually the least obvious person, isn't it? What do you say to Lavinia Philpott? Or Dr. Bachmann?'

'Either of those might do, I should think. But what about motive?'

'I expect we could think of one easily enough. If it was Lavinia, then perhaps the professor met her in India, and knows something to her disadvantage.'

'That's possible, I suppose. But what about Bachmann?'

'I don't know. Some sort of academic rivalry?'

'Yes, that's convincing enough,' said Freddy. 'I've heard about what goes on in these circles. You'd think most professors and lecturers were shrivelled old beans with brains full of algebra and nothing else—certainly no human feeling, but don't you believe it! I've heard stories that would make your hair stand on end. I don't suppose you've ever heard of the East Quadrangle Massacre which took place a few years ago at a very well known seat of learning? They hushed it up, you know, because understandably it was thought that the parents of impressionable young men might be somewhat reluctant to send their sons to a place in which one couldn't be quite sure of going to bed with the same number of limbs one had when one got up. The *Clarion* sent me to cover the story, but I was only permitted to write about it in the most veiled terms. At any rate, I can tell you categorically that if you care to accuse a well-respected professor of Greek of having misrepresented the emphasis of a particular phrase in his translation of the *Iliad*, then you had better do so from across the room—and preferably while standing by the door, all the better to make a quick escape. I see disbelief in your face,' he went on, as she shook her head smilingly at him. 'I promise you that every word of it is true. Still, though, we've got it all wrong, you know. In my business I see a lot of sordid doings every day, and sadly one finds that the murderer is usually the *most* obvious suspect rather than the least obvious one.'

'In that case, if somebody killed the professor it would have to be one of the Warehams, since it's their house party he's spoiling, and he keeps on hinting that they're hiding awful secrets, which I'm sure they're not.'

'And I'm quite sure they *are*,' said Freddy. 'We've all got secrets—even you, I'll wager.'

'Oh, I have heaps!' said Kitty charmingly. 'But the question is, are they deadly enough secrets to commit murder for?'

'I don't know, are they?' said Freddy.

She smiled into his eyes. She really was very pretty, and demure, too, in her chocolate-brown satin dress, set off with one simple amber necklace.

'Perhaps,' she said. 'But I should be a fool to admit it if so.'

'Then you'd better keep them to yourself,' he said lightly.

CHAPTER NINE

FREDDY WAS ONE of the last to turn in, for he was playing billiards with Goose and money had been staked upon the outcome. Eventually, however, he headed up to his room and fell into bed without ceremony. Under normal circumstances he would have slept like a top, but for some reason on this particular evening he took a while to drift off, and when he did he managed nothing more than a fitful doze. Some time later he awoke with a start, and wondered for a second where he was and what had woken him. Had he heard a noise outside the door? He switched on the lamp next to his bed and looked at his watch. It was after two. Someone was certainly outside in the passage, for he could hear what sounded like a man singing drunkenly, half under his breath. Freddy got up, threw on a dressing-gown and looked out. The landing was illuminated with dim lights on the walls, and he saw the retreating figure of his grandfather, tottering down the corridor some distance away. Nugs's room was in the other wing, and he was heading in quite the wrong direction for bed.

'What's the old villain doing now?' said Freddy to himself, and followed quietly, so as not to wake anybody. He soon caught up with Nugs, who had stopped singing and was now standing listening at a door, swaying slightly. From inside the room could be heard the sound of gentle snoring. Freddy thought he remembered that the room was Lavinia Philpott's, and knowing Lavinia, he was certain that Nugs was not there by invitation.

'What the devil d'you think you're doing?' he hissed.

Nugs jumped and whirled around.

'Eh? What's that?' he cried. 'Freddy, old chap! What are you doing up? I was just going back to bed.'

'But this isn't your room,' Freddy pointed out.

'What? Isn't it?' said Nugs, with a theatrical look of surprise which would not have fooled a child. 'Am I lost again?'

'You know jolly well you're not, you disgraceful old goat,' said Freddy. 'Now, lower your voice and come away before she screams the house down. Do you want to embarrass Bea again?'

Nugs wavered a second.

'Damn,' he said grumpily at last. 'You're no fun.' He turned away from the door with one last longing look, then brightened. 'I say, come and have a drink.'

'At this time of night?'

'I'm bored. At my age I don't sleep, and this party has been so utterly dreary so far—thanks to you—that I've had no excitement to tire me out enough to drop off. Go on, the night's barely begun. And besides, if you don't I shall merely go and cause a disturbance somewhere else,' he added.

'Oh, very well, then,' said Freddy, who was now wide awake. 'Just a quick one, to send me off to sleep properly.'

They went downstairs and into Cedric's study. Nugs sat in the best chair while Freddy poked about in a cupboard and brought out a bottle of whisky and some glasses. He was just pouring the drinks when Goose put his head around the door.

'I thought I heard someone up,' he said. 'Fill 'em up, then!'

Drinks were poured, and there was a respectful silence for some minutes as they worshipped at the altar of the Duke's best single malt. From out in the hall came the chimes of an ancient and venerable grandfather clock as it struck the half hour.

'What are you doing up, anyway?' said Goose at last.

'Preserving the virtue of Lavinia Philpott,' replied Freddy idly. The whisky had given him a pleasant, drowsy feeling. He believed he should go to bed shortly.

'Hmph,' said Nugs.

'It's just that I saw the door to your room was open, and thought you might be—you know,' said Goose.

'What?' said Freddy.

'Well, Iris is here, isn't she?'

'What's that to me?' said Freddy. 'Perish the thought, old boy—that ship has well and truly sailed.'

'Pity, really,' said Goose.

'Not at all. She's made her choice.'

'Yes, but I mean to say, she's obviously had some sort of temporary failure of the mental faculties if she's agreed to marry that dreadful stiff.'

There was a grunt of agreement from Nugs, followed by another silence as they all sipped their whisky.

'Let's go and play a joke on Ralph,' suggested Goose suddenly.

'Splendid idea!' said Nugs.

'What, now? I was going to go to bed,' said Freddy.

'What sort of a coward are you?' said Nugs. 'We'll go upstairs and put a pillow over his face.'

'That is *not* a joke,' said Freddy. 'I know things were different when you were a mere stripling and Napoleon was trampling all over the flower-beds, but nowadays the police tend to call that sort of thing attempted murder.'

'Nonsense,' said Nugs. 'We did it all the time in my day.'

'No, but look,' said Goose eagerly. 'I've had the most marvellous idea. There's a tailor's dummy in Mother's dressing-room. Mrs. Dragusha brought it. Let's dress it up in some sheets and pretend it's a ghost.'

'Don't be ridiculous—that won't fool him for a second,' said Freddy.

'Yes it will,' said Goose. 'We'll sneak the thing into his room then stand outside the door and make ghostly noises. You'll see—he'll be terrified. I expect he'll scream like a girl.'

It was a very crude and childish idea, and so of course appealed strongly to Freddy.

'Where did you say this dummy was?' he said at last.

'In Mother's dressing-room,' replied Goose.

So the plan was agreed. Freddy fetched the tailor's dummy and brought it to his bedroom, and Goose went to rummage about in the linen cupboard.

'Here,' he said, returning with an armful of sheets. 'This ought to do it. Where's Nugs?'

Nugs was located outside Lavinia's door again and escorted firmly away, while the gentle rumbling sounds that emanated from within indicated that she remained mercifully unaware of the repeated attempts upon her stronghold.

They draped the sheets over the dummy as artfully as they could, then stood back to regard their handiwork. In no sense did it look a convincing ghost.

'Frightful, perhaps, but not exactly frightening,' said Freddy at last.

'I see what you mean,' said Goose. 'All it will do is puzzle him. What can we do to make it better?'

'Tie a torch inside it?' suggested Nugs.

'It'll blind him, and he won't be able to see the ghost,' said Freddy.

'Not if we put more sheets on it to dim the beam,' said Goose.

More sheets were brought and duly heaped over the dummy, then Goose ran down to the library, returned with the torch, and dived under the mountain of linen. There was a certain amount of panting and struggling as the sheets did their best to entwine themselves around his neck.

'Ought to have done this first,' came his voice from somewhere inside the creation. 'There. Let's see what it looks like. Turn the light off.'

They did so, and Goose, from under the sheets, switched on the torch. The tailor's dummy glowed eerily in the darkness.

'We'll have to wrap the sheets more neatly, but it might just do the trick,' said Freddy.

They spent some few minutes fastening the torch tightly to the dummy and wrapping the sheets around it to fashion it into something more resembling human form, and then they were ready. Freddy picked up the ghost with some difficulty.

'Better make sure the coast is clear,' said Nugs, turning off the light again. He peered out. 'All right,' he whispered.

The odd party stepped out and headed across the passage with much suppressed laughter. Ralph's room was opposite Freddy's, and they stopped to listen at the door. There was no sound.

'Better just one of us,' whispered Goose. 'That'll be quieter. You do it, Freddy, then come back out and we'll make spooky noises until he wakes up.'

'Open the door, then,' said Freddy.

Goose did so, and Freddy crept in as silently as he could. He had to pick his way carefully, for Ralph's room was small and filled with heavy furniture, against which it was easy to bump, while some of the sheets had not been tied tightly enough around the dummy, and were showing signs of wanting to unwrap themselves. He stopped and glanced around, wondering where to situate the 'ghost' for the greatest effectiveness, and decided the foot of the bed would be the best place. He was preparing to set it down carefully when Ralph gave a great snort and turned over in bed. Freddy froze. The sound of regular breathing resumed. Freddy counted to three, then put down the dummy and was about to flee when he realized that the torch had somehow slipped round and was now pointing in the wrong direction. Sighing inwardly, he ducked down and groped under the sheets to right it—then nearly jumped out of his skin as the quiet of the night was rent by a piercing scream. The noise came from somewhere nearby, and gave Freddy such a fright that he straightened up suddenly and got his head and arms tangled up in the sheets. He thrashed, but only succeeded in imprisoning himself further. He staggered, embraced the dummy, twirled around with it in a series of steps that would have impressed any professional dancer, and then he and it fell backwards and landed on the floor with a resounding crash.

'What? What's that?' came Ralph's voice. 'Goose, is that you?'

A lamp was switched on, just as Freddy finally managed to extricate himself from his treacherous creation. He sat up to see Ralph half out of bed and eyeing him in wonder and suspicion.

'Oh, it's you. What the devil do you think you're doing?' said Ralph.

'Who screamed?' said Freddy.

'What are you talking about? And why are you rolling around on the floor with a tailor's dummy?'

Freddy ignored him and dashed out of the room, to find that Goose and Nugs had retreated farther down the passage in fright.

'What was that noise?' he said, just as Ro burst out of her bedroom, looking terrified. She saw Goose, Freddy and Nugs and let out a sharp breath of annoyance.

'Was that you?' she said. 'You scared me half to death, you idiots.'

'What do you mean?' said Freddy. 'Was that you screaming?'

'Yes, and I don't think it's very funny, frightening a person like that.'

'Frightening you?' said Goose. 'I should rather say it was the other way round. I almost died of shock when you screeched. What did you have to make a noise like that for?'

Ro stared.

'Do you mean it wasn't you?' she said.

'Wasn't us what? We were out here playing a perfectly harmless joke on old Ralph and you ruined it.'

'Oh, so that's what you were doing,' said Ralph, who had come out of his room.

A number of other people had also emerged, and were asking what was happening. Cedric was one of them.

'What's all this noise?' he said.

'There was a man in my room,' said Ro. 'He gave me the most awful shock. But it seems it was these three fatheads playing a joke.'

The Duke turned his gaze to Freddy, Goose, and Nugs, whose sheepish expressions at that moment did indeed appear to indicate their guilt.

'Remind me how old you are,' he said to Lord Lucian in a voice heavy with weariness.

'It wasn't—' began Goose, but Cedric was not listening.

'This is all very amusing, I'm sure,' he said, 'but if you must play silly jokes, I'd rather you did it without waking all our guests up.'

At that moment Freddy felt someone clutching his arm. It was Iris. He glanced at her in surprise and she let go quickly just as Daphne came out of her room and spotted them.

'Am I wanted for anything?' said Kitty Fitzsimmons languidly. 'It's frightfully chilly out here. If nobody's bleeding to death then I'll go back to bed, if you don't mind.'

'I, too, shall go to bed,' announced Dr. Bachmann. Mr. Wray, wrapped up warmly in a woollen dressing-gown and looking as though he were not exactly sure where he was, gave a little murmur of agreement and faded away.

'Yes, do,' said Cedric. 'Let's just hope we can all get back to sleep again. Mrs. Philpott—Mrs. Dragusha—ladies, I'm dreadfully sorry about the racket, but there's nothing doing here. Goodnight—goodnight.'

He was ushering everybody back into their rooms as he spoke. Once everybody had been chivvied away or gone of their own accord he glared round at the three conspirators and strode off back to his room in the East Wing. Nugs yawned and announced that he had had quite enough excitement and was now ready for his bed. Freddy and Goose stared at one another, then Goose said:

'Well, I suppose there's no use in standing around here all night. I believe I shall turn in.'

Freddy was about to reply when a door opened and Ro came out of her room again. She looked very cross.

'What have you done with the pearls?' she demanded.

CHAPTER TEN

'WHAT DO YOU mean?' said Freddy.

'Ha ha,' said Ro. 'You can stop pretending now. It isn't funny.'

Freddy and Goose looked at one another.

'We haven't got them, old girl,' said Goose. 'I told you, we didn't come into your room. We were playing a trick on Ralph.'

She stared.

'Then who was it I saw?' she said.

'I've no idea. Are you sure you didn't dream it?'

'Of course not! There was someone there, I'm certain of it. And now the pearls are gone. They were on my dressing-table and now they're not. Come and see.'

They followed her into her room. The dressing-table was scattered with odds and ends, but there were no pearls.

'They were just here,' said Ro. 'I know they were. I took them off before I went to bed.'

'Have they fallen on the floor?' said Freddy, peering underneath the table. 'No, nothing there.'

They hunted about for a few minutes, but there was no sign of the pearls.

'You're not teasing me, are you?' said Ro. 'I mean, you would tell me if you had them, wouldn't you? This isn't funny any more.'

'I swear we don't have them,' said Goose, and Freddy nodded in agreement.

'Then they've gone!' said Ro. She gasped and sat down suddenly, white-faced, as the enormity of the situation hit her at last. 'What am I to do?'

'Oh, Ro, why didn't you lock them away as you were supposed to?' said Goose reproachfully.

'I forgot,' she said, stricken. 'I meant to do it, truly I did, but it was late and I didn't remember until I was just drifting off to sleep, and I thought it wouldn't matter if it waited until morning. Then I woke up just now and saw someone creeping around my room. I screamed and he ran off, and I came out into the corridor and found you there, so I assumed it was you being an ass, as usual.'

'It wasn't,' said Goose. 'But then who was it in your room?'

'I don't know, it was too dark. Didn't you see him when he came out?'

'Nobody came out,' said Goose. 'Nugs and I were in the corridor the whole time. There was nobody else.'

'Then how did he get out of here?' said Ro.

'Through the secret passage, presumably,' said Freddy.

'What? In the dark, at this time of night?' said Goose. 'Why on earth should anybody do that?'

'How much are those pearls worth?' said Freddy.

'Hmm, I see your point,' conceded Goose.

'But this is simply awful!' cried Ro. 'What am I to do?'
She burst into tears.

'We shall just have to catch him, that's all,' said Freddy. There
was a pause as he stared hard at Goose, who looked as though
he did not relish creeping through a cold, dark passage in the
middle of the night.

'Er—yes, of course,' said Goose. 'We'll find him, Ro. I'll go
and fetch the torch.'

'Oh, please find him, and quickly!' said Ro. 'I'm going to be
in the most awful trouble if you don't.'

The torch was retrieved from Ralph's room (much to his
annoyance, for he had been on the point of drifting off to
sleep again when Goose barged in), then Ro pushed open the
secret door behind the tapestry to reveal the dark entrance to
the passage.

'Here goes,' said Goose in some trepidation, and he and
Freddy stepped inside. It took a minute or two to get used to
the dim torchlight, but eventually their steps became firmer
and they headed forward and then turned left. The way seemed
longer than it had that afternoon, and the air colder.

'Damn you, Freddy,' puffed Goose, as they went along. 'Why
did you have to tell her we'd do this? She's probably left the
pearls in the lav. or something, and we'll find them still there
safe and sound tomorrow morning.'

'I only hope you're right,' said Freddy.

'I mean to say, even if there was a burglar, he'll be long gone.
He's hardly likely to hang around here, is he? Why, I expect
he's miles away by now.'

'I doubt that very much,' said Freddy.

'What do you mean?'

'How did the burglar know about the pearls? And more importantly, how did he know about the secret passage?'

'Why, the story of the pearls has been in all the papers. And I should think half the county knows about the secret passage. It's not really secret, you know. As a matter of fact, it's quite famous.'

'Yes, but the papers have been talking about the ball at the Savoy,' said Freddy. 'All the stories I've read have implied that Ro will be wearing the pearls for the first time then. But who knew she'd be wearing them tonight?'

'Oh, I see what you mean,' said Goose, disconcerted. 'Well, naturally the whole house knew about it.'

'Including the servants?'

'I expect so. We're a talkative sort of family. But don't think for a moment any of them did it, as they're all perfectly honest.'

'Well, we'll see,' said Freddy.

'I say, you don't think whoever took the pearls might still be in the passage, do you?'

'I don't know. Perhaps.'

Goose stopped so suddenly that Freddy bumped into him.

'Perhaps we ought to have brought a weapon, in that case,' he said.

'Too late for that now,' said Freddy, who had just been thinking the same thing. 'Get on.'

They picked their way down the winding steps and turned on to the last straight. The darkness here was less dense, and

Freddy knew they must be coming to the door that led out into the library.

'He's left it open,' said Goose. 'Then he must have come this way after all.' He stepped out into the library and let out a sudden cry. 'Oh, Lord! Freddy! Look!'

By the urgency of his tone Freddy could tell that something was very wrong. He emerged from the passage and looked towards where Goose was pointing. The library was lit only by the moon which shone in from outside, and for a moment all Freddy could see in the pale glow was a pile of old clothes strewn across the floor. For one absurd moment he thought that somebody must have brought the tailor's dummy down here, but then the image rearranged itself in his head and he realized that the untidy heap of linen before him was nothing of the sort, but was a human being—or what was left of one.

'Why, it's Professor Coddington!' he exclaimed.

CHAPTER ELEVEN

THE PROFESSOR HAD fallen untidily, and was lying face-down, with one arm stretched out and touching a heavy desk that stood between him and the door. They stared at the sight.

'He must have been killed as he came out of the passage,' said Goose at last.

'It looks like it,' said Freddy. 'But what's this?'

They approached the body tentatively and shone the torch on it. In the professor's outstretched hand was something familiar, which glistened in the torchlight.

'It's the pearls!' exclaimed Goose. 'But what does it all mean?'

'I haven't the faintest idea,' said Freddy. 'Go and switch the light on, will you?'

Goose did so, and Freddy bent to examine the unfortunate Professor Coddington. He was wearing his night-things, and was wrapped in a dressing-gown. One of his slippers had come off as he fell, and was lying next to his right knee. Freddy looked along the body to the head, which bore an unpleasant dent, out of which something dark and sticky was oozing. Beside him, Goose jerked and made an involuntary sound of disgust.

'Brained!' he said. 'I suppose he's really dead?'

Freddy reached out gingerly and took the professor's wrist. 'Yes,' he said.

'But how did it happen? If he took the pearls then how did he die? Did he fall and hit his head, do you think?'

'Perhaps,' said Freddy doubtfully. He stepped towards the desk and examined the edges of it carefully. 'I don't think so, though. He certainly didn't fall against this, and what else could he have hit?' He looked around but could see nothing else which might have caused the injury. 'I can't see a sign of blood anywhere except his head. And besides, look at the way he's lying, face-down. If his feet had slipped from under him then one would expect him to be lying on his back, don't you think?'

'But he might have tripped over and fallen forwards, surely?'

'In that case, he'd have hit the front of his head, not the back.'

'Oh yes, of course. But if somebody did kill him, then who was it?'

'I don't know,' said Freddy. 'Look here, you'd better go and fetch your father.'

'All right,' said Goose, and bent to remove the pearls from the professor's hand.

'Leave them,' said Freddy. 'We oughtn't to move anything until the police arrive.'

'I don't care,' said Goose obstinately. 'I'm not leaving those pearls here for someone to come and take them again.'

He put the necklace in his pocket, then went to rouse the Duke again. Freddy was now quite alone in the library. He looked around. What had happened here? It was clear that Coddington's death had not been an accident, but in that case why did the professor have the pearls? Had he snatched them from the thief and been killed for his pains? But then, why had the thief not taken the necklace back before he escaped? It was all most perplexing.

It was eerily silent in the library, and it now struck Freddy that he was all alone with a murdered man. Who knew where the murderer was now? Perhaps he was lurking somewhere in that very room, in one of the alcoves, planning another desperate move. Freddy swallowed and looked around for something heavy. There were plenty of large books, but a book was not much use as a weapon. His eye fell on a table-lamp with a bronze base, and he went to pick it up, but it was much too unwieldy to be effective. Then he remembered the broken window. A sash weight would be the very thing. He went across to it, then stopped dead. On the sill lay three new sash weights, waiting to be installed in the window, but he was almost certain that there had been four earlier that afternoon, when all the guests had been in the library. He whistled quietly and took a closer look at the weights. They were clean and untouched. He picked one up. It must have weighed a good five pounds, and the lead felt cool and comforting in his hand. Cautiously, he moved around the library, peering around bookshelves and into alcoves, then started as he thought he heard something. Was that a creak overhead on the balcony? He moved back into the centre of the room and looked upwards, but could see nothing. The rail around the mezzanine floor was solid in places, where shelves had been built in. Perhaps somebody was hiding behind them. Freddy took a deep breath, then, shifting the weight to his other hand, cautiously climbed the stairs. Much to his relief, nobody was waiting at the top for him, and he traversed the entire length of the balcony, but it took only a few moments to see that there was no-one up here. He descended the stairs and went out into the hall. The big front doors were locked for the night, but there were any number of exits the assailant might have used. Freddy went into the small salon and tested the French windows. They were locked, too. He looked in one or two other rooms, but could find no sign that anybody had left the house.

He went back into the hall, and was just in time to see Goose hurrying down the stairs, followed by his father. Cedric's face wore an expression that was a mixture of irritation and resignation at having been woken up for the second time that night.

'What's all this nonsense?' he demanded. 'Goose is telling me some cock-and-bull story about a dead body. This had better not be another joke.'

'It's not! Tell him, Freddy,' said Goose.

'It's true enough,' said Freddy. 'Come and see.'

They went into the library. Cedric stood over the mortal remains of Professor Coddington and regarded him with disfavour.

'Damn the fellow!' he exclaimed at last. 'I knew it was a mistake to invite him. Now look what's happened. I expect we shall never hear the end of it.'

He spoke as though the professor had done this deliberately to annoy him.

'Shall I call the police?' said Goose.

The Duke yawned.

'Can't it wait until morning?' he said. 'He's dead, and a few more hours won't make him any deader. The Chief Constable rubs me the wrong way at the best of times, and I've had hardly any sleep. Another couple of hours and I might be able to face him without being rude.'

'But the murderer might still be in the house,' Freddy pointed out.

'Do you think so?' said Cedric in surprise, then sighed. 'Oh, very well, then. I suppose one can't just leave the fellow lying there cluttering up the place forever.'

He strode into the hall, where there was a telephone just outside the library door, and began barking into the receiver.

'He's coming as quickly as he can,' he said when he came back in. 'Wasn't too pleased to be woken up, I can tell you! He says we must keep everybody out of the library until the police get here.'

At that moment the door opened and Bea and Ro entered. Ro was wearing the pearls over her dressing-gown and was fidgeting with them, as though determined not to lose them again.

'I thought I told you to stay upstairs,' said Cedric. 'We can't have everyone milling about the place, trampling all the clues into the carpet.'

'No, but is it really true?' said Bea breathlessly. 'You were joking, weren't you, Goose?'

'Afraid not,' said Goose. 'He's here all right.'

'For God's sake don't go and gawp at him,' said Cedric testily, as his wife made a move towards the body. 'At least, not if you want to hold your breakfast down.'

'Is it that bad?' said Bea. 'Oh, poor Professor Coddington! And none of us liked him. It's all very unfortunate.'

'Ought we to get everybody up?' said Ro. 'If I went to stay at someone's house, I should like to be informed of any escaped lunatics running around the place. It's only polite.'

'You don't think he's going to do it again, do you?' said Cedric. 'I should have thought one murder a day was enough for anybody, however insane. And anyway, can we be absolutely certain there *is* a murderer at large? I shouldn't be a bit surprised to find out that Coddington fell over and hit his head while he was running off with the pearls.'

'But why *did* he have the pearls?' said Bea. 'I know he wasn't the pleasantest of people, but he didn't seem the type to steal. And a professor, too!'

'I don't know,' said Cedric. 'Perhaps he saw them close to and lost his head over them—had some kind of brain-storm, and decided he couldn't live without them. Who knows what goes on in people's minds?'

Freddy wandered over to the desk and stood, gazing down at the professor's body.

'I thought you said we'd better leave him alone,' said Goose.

'I've just had an idea,' said Freddy.

He crouched down next to the prone figure, averting his eyes from the unpleasant mess of Professor Coddington's head. The professor's dressing-gown had pockets in it. Freddy wriggled his hand into one of them and felt something hard and round. He brought it out. It was an eye-glass, of the sort used by jewellers. He regarded it thoughtfully then replaced it.

'I don't think he was stealing the pearls at all,' he said as he stood up. 'I think he just took them to have a closer look at them.'

'What on earth for?' said Bea.

'Don't you remember how interested he was in them at dinner? He said if he'd had his eye-glass with him he'd have examined them more closely. I think he took them to do just that, with every intention of putting them back.'

'But if he wanted to examine them, then why didn't he just ask? Why all this sneaking around in the dark?' said Cedric, perplexed.

'And if he just wanted to look at them, then why was he murdered, and who did it?' said Ro. 'Are you sure he didn't fall and hit his head?'

This question was to Freddy.

'It's possible, I suppose,' he replied. 'The police doctor will be able to tell us more, but if you ask me it looks like a deliberate blow. Besides, I was looking for a weapon earlier and discovered that one of these is missing.'

He picked up the sash weight, which he had put on the table next to him. Cedric stared.

'Good God!' he said in astonishment, and went across to the window. 'So it is. Do you mean to say someone whacked him over the head with the missing one?'

'It's easily heavy enough,' said Freddy. 'One smart tap would have been quite enough to crush his skull.'

'But where is it?'

'I don't know, but presumably somebody is wandering around the house with it now—unless they've already escaped, of course. I had a look in a few rooms, but none of the outside doors was unlocked.'

'He might have got out anywhere,' said Bea. 'What time is it? Nearly a quarter past four. The servants will be getting up soon and going in and out of doors. We shall have to ask them whether any of them were left open.'

'Go and get Spenlow up,' said the Duke to Goose. 'I don't see why he should be allowed to loll about in bed while we all run around wearing ourselves out. He can let the police in when they arrive.'

Goose departed to rouse the unfortunate butler, and the others waited. Freddy was sitting in an armchair, and found himself sinking into a doze. It had been a long night, and it looked as though there would be no staying in bed until eleven, as he would normally have done—not with a possible murderer on the loose, anyhow.

CHAPTER TWELVE

THE POLICE ARRIVED, consisting of three or four serious men and Sir Henry Rollison, the Chief Constable. He shook hands with the Duke and they went into the study. Meanwhile, an efficient inspector informed himself of the salient facts of the matter, then politely ejected them all from the library and asked the Duchess to keep the servants away. Day was beginning to break, and the shadows had become less fearsome, and so Freddy decided to take a little walk around the house to look for signs that whoever had murdered Professor Coddington had made his escape—although he did not hold out much hope of finding any, for it seemed perfectly obvious to him that the murderer was still somewhere in the house. Why would an intruder have been wandering around the library at night? Surely his first thought on entering the house would have been to rifle through drawers and cupboards, seeking valuables? And if there *had* been an intruder, then why had he not taken the pearls after attacking the professor? Freddy could make no sense of it. There was more to this than met the eye, he was sure of it.

At last he had tried all the doors he could think of and found them all locked, so he went back upstairs, washed and dressed, then came downstairs again. By this time the servants were up and Freddy was able to make a rudimentary breakfast. Goose was with his father, while Bea had disappeared somewhere and Ro had returned to bed, so Freddy was left to pass the time as best he could until the other guests rose.

By half past nine most people were up and had been drawn downstairs by the activity. The news had spread fast—for it was not to be supposed that the servants would keep such extraordinary happenings to themselves—and several of the guests gathered in the breakfast-room, eager to hear what had occurred. Having eaten so early Freddy was hungry again and had come in for seconds, and he found himself assailed on all sides by questions and exclamations.

'Why didn't you come and fetch me?' said an indignant Nugs. 'I missed all the fun.'

He was still grumbling when Cynthia came in and said crossly:

'Isn't that police inspector simply the limit? I went to the library to find out what was happening—wholly natural curiosity, I must say—and the constable at the door wouldn't let me in. Well, of course that was quite ridiculous, but he obviously wasn't going to give way so I told him Sir Henry wanted to speak to him in the study. He went off and I went into the library, but I couldn't see anything because the inspector spotted me immediately and asked what I thought I was doing there.'

I said I was one of the family and had a right to see what was going on, but he was obstinate, quite obstinate. Even when I told him I was a top reporter at the *Clarion* and asked whether he wanted to see the bad manners of the Dorset police all over the front page he didn't seem impressed, and chivvied me out of the room most impolitely. I shall have to have a word with Sir Henry later.'

'It is a pity you were treated so, but it is a difficult job they do there,' said Dr. Bachmann courteously. 'I believe we will be better off leaving them to their work.'

'Yes, but really—' began Cynthia, just as the Duchess came in. 'Oh, Bea, darling! What a thing to happen!'

Bea was looking strained.

'Yes, it is rather dreadful,' she said. 'Poor Professor Coddington!'

'Do they have any idea of what happened?' said Lavinia Philpott. 'Such a *polite* man. Who could have wanted to kill him?'

There was no answering that truthfully, so Bea contented herself with making a gesture expressive of puzzlement and dismay. She could not stop long, she said, but had merely come in to make sure that all her guests were suitably provided for. She went out just as Ralph came in, followed silently by Mrs. Dragusha. Ralph helped himself to breakfast, then sat down next to Iris, who had been sitting tearing a slice of cold toast into shreds.

'Jolly comfortable beds here,' he remarked. 'I slept like a top, despite all the interruptions. Funny how these stories get twisted, isn't it? One of the servants has just told me the most ridiculous story about a dead body. I told her not to worry herself, as it was just a silly joke, and sent her on her way. These girls are so easily thrown into a fright over nothing.'

'It's not a joke,' said Iris.

'My dear girl, I saw it with my own eyes,' said Ralph. 'I should think I know the difference between a dead body and a tailor's dummy. And I caught Freddy in the act—so you see, there's no doubt at all.'

'What are you talking about?' said Iris.

'Oh, Freddy thought it would be funny to try and scare me with a silly ghost rig-up that wouldn't have fooled a child,' said Ralph, in a maddeningly superior tone.

'It wasn't just me,' said Freddy, as Iris gave him an odd look.

'I don't know about that,' said Ralph. 'At any rate, I caught him in the act, but it seems as though the servants have somehow turned the story around and got it into their heads that there's a dead body lying about somewhere.'

'There is,' said Freddy. 'Somebody has killed Professor Coddington.'

It took some minutes to explain this to Ralph's satisfaction, and he stared.

'Good gracious!' he said, then adopted his most pompous manner. 'I hope this will be a lesson to you in future, Freddy. You're far too old to be playing silly jokes these days.'

'What's the joke got to do with anything?' said Freddy testily. 'How were we supposed to know that old Coddington was going to take it into his head to go sneaking around in the secret passage and run off with the pearls?'

At that there were several exclamations of astonishment around the table, for not all had heard this part of the story.

'Run off with the *pearls*?' said Cynthia, her eyes gleaming with excitement. 'Surely not! Do you mean to say the professor was a thief?'

'We don't know yet,' said Freddy. 'All we know is that he had the necklace in his hand when we found him.'

'Well!' breathed Cynthia.

'But why?' said Lavinia.

'Perhaps he wasn't a professor at all, but an impostor,' suggested Daphne.

Dr. Bachmann shook his head.

'No, no, no, this cannot be,' he said. 'I knew Professor Coddington very slightly, and this was the same man. It could not be a mistake.'

'I had no idea that academics were paid so little,' said Ralph.

'Oh dear,' said the quiet Mr. Wray. 'This is all very upsetting. It is not pleasant to discover that an acquaintance was not a good person, but I believe this may have been the case here. We must all pray for his soul.'

His words reminded Freddy suddenly of the conversation he had had with the clergyman the evening before. It seemed that someone, at least, had sensed the disaster that was about to befall them. Freddy wondered whether Mr. Wray had foreseen more of the event than he had told, and resolved to have a quiet word with him later.

Mrs. Dragusha looked aghast. She was wringing her hands.

'But this is terrible,' she muttered to herself. 'It is all my fault.'

'What do you mean, Mrs. Dragusha?' said Daphne. 'How could it have been your fault?'

Mrs. Dragusha glanced at her and came to herself.

'I have been very unwise,' she said. 'But I had not the first idea that he would—' She shook herself. 'I must go and speak to his Grace.'

And with that she stood up and hurried out.

'What did she mean?' said Daphne, looking after her in puzzlement, but nobody was listening, for they were all too busy speculating wildly about what might have happened the night before. Some said that the professor must have hoped to escape to London and sell the pearls there, while others thought he must have caught a thief in the act and died while retrieving the necklace. Lavinia declared she was certain that he must have been walking in his sleep and taken the pearls accidentally, then fallen and hit his head, but this idea was roundly pooh-poohed as being absurdly far-fetched. At that Lavinia bridled and said it was no more far-fetched than the idea that he had been murdered, for who could possibly have wanted to kill the poor man? Here she put a handkerchief to her eyes and began to sniff.

Freddy decided to leave them to it, and went out of the room. Iris followed him.

'Was all that true?' she said out in the hall. 'Were you really playing a joke on Ralph?'

'Yes,' said Freddy resignedly.

'But why?'

Freddy shrugged.

'Because it was three o'clock in the morning and there was nothing else to do.'

'Oh,' she said. She twisted a bangle around her wrist. 'I thought it might be because—'

'Because what?'

'Nothing. Ridiculous of you, though.'

'I suppose so,' said Freddy.

She looked as though she wanted to say something, but thought better of it.

'Well, don't do it again,' she said at last.

They were still standing together when Daphne came out of the breakfast-room. Iris turned on her heel and walked away.

'It seems I missed all the fun last night,' said Daphne. 'What did *she* want, by the way?'

'Nothing,' said Freddy as he watched Iris depart.

'She's the sort who likes to hedge her bets, you know,' said Daphne. 'You'd better watch out.'

'What?'

'Never mind. Come out for a walk and tell me what happened last night. The place is crawling with police and Lavinia's being even more insufferable than usual.'

They went out and wandered around the garden. The sun was out and there was a breeze, and it looked as though it would be a pleasant day. Daphne listened in astonishment as Freddy recounted the events of the night before.

'It's almost too much to believe,' she said. 'Do you think he died accidentally?'

'No.'

'Then somebody killed him. But in that case why didn't they take the pearls?'

'*That* is very much the question,' said Freddy.

'You say there was an eye-glass in the professor's pocket, and he did mention that he wanted to look at the pearls more closely—although I don't know why he didn't just ask.'

'I suspect he thought they were fake,' said Freddy.

'Really? But why?'

'Didn't you hear him at dinner? He said something of the kind then. I wonder whether he didn't suspect that the real ones had been pawned secretly. He was pontificating about aristocratic families and their secrets yesterday afternoon, and I shouldn't be surprised if he believed he was about to unearth yet another scandal. He probably thought he wouldn't be allowed to examine the pearls closely, and wanted to get all the *kudos* for exposing the necklace as a forgery, so he decided to take them without bothering to ask permission.'

'But the pearls aren't fake, are they?'

'I doubt it,' said Freddy. 'Cedric isn't short of money as far as I know.'

Daphne was thinking.

'The professor did seem the type to do that sort of thing, didn't he? He liked to find out secrets. I overheard him talking to Mr. Wray about something or other. What was it, now? Something about somebody's not having a legitimate claim to the dukedom.'

'Oh, the fourth Duke, you mean? That's an old story,' said Freddy.

'I don't know. It was something to do with John Wareham, I think.'

'That sounds like it. I'm a little hazy on all the facts, but he was the black sheep of the family—you know, the one who ran off to India and brought back the Belsingham pearls. I believe he spent some years plaguing the family with claims that he ought to be Duke rather than his elder brother, although I'm fairly sure nobody took him seriously.'

'Perhaps Professor Coddington thought he'd found out some new information that would have proved him right,' said Daphne.

'That would certainly set the cat among the pigeons. I wonder if that was it, then. I shall ask Mr. Wray,' said Freddy. 'Which reminds me—the old fellow said something very odd to me last night. He seemed to think he could sense danger approaching, or something of the sort. He has a gift for that kind of thing, apparently.'

'Really?' said Daphne. 'How very strange! Visions, do you mean?'

'That's what it sounded like, although he couldn't be any more specific than that. But he was convinced that something terrible was going to happen, and he was rather cut up that he couldn't do anything to stop it.'

'But it's hardly his fault, is it? I mean, he could hardly be expected to predict something like this. None of us could.'

'Well, quite. I'll bet he's kicking himself this morning, though, for not having prevented it.'

They heard someone hailing them, and saw Goose and Ro approaching them from the house.

'I wondered where you'd got to,' said Goose, giving Daphne an appreciative glance as he arrived.

'Are the police still here?' said Freddy.

'Yes,' said Ro. 'They're tramping around my bedroom and fossicking about in the secret passage.'

'It's all jolly queer, don't you think?' said Freddy.

'Of course it's queer,' said Ro. 'You don't think we have a murder every week, do you?'

'I didn't mean that. I was talking about the murder itself, and how it happened. It looks as though the professor was hit from behind just after he came out of the passage, but what was the killer doing in the library at the time? And was he waiting for Coddington to come out so he could kill him, or was he there for quite a different purpose? Have they found any sign that the murderer came from outside, by the way?'

'No,' replied Goose. 'I'm afraid it rather looks as though it was someone in the house.'

'I can hardly believe it!' said Daphne. 'One of us, you mean. Unless it was a servant.'

'I don't see which of *them* it could have been,' said Goose. 'Most of them have been with us for years.'

'Who was up last night?' said Freddy. 'Can we rule anybody out?'

'Let's see, now, what happened?' said Goose. 'Ro howled, then we all came out, then everybody went away again, and then Ro came out again five minutes later and said the pearls were missing. So obviously it couldn't have been you or I, Freddy. We were standing around in the corridor all the while, and can give each other an alibi. I suppose when Ro went back into her room after waking the whole house up, she might have chased him through the passage and brained him, then come back and raised the alarm about the pearls being missing.'

'Ass,' said Ro. 'Of course I didn't.'

'How long had he been dead when we found him?' said Freddy. 'It can't have been more than a few minutes, surely. Let's look at what happened. What time did you scream, Ro?'

'How d'you expect me to remember that?'

'I think it was about ten past three,' said Goose. 'We were outside Ralph's door at the time, and I remember I looked at my watch just before that, and it was just before ten past.'

'Very well, that's probably near enough,' said Freddy. 'Anyway, when Ro yelled I assume the professor realized he'd been rumbled and hot-footed it back into the passage. Then everybody came out of their rooms and went back in again when they found out there was nothing doing. Let's say everybody had gone back to bed by twenty past three. Then Ro came out a minute or two after that, and we spent five minutes hunting around for the pearls. We must have gone into the passage at about half past three and found the professor at twenty to four. Allowing ten minutes for Coddington to stumble back through the passage after Ro woke up and caught him, he must have died at about twenty past three, or certainly not much after. That leaves the murderer twenty minutes to make good his escape.'

'But it also means it can't have been any of the people who came out of their rooms,' said Ro. 'If the professor died at twenty past three, then most of them were still out in the corridor with us at that time.'

'Who came out?' said Freddy. 'We ought to make a list.'

'I can't remember,' said Goose. 'Does it matter?'

'Yes, because anyone who showed himself after Ro screamed can't have killed the professor, don't you see? Between ten past and twenty past three most of the guests were out of their rooms, asking what the devil was happening. But since we know Coddington must have died at twenty past, then none of those people can be the murderer.'

'I see what you mean,' said Goose. 'Let's think, then. We three, of course. Nugs and Ralph. You came out too, didn't you, Daphne?'

'Yes,' said Daphne. 'I didn't hear the scream, but I heard a racket outside my room so came out to see what was happening. Iris was up, I remember.' Here she glared briefly at Freddy. 'Mrs. Fitzsimmons came out, and Mr. Wray, I think. And the Duke.'

'What about Mrs. Philpott?' said Ro.

'She got up, too,' said Daphne. 'And so did Mrs. Dragusha. The Duke practically pushed them both back into their rooms afterwards.'

'So our society dressmaker wasn't scampering gaily about the place with a lead cudgel either,' said Freddy. 'Now, is that all? Wasn't there someone else? Ah—I remember: Dr. Bachmann was up too, wasn't he? I think that's everybody. Who's left without an alibi, then? Bea and my mother. They both sleep in the East Wing, so they have a perfectly good excuse for having stayed in bed. Not that I'm so partial as to believe my mother is incapable of murder, but even she's not the sort to go around whacking people on the skull without at least the glimmerings of a motive. And the same goes for your mother, I imagine.'

'Might someone have run downstairs afterwards?' suggested Ro. 'After they'd all supposedly gone back to their rooms, I mean. There might just have been time to get to the library and kill him that way.'

'I don't think so, because Goose and I stayed out on the landing,' said Freddy. 'We'd have seen them.'

'Not necessarily,' said Goose. 'What about the people who went back to the East Wing? Nugs was suspiciously keen to get back to bed, for one.'

'Don't tell me that old dodderer did it,' said Freddy. 'He couldn't possibly move fast enough.'

'I don't know—I've seen him get up quite a turn of speed when the dinner-bell rings,' said Goose.

'But why would he want to kill Coddington?'

'Well you must admit he was annoying,' said Goose. 'I'm sure we'd all have happily given him a tap on the noodle given enough provocation. I know I would.'

'Dr. Bachmann went back to the East Wing too,' said Ro, then had a sudden thought. 'What was he doing in the West Wing, anyway? He couldn't possibly have heard the scream from his bedroom.'

Nor could Cedric, thought Freddy, but said nothing, as it seemed obvious enough to him why the Duke had been wandering around in the wrong part of the house.

'Oh, by the way, Freddy, I forgot to say the police want to see you,' said Goose. 'I expect they want to question you and make sure our stories agree. See what you can find out from them,' he added, as Freddy prepared to depart.

'I shall,' said Freddy.

Chapter Thirteen

IN THE HALL Cynthia had button-holed Sir Henry Rollison, the Chief Constable, and was talking to him very fast of her theory that Professor Coddington had been killed by a gang of cut-throat thieves, and that they had all by the merest stroke of luck escaped being murdered in their beds.

'But it's true,' she was saying. 'I could give you a list of notorious criminals who are currently at large in London. They will stop at nothing, Sir Henry, nothing! Why, there is one in particular—nothing less than a desperado, I should call him—who did *something* in London—I forget what, exactly, but I'm sure it was quite dreadful. My son will be able to tell you his name—he works for the *Clarion* too, you know—one of their most valuable reporters. I dare say you've read his work—although on second thoughts, perhaps you haven't, since I don't suppose you get the London papers down here, do you? There you are, darling,' she said, without pausing for breath, as Freddy came in. 'Freddy, tell Sir Henry about that horrid man you were writing about last week, and convince him that he must have murdered the professor.'

Sir Henry was wearing a slightly hunted look, and Freddy thought he could see a sign of appeal in his eyes.

'If you're talking about Bert Dymchurch and his gang, then there's nothing doing,' he said. 'They were all found guilty and sentenced to ten years apiece.'

'Oh,' said Cynthia. 'Well, then, if he didn't do it, it must have been one of the other ones. Goodness knows, there are plenty of wicked people in the world. Now, Sir Henry—'

'You are Mr. Pilkington-Soames, yes?' said Sir Henry, not quite interrupting. 'I hear you and Lord Holme found Professor Coddington's body.'

'That's right,' said Freddy.

'Then you're the very man I should like to speak to. You won't mind answering a few questions, will you? Come and meet Inspector Trubshaw. I beg your pardon, madam.'

He led Freddy firmly into the study and introduced him to the efficient inspector who had ejected them all from the library earlier that morning. Inspector Trubshaw gave Freddy an appraising glance and asked him abruptly to sit down.

'I'd better go and speak to the Duchess,' said Sir Henry, whereupon, having escaped neatly from Cynthia, he departed through another door.

'Hallo, hallo, this is a to-do, what?' said Freddy. 'I dare say it ruined your breakfast when the news came in—I know it certainly ruined mine. Sorry for interrupting your Saturday, and all that.'

'I take it the professor wasn't a friend of yours,' said Trubshaw.

'Your deduction is correct, inspector. No, I'd never met him before yesterday. I don't think anybody had, as a matter of fact. I understand he was rather foisted upon the family.'

Trubshaw consulted his notes.

'You are a cousin of the Duke, I believe,' he said.

'Yes—well, my mother is, at any rate. I'm once removed, I think they call it—not that they've ever managed to remove me, although I'm sure they'd like nothing better at times. By the way, I ought to warn you before we start that I'm by way of being a reporter. I work for the *Clarion*, up in London, so anything you tell me is likely to end up in print, unless you put an embargo on it.'

'Is that so, sir?' said Trubshaw. Freddy noted the hesitation before the word 'sir.'

'Just a little friendly warning,' he continued. 'Some of my fellow press-men wouldn't have mentioned it at all, and then you'd have had the pleasure of seeing your own fatuous words in print the very next day, haunting you for the rest of your life—not that I suppose you say anything fatuous as a rule, but anybody can have an off-day.'

'Quite,' said Trubshaw dryly.

'I shouldn't have said anything myself at one time—in my earliest days, when I was naught but a boy, wide-eyed and wet behind the ears. But one or two mishaps soon taught me the proper practice.'

'I'm glad to hear it,' said the inspector. 'In that case, I'd be obliged if you'd keep things to yourself for the present—or at least, just report the main facts of the case. It's all bound to get into the papers sooner or later, but we don't want to give too much away at the moment.'

'Oh, not at all,' said Freddy. 'In any case, I expect old Cedric won't be too pleased to have the place over-run with reporters, which will happen once the news gets out. He only puts up with me on sufferance, but to have the whole boiling of them descending upon Belsingham will send him quite over the edge, I imagine.'

'Now then,' said Trubshaw, 'I have already spoken to Lord Holme, who has told me his version of events. I gather from him that you, he, and Lord Lucian Wareham were up late last night—er—' he looked at his notebook again '—*playing a joke* on Mr. Uttridge.'

'Ah, yes,' said Freddy. 'It all seems in rather bad taste now, given what happened, but I assure you that nothing disrespectful was intended by it—except to old Ralph, of course. But as it happens, I do believe we might have done you a good turn, since we appear to have given most of the house an alibi.'

'Oh?' said Trubshaw with sudden interest.

'Yes,' said Freddy, and explained his deductions.

'Hmm,' said the inspector thoughtfully. 'That is certainly very helpful. From what we know so far it seems that Professor Coddington was killed just as he came out of the secret passage and into the library, but if your story is correct, then at that same time you, Lord Holme, Lord Lucian, Lady Rose, the Duke, Mr. Uttridge, Miss Bagshawe, Miss Garthwaite, Mrs. Fitzsimmons, Mrs. Dragusha, Mrs. Philpott, Mr. Wray and Dr. Bachmann were all on the landing outside her ladyship's room.'

'Yes,' said Freddy, as the inspector made a note. 'You'll have noticed that the only people who are let out are the Duchess and my mother. Of course, I naturally incline to the view that nobody in my family had anything to do with it, but in any case neither of them, as far as I am aware, had any connection to the professor or any desire to do him harm.'

'What about these pearls?' said Trubshaw. 'I understand they had gone missing, and you found them clutched in Professor Coddington's hand.'

'That's quite right. I told Goose—Lord Holme, that is—not to touch them, but he was determined to put them away safely, and I can't say I blame him. They're worth a fabulous sum, you know, and oughtn't to be left lying around. But that was the only thing we disturbed, I promise you,' he said, forgetting for a minute that he had also searched the professor's pockets. 'Goose went off to put the pearls away and I stayed with the professor until the Duke came down and called the police.'

'Did you see anybody while you were there?'

Freddy shook his head.

'Not a soul. I don't mind telling you I got into rather a funk for a minute or two, though, thinking that the murderer might be lurking somewhere in the library, so I picked up a handy weapon to protect myself with should it prove necessary.'

'The sash weight,' said Inspector Trubshaw. 'Yes, we found it on a table. Did you take only one?'

'Ah, you spotted that, did you? Yes, just the one.'

'We found two others on the window-sill. According to her Grace, there ought to be four.'

'It seems obvious enough what the fourth one was used for,' said Freddy. 'I don't suppose you've found any sign of it?'

'Not so far,' said Trubshaw.

'Pity,' said Freddy. 'This is a big house and it would be an easy enough thing to hide. That's if it is in the house at all. I take it there's no possibility that the murderer took himself off across the fields?'

'Not that we can see,' said the inspector cautiously. 'None of the doors was found open this morning.'

'An inside job, perhaps? Might one of the servants have passed a key to the murderer to let himself in and out with?'

'We are pursuing inquiries of that nature among the servants,' said Trubshaw.

'Of course, the real sticking point is the pearls,' said Freddy. 'Under any other circumstances it would look as though he'd been killed for them, but since they weren't taken that can't be the motive. I take it you've realized that Professor Coddington only took the pearls to have a closer look at them?'

'His Grace was of that opinion, yes,' conceded the inspector. 'It seems a strange way of going about things.'

'Yes, but Coddington was like that. Awfully full of his own self-importance, you see. I think he was on some kind of crusade to expose wrongdoing wherever he detected it, and he had a particular bee in his bonnet about aristocratic families misbehaving. Naturally, in a family such as this one, which has a history going back centuries, there are bound to be all sorts of dirty secrets tucked away in drawers and behind the panelling, but it seemed he'd fastened upon the Belsingham pearls. He kept on talking about how many people had been killed for them.'

'Killed?' said the inspector, startled.

'Oh, it was a long time ago, back in India,' said Freddy cheerfully. 'One of my ancestors slaughtered a thousand people and did a spirited breast-stroke through a lake of blood with a dagger between his teeth in order to steal the pearls, or something of the sort. All pretty ghastly, but not exactly something one can blame old Cedric for. But it seemed the professor disagreed, to judge by the number of times he mentioned it.'

'I see,' said Inspector Trubshaw. He looked as though he did not know quite what to make of Freddy.

'To be perfectly frank, he was a bit of a blister,' went on Freddy. 'You know—the sort of guest who turns up to a party and makes everybody feel uncomfortable. I had an aunt like that, once. We'd all be skipping merrily around in a country dance, and she'd stand at the side watching, then take advantage of a pause in the conversation to inform us airily that we were dancing on the site of an ancient plague-pit and mass burial ground, and that the spirits of the dead had woken up and were dancing with us, invisible to the eye. It tended to put a damper on things. Still, Professor Coddington was unknown to nearly all of us before he came, and irritating as he was I'm sure most people would have preferred to avoid him rather than kill him outright.'

'Well somebody killed him,' said Trubshaw. 'And we must find out who.'

'I say,' said Freddy. 'I've done a little of this sort of thing in London—detecting, I mean. I dare say you remember the

Dorothy Dacres case—I was in on that from the start, helping Scotland Yard, and they were good enough to acknowledge that I gave them some invaluable assistance. They're quite used to my buzzing around them these days, so what about it? If the Metropolitan Police think I'm not a completely useless degenerate, then perhaps I can be of help to you too. I could ask people questions, and find out things, and generally snoop around. People might tell me things they wouldn't tell you, for example. Not that the Duke is harbouring a house full of criminals, or anything like that, but people are often very wary of the police and prefer to give them a wide berth if possible. I'm sure you've found that yourself at times.'

Inspector Trubshaw stiffened and regarded Freddy with an expression that was less than friendly.

'Kind of you, sir,' he said, 'but I'd be obliged if you'd leave that sort of thing to us. I expect Scotland Yard know what they're doing—' (here he looked Freddy up and down, and his gaze said as clearly as anything that he believed Scotland Yard had taken leave of their senses) '—but down here in these parts we're not in the habit of allowing enthusiastic amateurs to join in our investigations. If you have any evidence for us, I'll be more than happy to hear it, but if you'll take my advice, you'll leave the investigating to the police.'

'Oh, certainly,' said Freddy. 'That's put *me* in my place,' he said to himself five minutes later, as he came out of the study. 'Pity. Trubshaw seemed friendly enough to start with, but I suppose my face didn't inspire him with confidence. Hardly surprising,' he continued, as he caught sight of his reflection in the glass of a picture. 'Half a gallon of single malt and an all-nighter chasing after an escaped murderer don't exactly do much for the complexion. Still, I don't see why I shouldn't do what I can to find this fellow. Good stories have been a little thin on the ground lately, and this promises to be a particularly juicy one—always assuming one of my relations didn't do it. But who *did* kill him? It's a facer, all right. One doesn't like to think a member of one's family might be capable of such a thing, but somebody must have done it, if he really didn't fall over and kill himself.'

He stopped in the hall and stared absently at the grandfather clock, as he tried to picture the sight that had greeted him last night when he stepped out into the library. The door to the secret passage had been open, and the professor had been sprawled on the floor, parallel with the bookshelves, three or four feet to the left of the passage door as they came out. Freddy screwed up his eyes and tried to remember how Coddington had been lying. His right arm had been outstretched, his hand clutching the pearls, but what about his left arm? Freddy thought he remembered it had been bent under him, as though the professor had put out a hand to save himself when he fell. But there was something wrong with the picture, something missing, Freddy was sure of it. Then he realized what it was, and raised his eyebrows.

'Now, that's dashed odd,' he said to himself. 'Why didn't he have a torch with him? I don't go in for night-time robbery much myself, but I should have thought a torch would be an essential piece of equipment for marauding about in secret passages. What on earth was he thinking?'

CHAPTER FOURTEEN

CEDRIC WANDERED INTO the hall, looking lost.
'Hallo, Freddy,' he said glumly. 'They've thrown me out of my study. Now where am I to go? The police are in the way and the servants are confused, and I can't even sit down in an armchair without someone telling me they were just about to beat the cushions and making me get up again.'

'The guests are mostly in the small salon,' hinted Freddy.

'Then I shall avoid the small salon at all costs,' said Cedric. 'As a matter of fact, I'd be quite happy if all my guests would go home now and never talk to me again. I've already spent half the morning agreeing politely that yes, this is a terrible business, and no, I don't know anything and I don't suppose the police would let me say anything if I did, and please not to worry, because I'm fairly sure we're all reasonably safe in our beds. But even then I don't know if that's true. For all I know Mrs. Dragusha and Dr. Bachmann are here in disguise, and are really a pair of homicidal maniacs sworn to wipe out the entire Wareham family and everybody who knows them.'

Freddy coughed suddenly, and Cedric turned round to see the dressmaker herself approaching them.

'Ah, hallo, Mrs. Dragusha,' he said hastily. 'I hope you haven't been too disturbed by this whole business. Terribly upsetting, what?'

'Please, your Grace, I have been looking for you all morning, for I must speak to you,' said Mrs. Dragusha. She was rubbing her hands together nervously, and there were deep lines between her brows.

'Certainly,' said the Duke politely. 'Is it about the murder? Shouldn't you prefer to talk to the police? They know more about it than I do.'

'No!' she exclaimed. 'Not the police. It is much better that we keep this private, between ourselves. You will understand why when I tell you all.'

Here she threw a look at Freddy which said as clearly as anything could that she wanted him to go away. Cedric in turn threw a look at Freddy which said clearly that he had better not leave. Freddy stayed.

'Very well, then, what is it?' said Cedric, then added, 'I'd take you into the study, but I'm afraid the police have thrown me out.'

Mrs. Dragusha saw that she had no alternative but to speak here and now or hold her peace.

'It is about the pearls,' she said. 'Everyone is saying that the professor took them. Is that true?'

'Yes, he did,' said the Duke.

'Did you get them back?'

'Fortunately, yes,' said Cedric. 'They're firmly under lock and key now, and quite safe.'

'Have the police asked to see them?'

'Only to look at them quickly and see that all was in order,' replied Cedric, glancing at Freddy in surprise.

'That is good—or at least, it ought to be,' said Mrs. Dragusha. 'One does not wish to cause a scandal, and I am nothing but grateful to her Grace and her ladyship. They have been very good clients, and have been kind to me and brought me much business. Please understand that I tell you this as a warning, that you might act, and not out of any malice or wish to advantage myself.'

'I don't understand,' said Cedric.

Mrs. Dragusha's distressed expression became more pronounced.

'This is all my fault!' she said. 'In the usual way of things I am very discreet, and I do not know why it should have been different yesterday, but I am afraid that without thinking I let it slip to Professor Coddington that I believed the pearls were not real. He was most interested in what I had to say, and I believe he may have decided to take the necklace in order to examine it and see whether what I had said was true. It is most unlike me to be so unguarded, and I fear the professor has paid the price for it—although you may be sure that I was very far from thinking that he would do such a thing.'

'You—what?' said Cedric, astounded. 'You told him the pearls weren't real? Why?'

A look of embarrassment passed across the dressmaker's face, and she turned her eyes away from the Duke.

'I am not certain—perhaps I am wrong,' she said. 'But it first came to me two days ago, when we were doing the final fitting for her ladyship's dress and she took out the pearls to try on. There was something about them that caught my attention. My brother, you see, is an expert in such things. He has a business, importing precious stones. It was he who sold the famous Freiburg diamond to the Earl of Ashfield, and had it set for the Countess, and it was he, too, who helped me in my business when I first came to this country. He introduced me to the Countess, who was pleased with my work and was kind enough to speak of me favourably to other ladies. My brother deals in all kinds of stones, but his great passion is rare pearls, and he has taught me a little about them over the years—although I am far from having the same knowledge of them that he has. But I know enough to have an inkling of the difference between real and false, and when I saw the Belsingham pearls there was something that did not sit quite right with me, and I had the strongest feeling that I was not looking at the real ones. As Professor Coddington himself said, I know that some families prefer to keep their valuables locked away for safety, and display only copies in public—' Here she paused and glanced at the Duke '—but I see from your face that that is not the case here.'

'Certainly not,' said Cedric. 'Good Lord! You can't mean to say the Belsingham pearls aren't real?'

'I cannot be sure,' said Mrs. Dragusha. 'I have only a suspicion.'

'But that's impossible! They've been kept in the safe for ten years at least, since Aunt Ernestine gave them up and told us to keep them for Ro. How could they be false?'

'Have they been taken out or re-set at all?' suggested Freddy.

'Why, yes, Bea and Ro took them to Keble's last year to have a new clasp put on, as the old one was broken. You're not suggesting the exchange took place then?'

'Might they have been left lying around accidentally?' said Mrs. Dragusha. 'I do not believe for a second that the Duchess would have mislaid them, but young ladies can be careless sometimes—'

She left the suggestion hanging delicately in the air. Freddy and Cedric looked at one another.

'You have to admit Ro has been known to lose things,' said Freddy.

'But it isn't a question of losing things,' said the Duke, who seemed as though he were about to begin spluttering indignantly at any moment. 'If those pearls are fake then it would have to have been a deliberate exchange. Mrs. Dragusha, are you suggesting that my daughter sold the pearls and is passing off a copy as real?'

'No! Not at all!' exclaimed Mrs. Dragusha in alarm. She wrung her hands. 'That was far from my thoughts, please believe me, your Grace. I thought only that somebody might have taken advantage of her good nature. There are people who hover about young women and pretend friendship, when really they want only to deceive, and it is known that some of her ladyship's acquaintances are not of the highest quality. Do not blame her—I could tell you other similar stories in which insinuating people have stolen valuable objects from ladies— yes, and gentlemen too—of the aristocracy. I have seen it with my own eyes in other great houses, although naturally one must pretend to be unaware of what has happened. There is always someone who will take advantage of a kind heart. But I never should have spoken had it not been for the fact of what I accidentally said to Professor Coddington. Now he is dead and it is all my fault, and it seemed to me that to prevent more trouble I ought to warn you in advance of the possibility that the pearls might not be real, just in case the police decided to look at them more closely. I do not suppose you wish to have the truth made public if the pearls *are* false. That is why I tell you this now.'

Cedric stared at her, aghast.

'I can't believe it,' he said feebly at length.

'It may be that I am wrong,' said Mrs. Dragusha. 'But whether I am or not, you may be assured that I shall say nothing of all this. My business depends on my discretion, and I have already made one mistake for which I will never forgive myself. But now the police are here it is right that you should know.'

She made to leave, but Cedric said:

'Just a minute. You say your brother knows about pearls?'

She nodded.

'Can he keep his mouth shut? Would he be prepared to come down here immediately and have a look at the Belsing-ham pearls?'

'I do not know,' she said doubtfully. 'Philip is always very busy. But there is no harm in telegraphing him to ask. It may be that he will not be at home, for he has many important clients, but if he is, and if I can impress upon him the urgency of the matter, then perhaps we can bring him here. You may be certain that whatever the case, he will say nothing to anyone.'

'Very well, then,' said the Duke. 'Please telegraph him and tell him to come at once if he is able.'

'Of course,' she said. 'I will do everything in my power to persuade him, and if we are very fortunate he will tell you that his sister is a very stupid woman and that the pearls are real.'

'Don't say a word to anyone,' said Cedric to Freddy, as Mrs. Dragusha went off to send the telegram. 'Not even Ro. It may be that this is all a mare's nest, and we don't want to stir things up unnecessarily.'

'I won't say a thing,' promised Freddy.

Cedric sighed in exasperation.

'I think I shall take a turn in the garden,' he said. 'If anybody wants me I shall be drowning myself in the fountain.'

'Do it in the bath instead,' said Freddy. 'The water will be warmer.'

Cedric made a huffing sound that might have denoted sardonic amusement, and went off.

Chapter Fifteen

THERE WAS STILL an hour to go until luncheon, and the weather was fine, so Freddy decided to follow Cedric's example and go outside again. He went into the morning-room, intending to go out through the French windows, and found Bea standing by them, looking out into the garden. Freddy followed her gaze and saw the Duke hastening after Mrs. Fitzsimmons. Kitty turned and smiled as Cedric joined her, and they proceeded along the gravel walk together. Bea glanced round and saw Freddy.

'She's very pretty,' she said with a sigh.

'No substance, though.'

'That's never stopped anyone before,' said Bea with some bitterness.

'I'm sorry, old girl,' he said sympathetically.

'Men are such beasts at times,' she said.

'I know we are. I'm afraid we can't help it. But he'll get over it, you'll see. Go and flirt with Dr. Bachmann. He's out there in the garden with Mr. Wray, and he's been casting longing glances at you ever since he got here.'

'Will that work, do you think?'

'Probably not, if Cedric's got it badly. But I don't see why he ought to have all the fun.'

She gave a wan smile.

'You're very kind, but there are so many things to do. The police have been here all morning and I suppose we ought to offer them some sandwiches, at least.'

'Have they taken Coddington away yet?'

'Yes. They're just making sure they've collected all the evidence they need, then they say we can have the library back.'

'That's good news.'

'Yes, it is, although they've started making noises about not letting anybody leave, which will be awkward.'

'I dare say it'll just be until they've questioned everyone,' said Freddy. 'They'll want to take names and addresses, just so they don't accidentally let the murderer escape.'

She shuddered.

'Don't! It's almost too much to believe that somebody did it deliberately. I'm half-hoping the police surgeon will say the professor somehow did it himself, or that it was an accident. A death in the house is bad enough, but anything's better than deliberate murder.'

'I suppose it is,' said Freddy. He wanted to say something reassuring, but could think of nothing, and after a moment Bea said she must go and see to the sandwiches, and left.

Outside, Iris and Ralph were walking on the lawn with Goose and Daphne. Freddy decided to join them, but they were some distance away, and by the time he arrived at the place where he had seen them last they had vanished. He wandered about for a few minutes until he found himself by the kitchen-yard, which was bustling with servants running to and fro. He did not wish to be in the way, and so retreated a short distance to where a grassy area sloped down gently to a lake surrounded by trees. The view from here was very fine, and he sat down on a bench and lit a cigarette, with the intention of idling away a few minutes pleasantly.

'Got another of those?' said a voice, and Valentina Sangiacomo plumped herself down on the bench next to him without invitation or ceremony. He obliged, and she settled back to smoke and enjoy the view, with every appearance of having all the time in the world.

'Oughtn't you to be darning a stocking or folding some unmentionables?' he said.

'Not I,' she replied. 'I'm all done for now. She'll be wanting me soon, though. So what's all this, then? You lot been chasing each other around in the dark? Evening-parties wearing a bit thin these days? I must say, I can think of better ways to entertain myself than by whacking some aggravating old codger over the head with a five iron.'

'Professor Coddington was a very well respected academic,' said Freddy severely. 'And it was a sash weight, not a five iron.' She flashed him a grin.

'Go on with you,' she said. 'Well respected, indeed! Do you think we know nothing? We see what goes on—probably more than you do. He got on all your nerves, didn't he?'

'He was something of a wart,' admitted Freddy.

'I'll say! He put all the servants' backs up, too, ordering them around like he was so high and mighty.'

'Well, that is what you're there for,' said Freddy reasonably.

'P'raps. But there are ways of talking to people that won't earn you a gob of spit in your soup.'

'Good God!' exclaimed Freddy in disgust. 'I shall never have soup again.'

'Oh, you're all right,' she said cheerfully. 'Nobody has a bad word to say about you that I can tell.'

'I'm glad to hear it,' said Freddy. 'So you've all been talking about this affair, then, have you?'

''Course we have.'

'And what conclusions have you reached? Have you identified the culprit to your satisfaction?'

'Not exactly. It's all just rumour at the moment, and you know how things get twisted. But I did hear you and his lordship were the ones to trip over the corpse.'

'Yes, we were.'

'Go on, then, tell me what happened. The Duchess's maid is looking down her nose at us all because she thinks she knows the whole story, but I'm sure she must have got things wrong.

Tell me something she doesn't know so I can go back in and get one up on her.'

'I applaud your brutal honesty where others would claim purely altruistic motives for their curiosity,' said Freddy.

She made a face at him, and he told her as much as he thought the police would allow.

'You think he half-inched the pearls just because he wanted to have a look at them?' she said in some disbelief.

'I realize it's a difficult idea for you to grasp, but yes,' said Freddy. 'That does seem to be what happened. He was very interested in their history, you see, and it's only natural that he should want to examine them more closely in that case.'

He said nothing about the suspicion that the pearls were fake.

'Nosy old devil, was he?'

'That's about the size of it,' agreed Freddy.

'I gathered as much. So half the house was wandering around in the West Wing corridor when he was killed. What about the other half?'

'As a matter of fact, there are only two people left once those have been eliminated—the Duchess and my mother.'

'That's a good thing—not that her Grace and your mother are under suspicion for murder,' she added hurriedly. 'I meant the fact that most people can prove they didn't do it.'

'True, but that leaves us without any idea of who killed him. What about the servants? Anything doing there?'

'You think one of them did it?' said Valentina.

'I don't know. Do you?'

'I doubt it,' she said. 'They'd have had the sense to take the pearls off him, wouldn't they?'

'One would think so, yes.'

'The police have got there before you, anyway. They've been in the servants' hall all morning, asking questions. They wanted to know whether anyone was up at that time.'

'And were they?'

'Hardly. Most of 'em are worn out by bedtime. You'd long for your bed too if you had an early start and an eighteen-hour day to look forward to.'

'I dare say,' said Freddy. He stroked his chin, thinking.

'No, I can't see any reason for it,' muttered Valentina, as though to herself.

'Any reason for what?'

She glanced at him.

'Killing him. Without touching the pearls, I mean,' she added.

'I wonder why they did it, then.'

'I expect he irritated someone past all bearing,' she said. 'Want me to find out who it was?'

'Do you think you could?'

She shrugged.

'No harm in trying, is there? I can speak to the other servants. And I'm good at finding things.'

'That could be useful,' said Freddy. 'I'd like to know what happened to the missing sash weight. It's a pity we can't go and search all the bedrooms.'

'Won't the police do that?'

'They ought to, but I fear they may be slightly blinded by the fact that we're all the guests of a duke. Cedric's as unaffected as they come, but there's no denying the weight of a title, and if they happen to catch him in a bad mood when they propose searching the rooms and he makes an objection, then it might put them off.'

'You think they won't want to arrest one of the nobs?' said Valentina.

'I think they'd be relieved if it turned out to be a servant, certainly,' he replied.

'Or one of the foreigners. I don't think much of that dressmaker's chances, then. Or Dr. Bachmann's.'

She looked at him as though to see what he thought of that.

'Mrs. Dragusha was out of bed at the same time as the rest of us, so I doubt she's in any danger,' said Freddy. 'But Dr. Bachmann, now—that's a different matter.'

'Oh? What's he done?'

'I don't know, but he was milling around in the West Wing corridor with the rest of them after Ro screamed.'

'So?'

His bedroom is in the East Wing, and he couldn't possibly have heard the scream from there. So the question is: what was he doing out of bed at that time?'

'I'd have thought that was obvious enough,' she said. 'Why do any of you lot go creeping around in the middle of the night? I've heard you're not above that sort of thing yourself. You caused all sorts of an uproar last time you were here, they tell me.'

'It was all an unfortunate misunderstanding,' said Freddy delicately.

'Not from what I've heard. You and Lady Someone-Or-Other were where you oughtn't to have been when you oughtn't to have been, and I don't suppose it was accidental. Mrs. Bates still gives you a wide berth to this day after the shock you gave her.'

'Hmph,' said Freddy. 'Then perhaps that will teach her to mind her own business in future.'

'Anyway, Dr. Bachmann is one thing, but I notice you didn't mention the Duke was up too last night.'

Freddy was surprised for a moment, but then remembered whom she worked for.

'Yes, his Grace was up, as you so impertinently point out, and I'll thank you to forget it,' he said. 'You seem to know all about that, and I won't inquire further. But Dr. Bachmann has no good reason that I know of to have been out of bed at that time.'

'Do you think he did it, then?'

'It doesn't make a lot of sense, but it's just remotely possible that he ran downstairs after everybody had gone back into their rooms, found the professor coming out of the secret passage in the library and killed him. Why, I don't know.'

'If he did it then perhaps there's some evidence of it in his room,' said Valentina.

'Perhaps, although the only thing I can think of is the sash weight—and why would he be stupid enough to take it back to his room with him?'

'There you have me. But if you want, I can have a look for you.'

'You? But won't you get into terrible trouble if you're caught?'

'Oh, I won't do it myself,' said Valentina. 'I'll get a friend of mine to do it.'

'A friend?'

'He's a footman here, but he's valeting Dr. Bachmann this weekend because he doesn't have his own man.'

'But will he be discreet?'

'He'll do anything I tell him,' she said complacently.

'I see,' said Freddy, amused. 'It's like that, is it?'

'There's no need to look so superior,' she said. 'Servants have lives too, you know.'

'I still can't quite see you as a servant,' said Freddy. 'You're not the type.'

'No,' she conceded. 'I'm not. I like to do what I like. But sometimes there's no harm in earning an honest living—for a little while, at any rate.'

'Then while you're doing that will you talk to the other servants and find out if they know anything?'

'If you like. It'll be mainly gossip, though.'

'You never know. There might be something useful in among the chaff.'

'Well, we'll see.' She put out her cigarette and stood up. 'I'd better go or I'll miss lunch. I'll see you later.'

Freddy watched her go, and suddenly realized she had not asked him for any money, which was unlike her. Presumably she was too swept up with the excitement of the night's events and had forgotten. Still, perhaps she would find out something useful, for everything was still a mystery so far.

Chapter Sixteen

A
S IT TURNED out, Mrs. Dragusha's brother was only
too happy to drop everything and come down to Dorset
to see his Grace. He took the first express from Waterloo and
was with them by tea-time. The police had gone away, but were
expected to return that evening or the next day, and Cedric took
advantage of their absence to usher the jewel-dealer into his
study for a conference which he hoped would remain private.
Thinking that a witness might be useful, he invited Freddy to
join them, since he already knew the story and there was no
sense in spreading it further if it turned out to be a false alarm.

Mr. Laurentius was a solemn little man who looked as
though he were constructed mainly from starch, such was his
air of respectability. He refused all offers of refreshment and
sat almost comically upright, in the most uncomfortable chair
in the room (his own selection), listening to the Duke's story.
Since Cedric was still confused and upset by what Mrs. Dragusha had told him, he did not tell a good tale, and Freddy was

forced to take the reins. Mr. Laurentius listened carefully, his head on one side, then pursed his lips.

'You have done well to call me,' he said. 'Bettina told me she suspects the pearls are fake. It is true that she is not an expert, but I have taught her many things over the years, and it is possible that she may be right—although let us hope she is not. But if she is, it will not be the first time such a thing has happened. I have encountered many similar instances over the years. You would be surprised, your Grace, at how many noble families have been forced to sell their valuables in order to make ends meet and—how do you call it—keep up appearances.'

'That is not the case here, however,' said the Duke stiffly. 'We're not quite at the soup-kitchen yet, and there is no reason for anybody to have sold the pearls.'

'No indeed,' said Mr. Laurentius hurriedly. 'I meant to suggest no such thing. I was talking of other families, naturally. If the Belsingham pearls do unfortunately prove to be false, then there may be any number of explanations for it that do not reflect badly upon anybody in your household.'

'Yes, well, there's no use in talking about it until you've given us your opinion,' said Cedric, slightly mollified.

'Then the pearls, please,' said Mr. Laurentius. He sat up even straighter, if that were possible, and watched expectantly as Cedric brought out the enamelled box to which the pearls had been returned that morning. 'Hm,' he said, as the necklace was lifted out of the box and handed to him. He took it and began to examine it with great interest. 'Hm,' he said again, non-committally, then gave a little click of the tongue. 'I see the clasp has been mended. Is it recent work?'

'Last November,' said Cedric.

'It might have been done better,' said Mr. Laurentius, 'but no matter.'

He peered at the pearls, held them up to the light, then brought out an eye-glass and applied it to his eye. Freddy and Cedric watched him intently, but his face gave nothing away. At last, he handed back the pearls with great ceremony and said:

'That is very interesting.'

'Are they real?' said Freddy, who could bear it no longer.

Mr. Laurentius turned to him.

'Most certainly I should say not,' he announced with decision. 'They are a very clever forgery—yes, very clever indeed. I should like to meet the man who made these. But most assuredly they are not real. I am sorry,' he said to the Duke. 'I think this is not the answer you wished to hear.'

'No,' said Cedric weakly. 'Quite the last thing I wished to hear, in fact.'

'I cannot say what has happened, or why you are now in possession of these instead of the real Belsingham pearls. Of course, I am but one man, and—even though the Earl of Ashfield was pleased to favour me with his custom—it may be that I am wrong. I should suggest you go up to London as soon as you can and seek a second opinion on the matter.' The Duke made a dismissive noise, but he went on, 'No, but I insist. This is an important question, and too great a responsibility for one small jeweller. As for what you can do afterwards, I do not know. It may be that you prefer not to tell the police, but naturally I place myself at your disposal to assist in any way I can.'

'Thank you,' said Cedric. 'I don't mind saying that this has all come as rather a shock.'

'I understand,' said Mr. Laurentius. 'Then it is better that I take my leave now, for you will have much to consider. You know your household better than I do, and perhaps you will have an idea of what has become of the necklace. Here is my card. Do not hesitate to summon me again if you require any further assistance or advice.'

'You won't say anything, of course,' said Cedric.

'You may depend on my discretion,' said the little man, and with a stiff bow departed.

Cedric gazed around him as though not quite sure where he was, strode once up and down the room, then turned and made an expressive gesture with his arms that made him look not unlike a windmill.

'Now what shall we do?' he demanded. 'Of all the—'

He snatched up the pearls and squinted at them, then handed them to Freddy.

'Do they look false to you?' he said.

'There's no use in your asking me,' said Freddy. 'I know less about pearls than you do, I imagine.'

'But who swapped them? And how did they get close enough to the necklace to have such a good copy made? It's been locked up in a box in the safe since last November.'

'That's easy enough to answer,' replied Freddy. 'The Belsingham pearls are famous the world over. They've been on public display and there are photographs of them all over the place, in newspapers and magazines. Why, anybody who wanted to make a copy would have plenty of material to work from.'

'But when was the exchange made? Can we be sure that the real ones weren't snatched from Professor Coddington and substituted for the fake ones by our murderer?'

Freddy looked doubtful.

'It doesn't seem very likely, does it?' he said. 'Why go to the bother of having a forgery made only to draw attention to yourself afterwards by whacking someone on the head in order to get the real ones? All the murderer has done is to make us look closely at the pearls and find out they're false, when presumably the intention was to have the exchange go unnoticed for years. Remember Mrs. Dragusha already had her suspicions on Thursday, before the guests had even arrived, so the substitution must have taken place some time ago.'

'True,' said Cedric.

'If I were you, I should speak to the people who mended the necklace for you last November. Are they to be trusted?'

'It was Keble's,' said Cedric with dignity. 'They have a Royal Warrant. If the King trusts them then who am I to argue?'

'But they have people working for them. Even the most reputable company might accidentally employ the occasional bad apple. Every man has his price, they say. I should speak to them discreetly if I were you—but in the meantime, assuming they had nothing to do with it, perhaps we ought to try and find out when the pearls might have been exchanged.'

'They couldn't have been—not unless someone took them out of the safe,' said the Duke. 'But the only people who ever have the keys are Spenlow and I, and I should as soon believe that I did it myself in my sleep as suspect Spenlow of being a thief.'

'Don't you ever give the keys to Bea or Goose or Ro? Or might they have been left lying around?'

'Certainly not,' said Cedric. 'I'm very careful with them.'

'Then in that case, it seems most likely that they were swapped when Bea and Ro took the pearls to London last November—either that, or some time the day before Professor Coddington was killed.'

'Hmm. If Mrs. Dragusha had already spotted they were fake on Thursday, then that narrows it down considerably,' said Cedric. 'The only people who were here then apart from ourselves were Mrs. Dragusha herself and Iris Bagshawe.'

'Ah,' said Freddy, taken aback.

Cedric sighed heavily.

'We'd better have it out with Ro,' he said. 'I have the awful feeling that the Farleys have something to do with all this.'

'The Farleys? I seem to recognize the name. Who are they?'

'They're a married couple who attached themselves to Ro for a while until we put a stop to it. They're older than she and not the sort of people I want my daughter associating with. They're fast, shady and plausible with it. As far as I've been able to discover nobody knows where their money comes from, which naturally gives rise to all sorts of suspicions. Ro palled up with the woman—Pamela Farley, I think her name is—last year. Silly girl's always been far too trusting. She lent Mrs. Farley a diamond necklace which she took far too long to return—we were rather worried we'd never get it back, as a matter of fact, as she skipped off with it to Le Touquet or some such place for a few weeks.'

'Ah, yes, I did hear something of it,' said Freddy.

'I have no idea why Ro thought it was a good idea to scatter her valuable jewellery around among her friends like confetti, but suffice it to say we told her in no uncertain terms to stop it. She promised she wouldn't do it again, but who knows what young people get up to these days? Oh, Lord!' Cedric went on in sudden dismay. 'If it's true that the Farleys are up to no good then I suppose that means we'll have to get someone to look at the diamonds, in case they're fake too. Damn the silly girl! Why does she have to get herself mixed up with these sorts of people?'

'You'd better ask her yourself,' said Freddy. 'Shall I fetch her?'

'Yes, do. And Bea too,' said Cedric. 'She'll have to hear this.'

The Duchess and Ro were summoned to Cedric's study, and arrived quickly.

'What is it?' said Bea eagerly. 'Have they arrested someone?'

'No,' said Cedric. 'Sit down, both of you. I've something rather serious to tell you.'

He proceeded to do so, watching Ro intently all the while. She looked astounded at the news that the pearls were fake, but showed no sign of any other consciousness, and when questioned as to whether she had seen her friends the Farleys when she and her mother had taken the necklace to London, denied absolutely that she had shown them the pearls, or that they had ever been in the same room as them.

'But you did see the Farleys?' said Cedric.

'Why, yes, I believe I did,' she said uncomfortably. 'Just for a short while, you know, one evening.'

'Oh, Ro,' said her mother reproachfully. 'Is that what you were doing when you were late for dinner that night? And you'd promised so faithfully to keep away from them.'

'They're friends of mine, and it would have been terribly rude to drop them flat,' said Ro.

'They're not your friends,' said Cedric. 'I should have thought you could recognize a pair of spongers when you saw them. I know the type—London is full of them. They prey on young, wealthy men and women who are too naïve to know better.'

Ro was beginning to look mutinous.

'Are you absolutely sure you didn't show them the pearls at any time?' said Bea. 'Where did you meet them?'

'They called for me at Claridge's,' said Ro.

'Did they come up to your room at all?'

'Well, yes, just for a few minutes, but they couldn't have done anything because I didn't have the pearls, did I? Don't you remember? It was you who had them in your room.'

'Ye-es,' said Bea slowly. 'But we had the rooms with connecting doors. It would have taken a matter of seconds for one of them to slip into my room and exchange the necklaces.'

'But the pearls were locked in their case,' said Ro.

'If they're used to this sort of thing then they might have picked the lock,' said Cedric.

'Is this the case?' said Freddy, who had been peering alternately at the pearls and the enamelled box. He squinted at the lock. 'It doesn't look as though it's been forced at all,' he said at last.

'See?' said Ro.

'There are ways,' said Cedric darkly.

'Did the Farleys know we had the pearls with us?' said Bea. 'Did you tell them?'

'I may have done,' said Ro. 'But they didn't take them!' she suddenly exclaimed. 'I promise you they couldn't have.'

And that was all they could get out of her. She maintained obstinately that the Farleys had neither seen nor been anywhere near the Belsingham pearls during the visit to London, and finally left the room in high dudgeon, leaving everyone else to gaze at each other uncomfortably, for it seemed that either Ro was telling untruths or that she had been very careless in her choice of friends. The fact remained, however, that the Belsingham pearls were missing, and nobody knew where they were.

CHAPTER SEVENTEEN

A FTER HE LEFT the study, Freddy went in search of Ro, and eventually found her in the garden, sitting on the edge of a fountain and smoking furiously.

'Do you mind if I have a word?' he said.

'Not if it's about the pearls,' she replied.

'Well, it is, but I haven't come to pitch into you, I promise.'

'What is it, then?' she said grudgingly.

'I know old Cedric has a bee in his bonnet about the Farleys, so he wasn't thinking too much about what might have happened this weekend. I just wondered whether the pearls might not have been taken last November at all, but on Thursday. That's when they came out of the safe, isn't it?'

'Yes,' said Ro.

'Who gave you them?'

'Father, of course. I asked if I might have them to try on with my new frock, and he agreed, but told me to be careful with them. And I was!' she said fiercely. 'I'm not as careless as people seem to think.'

Freddy refrained from pointing out that she had left what they now knew to be the fake pearls lying on her dressing-table when she had gone to bed the night before, and merely said:

'What did you do with them when you got them? Try and remember. Were they in your sight all the time?'

'Yes,' she said. 'I took them upstairs and locked them in my drawer until I needed them. Then I tried on the dress and Mrs. Dragusha stuck some pins in me, then I put on the necklace.'

'And you were the only person who touched it?'

'Yes,' she said, then remembered something. 'Oh, no—Iris tried it on too.'

'Iris?' he said quickly.

'Yes, but not properly. She only held it around her neck for a second and looked in the glass, then she took it off and handed it straight to me. I put it on and preened for a bit, then took it off and put it back in the box.'

'Who else was in the room? Only Mrs. Dragusha?'

'Yes. She wouldn't touch them—said they were bad luck.'

'What did you do with the box then?'

'I put it on the dressing-table—just for a few minutes, while I showed them both the secret passage. Then Mother came in and I picked the box up and took it back downstairs to the safe.'

'And you're sure no-one went near the pearls at any other time?'

'Quite sure.'

'And nobody except your mother came in while you were looking at the secret passage?'

'Nobody at all,' she said firmly.

Freddy could see no reason why she should lie about it, since the blame for the necklace's disappearance had been placed squarely on her shoulders, and she must surely realize that it would be to her advantage to create uncertainty on the matter. She must have read his thoughts, for she said ironically:

'Kind of you to try and get me off the hook, but there's nothing doing, I'm afraid.'

'Sorry, old thing,' he said. 'I wish none of this had ever happened.'

'So do I. I wish I'd never set eyes on those beastly pearls, in fact. They didn't suit me anyway.'

'Yes they did,' said Freddy. 'You looked splendid.' He saw a tear trembling in the corner of her eye. 'Poor you,' he said sympathetically. 'Not much of a birthday party, was it?'

She let out a sound that might have been a laugh or a sob.

'I've had better,' she agreed.

'Have you any idea of what might have happened to the pearls?'

She shrugged.

'None at all. I know it wasn't the Farleys, although I dare say Father will never believe it. I suppose he'll be putting the police on to them now. Poor Pam—and she hasn't been at all well lately, either. As a matter of fact, though, I did wonder whether someone at Keble's mightn't have exchanged them.'

'Yes, I'd thought of that myself,' said Freddy. 'That will be for the police to find out—always supposing Cedric reports it.'

'If he doesn't we'll know for sure he thinks it was my fault,' she said glumly.

Freddy left her to brood and went away, turning the mystery over in his mind, although at present he could make no sense of it. He did not have long to reflect before he saw Mr. Wray walking towards him in company with Dr. Bachmann. They were talking about botany, and Mr. Wray was listening courteously as Dr. Bachmann enumerated some of the many fine specimens of water-plant he had collected as a student many years ago during a holiday in Austria.

'Hallo, hallo,' said Freddy. 'It seems everybody is keen to take a turn in the fresh air today.'

'And why not?' said Mr. Wray. 'The weather is so pleasant and the gardens here so very fine that I could not resist the opportunity to show some of their beauties to Dr. Bachmann here.'

'Oh, certainly,' agreed Bachmann, then lowered his voice. 'Besides, I know we must remain at Belsingham while the police investigate, but one does not wish to get in the way, or be *de trop*, as they say, so this seemed the wisest place to come. But Mr. Wray is right—one does not often see such magnificent grounds.'

'Or such a magnificent house,' said Mr. Wray. He turned back and extended a hand to encompass the imposing outline of Belsingham, which was shown to particular advantage at that moment, bathed as it was in the late afternoon sunlight. 'I have been here some weeks now, and have had an opportunity to explore the place thoroughly. The Duchess has been kind enough to show me some of the rooms, and some of the secret nooks and crannies, which are not often shown to guests. In a place of this size, there must inevitably be some parts of the building which are so rarely entered that even the servants know little of them. And such fine works of art! Far more than can be displayed in the few rooms that we have seen this weekend. I have spent many a happy hour absorbed in the contemplation of undiscovered works by several of the Old Masters. There is quite a collection here. The library is a great treasure-trove, too, especially for anyone who has an interest in the history of Belsingham. There are a number of quaint old works that relate the story of the house, and I have learnt much about it. I have also done a little reading about the history of the Warehams—who are one of our most noble aristocratic families, in my opinion.' (Here he made a little bow to Freddy.) 'I have been most fascinated to learn of the great things they have done for the benefit and the glory of England.'

'You make me feel ashamed of my ignorance,' said Freddy. 'I have to admit I've always found all this family history stuff rather dull, but perhaps that's a mistake on my part.'

'It is indeed,' said Mr. Wray. 'I can highly recommend spending an hour or two in the company of your ancestors, as they are anything but dull.'

'Professor Coddington was interested in the history of the Warehams too, I think,' observed Freddy.

'Yes, I believe he was,' replied Mr. Wray distantly. 'Although I am not convinced that his motives were of the purest.'

'What makes you say that?'

'Why, he seemed unduly concerned with unearthing stories which I am sure the family would not want to get about, for they cast a bad light upon them which is quite undeserved. He knew I had read one or two books on the subject and asked me a number of pointed questions, although naturally I refused to indulge him.'

'He tried to pump you, did he?' said Freddy. 'What did he want to know?'

'Nothing of any consequence,' said Mr. Wray. 'Certainly nothing that would stand up to academic examination, at any rate. I was polite, of course, but I could not help hinting that I thought his curiosity somewhat impertinent, especially when he had been so graciously invited to Belsingham by the Duke himself. I understand that we are all less formal these days, but good manners will never go out of fashion, and I do believe the professor had forgotten his.'

His demeanour had become very stiff, and Freddy regarded him with some amusement. Evidently here was another who had not found Professor Coddington's company particularly congenial. Dr. Bachmann had gone to examine an unusually luxuriant species of rose-bush, so Freddy took the opportunity to say:

'By the way, it's rather odd what happened to the professor after our conversation last night, don't you think?'

Mr. Wray gave a deep sigh and shook his head.

'I half-hoped you had forgotten that, Mr. Pilkington-Soames,' he said. 'I assure you I have been most distressed by the whole affair.'

'Is this the thing you feared?'

'I do not know what I feared, although I will confess that I felt it had something to do with Professor Coddington. But never did I imagine it would be anything so dreadful as this.'

'How could you have? I must say, though, that if you'd asked me which of us was most likely to be murdered, I should have fastened upon him as the prime candidate.'

'Yes, indeed,' said Mr. Wray sorrowfully. 'It is not for us to judge, but I am very much afraid he may have brought it upon himself.'

'Well, I'm all for judging anyone who thinks he has the right to go about lifting other people's valuable heirlooms on a whim, although personally I'd have thought that an ignominious ejection from the house was a more appropriate punishment than a heavy object to the cranium—speaking of which, has your headache gone now?'

'Ah, yes, it has eased somewhat,' said Mr. Wray cautiously.

'Excellent. Then I suppose we needn't expect any more murders for the present,' said Freddy. 'I do beg your pardon,' he added, as he saw Mr. Wray's expression. 'I can't help being facetious at times. It's a habit of mine, and it's got worse since I became a reporter, as that sort of thing is positively encouraged at the paper, but sometimes one forgets that it's not welcome everywhere. Still, I'm glad to hear you're on the mend.'

Mr. Wray made a gracious reply. They were then rejoined by Dr. Bachmann, who had overheard something of the conversation.

'I am very sorry for the Duchess,' he said. 'It is most regrettable that she should have to suffer such a terrible event in her own house.'

'Oh, yes,' said Mr. Wray, returning to his customary warmth of manner. 'She is a delightful woman—quite delightful! Indeed, I cannot praise the family highly enough. I know there are those who wish to see them discredited, but fortunately they are in the minority. You know the Duke and Duchess well, I believe?'

'Yes,' said Bachmann. 'The Duke and I were friends at Oxford many years ago, when he was still plain Cedric Wareham, and we have continued to write to each other over the years. I also knew Mrs. Wareham, as she then was, and I have been pleased to find that she is still as kind and unaffected as ever.'

'Most unaffected indeed. The Duchess in particular has shown me nothing but courtesy ever since I arrived. Nothing is too much trouble for her. Which reminds me—this morning I heard that the repairs on my house are almost complete. This is good news, of course, but I confess that I shall be sorry to leave Belsingham, for the Duke and Duchess have made me feel quite at home—quite at home.'

'I wonder when the police will allow us to leave,' said Dr. Bachmann.

'Soon, I dare say,' said Freddy. 'Once they've finished asking everybody questions. Have they spoken to you yet?'

'Yes,' replied Bachmann. 'I had nothing of use to tell them, alas. I heard Lady Rose scream, as did everybody else, and came out into the corridor, but then I returned immediately to bed. I saw nothing of the professor.'

'You heard the scream from the East Wing, did you?' said Freddy.

Bachmann hesitated.

'No, I was already up. I could not sleep, so I decided to take a turn about the house. I often do the same at home—although naturally it does not take nearly so long to walk around my own little house.'

'But you didn't go downstairs?'

'No. I only got as far as the head of the stairs. I do not know where I should have gone after that, but I happened to glance along the corridor of the West Wing and saw something that arrested me for several moments—a ghostly apparition, floating along the corridor. Once I had got over my shock I realized somebody was carrying it, and that there must be a game afoot, but for a moment I was quite frightened. I understand it was some of the young men of the house playing a joke.' He regarded Freddy with a twinkle in his eye. 'Then Lady Rose screamed and so I came to see what was the matter.'

Mr. Wray shivered.

'It is getting a little cold,' he said. 'The clouds have come over. Perhaps we might go indoors.'

Dr. Bachmann agreed, and the two of them departed. Freddy was just about to go and look for Daphne, who had been mysteriously elusive for most of the afternoon, when he spied Lavinia Philpott by a raised flower bed, pulling at weeds in a ruffled sort of way. She moved to pick up a heavy plant pot and he hastened forward to help her, but she lifted it effortlessly in her strong arms and arranged it in a better position.

'Hallo, Mrs. P,' he said.

She straightened up and drew a breath, and he prepared for an outburst.

'I've just had a most trying interview with the police,' she said indignantly. 'I told them I wasn't accustomed to this sort of thing, and asked them how they could possibly think that I had anything to do with Professor Coddington's death, but they were quite implacable, and insisted on asking me a lot of rude questions.'

'Dear me,' said Freddy. 'What sort of questions?'

'About our life in India, and what exactly we were doing there. Someone overheard the professor say he knew India very well, you see, so they kept asking me whether I'd known him when Mr. Philpott was alive, and whether there was anything he knew to my disadvantage. Well, naturally, the very idea is absurd! I'd never even heard of Professor Coddington before I came to Belsingham. He *said* he'd been to Mahjapara, but it's a big place and I certainly never met him. And the suggestion that I might be hiding all sorts of secrets is pure impertinence, if you ask me.'

'I shouldn't worry about it,' said Freddy. 'They asked me a lot of silly questions too. They have to do it, just so they can eliminate people from the inquiry.'

'That would be all very well if one didn't have the feeling that they were trying to trip one up,' said Lavinia. 'I don't know what they expected me to admit, but I felt as though they thought I was lying all the while.'

'Yes, they do have a way of making one feel guilty, don't they? Never mind—they can't arrest you just on a suspicion.'

Lavinia let out a little shriek and put a hand to her ample bosom.

'Arrest me? What a dreadful thought! I should die if they arrested me, I know I should! Goodness me! What would people think?'

She seemed unduly appalled at the idea, so much so that the thought darted involuntarily into Freddy's head that perhaps this was not her first encounter with the police. But there was no reason to suppose she had had anything to do with the murder, since Freddy had seen her with his own eyes out in the corridor with the others, and so he said curiously:

'What do you think happened to Professor Coddington?'

At that she sniffed.

'I'm sure I don't know,' she said. 'Why should I have an opinion on the matter? Naturally, I feel every sympathy for the Duchess, but one doesn't expect this sort of unpleasantness in the house of a duke, does one?'

Freddy wanted to ask why a duke should be any more immune to murder in his house than a man of lesser stature, but she had not finished. She went on:

'Why, Lady Turpin would never have allowed such a thing to happen in her home! She was quite the hostess, you know—a great beauty, of course, at the very head of our little society back in Mahjapara—and at her dinner-parties everything had to be just so—everything in exactly the right place on the table. She confided to me once that she even changed the colour of the napkins to match her dress. Quite the most painstaking attention to detail! And she served ten, twelve, even fourteen courses at some of her larger parties. Her evening entertainments were attended by all the most important English people in the area—although there was one odd little Danish man who was occasionally invited—oh, and Mrs. O'Reilly too, but she was the cousin of an earl, so one let it slide and did one's best to ignore the accent.'

'Naturally,' said Freddy.

'But to be woken up in the middle of the night like that! I don't sleep at all well, you understand. I should have suffered it without complaint, but my doctor *insisted* I take a preparation of his own devising—all perfectly innocuous, and only for a short while—I was very firm about that—and I must say it has been miraculous in its effects. Usually I take just two drops and sleep soundly until morning, but with all the commotion last night the mixture did not do its job, and I was roused from my bed along with everyone else. One doesn't like to be seen in dishabille, but fortunately this is a *respectable* household, and so I knew there was nothing to fear—and all the other women were up, anyway. I must say, however, that Mrs. Fitzsimmons was quite unsuitably attired for the time of year—I was just about to step forward and warn her that she was likely to catch a cold in that flimsy silk nightgown of hers, when Mr. Wray came out of his room unexpectedly and made me jump, so it slipped my mind. Poor thing, I believe he took a bigger fright than I did—he clutched the door handle as though for dear life and looked as though he had half a mind to run back inside— but that's nothing to the shock we all got the next morning when we heard the professor had been killed! I declare this is *not* the sort of thing I am used to, and I am accustomed to mix with some *very* exalted company—'

She stopped, as though she had forgotten what she had been about to say. Freddy waited, but she did not continue, and instead turned to look towards the house, a puzzled expression on her face.

'What was I saying?' she said at last.

'Something about flimsy silk nightgowns,' he hazarded.

'Yes, well whatever it was, this has all been most unsettling. I don't wonder I forget where I am and what I'm doing half the time—and I'm not the only one to be confused, I'm sure of it.' She began pulling at the weeds again, and Freddy took the opportunity to make some suitable remark and effect his escape before he could be subjected to a list of all Lavinia's titled friends. Daphne was nowhere to be seen in the garden, but as he looked back at the house he thought he saw someone wearing a pale frock standing just inside the French windows, and so decided to go in that way, but when he entered he found not Daphne but Iris, who was sitting coolly on a sofa, although she had certainly been watching him through the window only a moment before. He was about to pass through when she said:

'Well? Aren't you going to tell me what you've been finding out?'

'What do you mean?'

'You've been nosing around, haven't you? I know you—you can't resist a mystery. I'll bet you've been asking people all sorts of questions.'

'Perhaps one or two,' he admitted.

'Have you found out who did it?'

'Who did what?' he said without thinking.

'Why, who killed Professor Coddington, of course! What else?'

'Ah, yes. I haven't the foggiest. Most of the house was up and yet no-one was anywhere near the professor, so I can only conclude that nobody killed him, and that something heavy fell on his head and then rolled away.'

'Don't be absurd,' she said. 'Somebody must have done it. It wasn't me, in case you were wondering.'

'I never thought for a second it was,' he said.

'I might have bashed *you* on the head, but not Professor Coddington,' she said, with a gleam of mischief in her eye.

'I expect Ralph would say the same.'

'Oh, Ralph,' she said dismissively. 'There wasn't the slightest use in your playing that trick on him, you know. He hasn't a sense of humour and wouldn't see the joke. He didn't kill the professor either, by the way.'

'No, I don't suppose he did,' said Freddy.

'He wouldn't have the imagination. And besides, he has no motive.'

'And therein lies the difficulty,' said Freddy. 'Nobody seems to have a motive.'

'Apart from everyone in your family.'

'What do you mean?' he said, surprised.

'Why, didn't you hear him? He was talking about all sorts of dire secrets that ought to be exposed to the world for the good of humanity.'

'But that was all nonsense,' said Freddy. 'Nobody really believed him. And there are no secrets in this family that anybody cares about. Not really.'

'Are you quite sure?' she stood up and came across to where he was standing. 'What about the pearls?' she said quietly.

'What do you know about that?' he said quickly, and she laughed.

'I'm not stupid. Mrs. Dragusha has been dropping hints all over the place since she got here, and then that little man came who looked like a pawnbroker. They're not the real pearls, are they?'

'No,' he admitted after a moment. 'They're a clever forgery, it seems.'

'Then what happened to the real ones? I thought they'd been locked up for months. How could anybody get at them?'

'There are a number of possible explanations,' he said non-committally.

'Yes, and one of them is that I took them, isn't it? Don't look like that—you must have thought it.'

'I promise you the idea never entered my head,' he said.

'Then you're an awful fool,' she replied. 'You must know I tried them on the other day. As far as I know I'm the only person outside the family to have touched them since they came out of the safe. If someone has taken them then who more likely than Lady Rose's poor, envious friend who has no valuable jewellery of her own?'

'You're not envious, are you?'

'Horribly,' she said. 'I like pretty things as much as anybody, and I shall never own anything half so beautiful or fabulously expensive. How can you be sure I wasn't seized by a sudden temptation and took the opportunity to pocket them the other day?'

'What, and then replace them with a forgery?'

'Perhaps I have a lot of shady friends,' she said solemnly. 'You haven't seen much of me lately, have you? How do you know Ralph isn't secretly running a gang of international thieves who rampage around the houses of the aristocracy, stealing anything they can get their hands on? Perhaps I only agreed to marry him because I knew he'd shower me with stolen jew-ellery and fur coats.'

She glared grimly at him. It was not in the least convincing.

'Idiot,' he said. 'I might believe it of you, but not of Ralph.'

Her face relaxed and she let out a peal of laughter.

'Can you imagine it?' she said. 'Poor Ralph, I oughtn't to make fun of him, but he does invite it, rather.' They smiled at one another, then her face turned suddenly serious. 'Do you promise you don't suspect me?'

'Not at all.'

'Good. I should be awfully upset if you did.'

She frowned, then stepped closer and brushed some ciga-rette-ash off his jacket.

'That's better,' she said, then gave him another smile and went out.

Chapter Eighteen

WHEN FREDDY CAME out into the hall, he heard a voice say, 'Psst!' He looked about him and saw Valentina Sangiacomo standing in the shadow of a large bust of Plato, glancing around.

'What is it?' he asked.

'I might have something for you,' she replied in a low voice. 'But I haven't got time now—the dressing-bell's about to go and she'll want me. What about after dinner? Come round to the kitchen-yard.'

'All right,' he said.

Someone came through the hall just then and she whisked herself away, while Freddy went up to his own room to dress.

The men sat late that evening, and it was some time before Freddy could get away. As soon as he could, he hurried around to the kitchen-yard, fearing that she might have given it up and gone back inside. It was chilly, with a light rain, and he found her standing in the shelter of a doorway.

'Mightn't it have been better to meet inside?' he said.

'Only if you want to get me into trouble,' she replied. 'They don't like us fraternizing, or didn't you know that?'

'Of course I knew, but I didn't think it was the sort of thing you cared about.'

'Well, perhaps,' she said. 'Anyway, do you want to hear this or not?'

'Yes. What did your young man get?'

She grimaced.

'The big lump was no use at all, so I had to get him to keep a look-out and go in myself in the end. First things first—I didn't find the sash weight.'

'I didn't really expect you to,' he said. 'The murderer was hardly going to leave that lying around.'

'No, but there was no harm in looking. At any rate, while I was in there, I thought I'd better have a squint at his things to see if he was hiding anything else. There wasn't much, but I did find something.'

'Oh? What?'

'I'm not exactly sure,' she said. She put her hand in her pocket and brought out an envelope bearing an impressive official seal. Freddy took it, and saw it was from a well-known Swiss university.

'I didn't mean you to steal anything!' he exclaimed.

'How was I to know what it said if I didn't take it?' she said.

'But if you don't know what it is then why *did* you take it? It's probably something quite ordinary.'

'Ah,' she said significantly, 'but I don't think it is. One of the maids was talking about it today. He was reading it yesterday evening and she said it upset him. She was seeing to his fire, when he came into his room reading it and muttering to himself in a foreign language. He looked all shaken up, she said.'

'Now you come to mention it, I did see him looking upset about something myself last night,' said Freddy, remembering. 'I wonder whether it was the same thing.'

'Well go on, then, have a look at it.'

'It's in French,' he said, taking the letter out of the envelope. 'I seem to recall sleeping through most of my French lessons at school. I believe you gave me this just to test me.'

'Hardly. What does it say?'

It was too dark to see much, so he moved towards a brightly-lit window and read through the letter with a frown. His French was a little rusty, but the purport of the missive was clear enough. He whistled.

'Well, well,' he said. 'It appears he was sacked from the university for plagiarism.'

'For what?'

'Copying someone else's work.' She stared uncomprehendingly, and he went on, 'At school you'll get a thrashing for it, but in academia they'll strip you of your titles and drum you out of the university, and your name will be ruined. It rather looks as though that's what happened in Dr. Bachmann's case. This is a letter in reply to his appeal against the sacking. It's all very apologetic and regretful, but it says they've examined the facts, and while there are some small grounds to suppose that he mayn't have been guilty, the evidence weighs too heavily against him for them to reconsider. No wonder he was looking a little peaky last night. Hmm—hmm. Now, what else does it say?'

He read on.

'It doesn't sound as if this has anything to do with the murder,' said Valentina, but Freddy gave an exclamation.

'Look!' he said.

'There's no use in showing it to me—I won't understand a word.'

'No, but look! Do you see a name you recognize?'

She peered at the letter.

'Horace—what's that? Coddington.' She glanced up. 'Where does he come in, then?'

Freddy was still reading.

'By Jove!' he said at last. 'It seems Bachmann asked for the name of the person who accused him of plagiarism, and they've obliged.'

'Professor Coddington?'

'Yes! It was Coddington who reported him in the first place and got him sacked!'

'What a sneak!' she said. 'People ought to mind their own business.'

'Quite. But the fact is, he ruined Bachmann's reputation, and if that's not a motive for murder then I don't know what is. He must have found out for the first time yesterday that Coddington was the man responsible for his misfortunes. What's more likely than that he took a heavy object to him in a fury? I should probably do the same thing myself in the circumstances.'

'But I thought everyone had an alibi for the murder,' she said.

'Yes, that is a facer,' said Freddy. 'I wonder, though—I shall speak to Cedric. He was up last night too, and their rooms are both in the East Wing. Bachmann *said* he was going back to bed after all the commotion, but perhaps he didn't. We've been assuming that the professor died at twenty past three at the hand of someone lying in wait for him, but he might have died a few minutes after that, because we didn't find him until about twenty to four. Perhaps Bachmann, instead of going back to his room, dashed downstairs when Goose and I weren't looking, and intercepted Coddington just as he came out of the secret passage.'

'But how did he know it was the prof creeping about in her ladyship's room?'

'I couldn't tell you,' said Freddy, scratching his jaw in perplexity. 'It's not very satisfactory, I know, but I don't like to reject such a strong motive out of hand. It's the only one we've found so far. Look here, you'd better put this back before Bachmann discovers it's missing. I don't suppose you found anything else, did you?'

'Like what? The real pearls, do you mean?'

'Why do you say that?' he said, staring.

'Because everyone's saying the ones you've got now are a copy.'

'Is nothing secret in this house?' he said in exasperation.

She gave him a pitying look.

'They say that little man was an expert come to look at the necklace,' she said. 'I take it he gave you bad news?'

'Yes, as a matter of fact, he did,' said Freddy. 'But you'd do well to keep it quiet. The family don't want any scandal, and this would be a big one.'

'What happened to them?' she said. 'Did her ladyship pawn them?'

'I doubt it. It seems to be more a case of leaving them lying around accidentally.'

'Does she do that a lot?'

'More than she ought to, certainly.'

'Maybe that'll teach her, then,' said Valentina. She appeared only half-interested in the subject. 'What time is it?' she said suddenly. 'I'd better get back inside before I'm wanted.'

'Make sure you put the letter back before Dr. Bachmann goes up to bed,' warned Freddy.

'I will,' she said, and was gone.

The drizzle was becoming heavier, so he went back into the house through the kitchen, much to the consternation of the servants, then made his way to the billiard-room, there to practise some shots and think about what he had just learned. One person in the house was now known to have had a clear motive for killing the professor, but could Bachmann have done it? His story about not being able to sleep had sounded a little thin. Might he have been out of bed for quite a different reason? Might he, in fact, have risen with the express purpose of revenging himself on the man who had been the direct cause of his disgrace? Freddy tried to think how it might have happened. Presumably Bachmann would have gone to the professor's room first, and would have found him absent. What would he have done then? He would have wandered along the corridor to search for him, most likely—just as he *had* done, in fact. Perhaps Bachmann had been standing at the head of the stairs, wondering whether to go down and look for Coddington, when Ro had screamed and he had come into the West Wing corridor to find out what was happening. That was pretty much the story he had told Freddy, in fact. So far, so good, but there things became less certain, as Valentina had pointed out. Had Bachmann waited for everybody to return to their rooms, then run downstairs to the library and done the deed quickly? Had the sash weight been in his plans all along? Or had he seized upon the nearest weapon and struck? No, thought Freddy—that did not seem possible. The weights had been lying on the window-sill, far from the door to the passage and where the professor had been found. To pick up a weight Dr. Bachmann would have had to walk thirty feet across the room. If he *had* done the deed then it must have been deliberate and premeditated, then. But again, how did Bachmann know the professor would be coming out of the passage into the library? He could not have known that the man in Ro's room was Coddington—since at the time everybody had been assuming it was Freddy, Goose and Nugs playing a joke—and therefore could not have known he was intending to escape through the secret passage. None of it seemed to make sense.

Wrapped up in his ruminations, Freddy realized he was missing every shot, and so gave it up and went into the small salon, where the other guests were all now gathered. The first thing he saw was Dr. Bachmann talking to Bea. She looked as though she were enjoying the attention. Kitty Fitzsimmons was talking to Mrs. Dragusha, but Cedric was nowhere to be seen, and Freddy was about to withdraw when he was seized upon by his mother, who had been holding herself in all day and wanted to give vent to her feelings. The matter for offence was chiefly her treatment at the hands of the police, who had unaccountably failed to appreciate Mrs. Pilkington-Soames's standing in the family and her position as society reporter at that august London publication, the *Clarion*.

'If I didn't know better, I should say that Sir Henry had been trying to avoid me,' she said. 'He seemed *most* unwilling to give me any useful information. All I asked was whether they expected to make an arrest soon in this case, and whether he thought the reputation of the Dorset police had suffered after their ignominious failure to catch that horrid man who drowned his wife in a horse trough—what was his name again?—you know, that ferrety little shopkeeper with the wart on his chin—quite obviously a murderer to look at him, and yet it seems the Dorset police disagreed, because he wasn't caught until he moved to Suffolk and tried the same trick again—but as soon as I brought the subject up Sir Henry made some excuse and practically *ran* in the opposite direction. And Inspector Trubshaw was most impertinent, too.'

'Was he? What did he say?' said Freddy with interest.

'Never mind,' said his mother, turning slightly pink. 'But it was most disrespectful. At any rate, they ought to have been consulting me about this murder, since I'm by way of being an expert, but instead I've had to spend the afternoon listening to Lavinia Philpott talking about someone called Lady Turpin, whom I imagine she invented.'

'Lady Turpin? The wife of Lord Turpin, the tea magnate, do you mean?' said Freddy, looking around to make sure that Lavinia was out of earshot, since his mother was not too particular about talking about people in their hearing.

'Oh, one of these new creations, is it? Then I shouldn't be a bit surprised if Lavinia scraped the acquaintance by force.

It was nice of Bea to take pity on her and invite her here, but really, she has no idea how to behave in polite company. Why, I could hardly bear to watch her at dinner tonight.'

'Nonsense, she eats perfectly correctly,' said Freddy.

'But you can't deny she's awkward. I found her peering into the linen cupboard when I came up to dress tonight, and had to explain to her that if one needs an extra blanket then one asks a servant to fetch it. I said it kindly, of course, but she didn't seem to be paying attention. Anyway, she's insufferable. It's such a shame Daphne is stuck with her.'

'I thought you didn't like Daphne.'

'Well, perhaps she's not quite as bad as I thought,' said Cynthia graciously. 'She was most complimentary about my dress and was the only person to notice that I'd chosen this peridot ring specifically to match the colour of my eyes. You really ought to try and keep her away from Lavinia as much as possible, before the damage of her influence becomes irreversible.'

There was no suitable reply to that, so Freddy did not argue. He eventually effected an escape, and went to look for Cedric. The Duke was in his study, sitting in his favourite chair and gazing into a glass of whisky.

'Oh, it's you,' he said, as Freddy came in. 'Has Bea sent you to fetch me?'

'No, she's talking to Dr. Bachmann.'

'Hmph. He was always sweet on her, and I expect nothing's changed. She's still a good-looking woman. I ought to be in there making merry with my guests, oughtn't I? But somehow

I can't summon up the enthusiasm, what with one thing and another.'

'Are the police coming back?' said Freddy.

'Tomorrow, they said,' replied Cedric. 'Although I should far rather they stayed away. Nobody's trotted forward conveniently to confess to the murder, and I still haven't decided whether or not to tell them about the pearls.'

'I'd say better not, at least until you've spoken to Keble's and done a little investigating on your own account.'

'Yes, perhaps you're right. Lord knows we don't want a scandal.'

'Listen,' said Freddy. 'There's something I've found out, and I'm not certain what to do about it. It might have something to do with the murder.'

'What is it?'

'It's Dr. Bachmann,' said Freddy, and proceeded to tell Cedric what he had found out, although without mentioning the part Valentina had played.

'Do you mean to say you went rifling through his things?' said Cedric indignantly. 'That's not playing cricket, is it? Freddy, I'm surprised at you.'

'I didn't just do it on a whim,' said Freddy. 'Bachmann was one of the people who appeared in the corridor during all the uproar, but his room is in the East Wing. Nobody who sleeps there could possibly have heard the scream, so I just wondered what he was doing up, that's all. It was a natural suspicion given the circumstances, you must agree.'

Cedric opened his mouth to object, but then closed it again, perhaps realizing that it was as well to keep quiet, given his own unwarranted presence in the West Wing corridor that night.

'So, given that Dr. Bachmann had an excellent reason to hold a grudge against Coddington,' continued Freddy, 'I naturally wondered whether he might possibly have committed the murder. The only way that he could have done it as far as I can see would have been to hare downstairs after everybody had gone back to bed and do it quickly then, so I wanted to ask you whether you saw him go back to the East Wing last night. If not, then it might be a good idea to ask him where he was.'

'But he's an old friend of mine,' said Cedric. 'He couldn't possibly have done it. And even if he could have done it he couldn't have done it.'

'What?'

'I mean, not then. I saw him go into his room, you see. We said goodnight to each other.'

'Might he have waited a moment then come out again?'

'I doubt it,' said Cedric. 'His door squeaks appallingly—as a matter of fact, I've been meaning to speak to one of the servants about it. It took me a while to drop off when I went back to bed, and I'm pretty sure I'd have heard him if he'd come out of his room again.'

'Bother,' said Freddy. 'And it was such a beautiful theory. But ought we to tell the police about it?'

'*You* may, if you like. But I should like to know how you propose to explain what you were doing scrabbling around in Bachmann's underthings.'

This was a fair point, Freddy was forced to admit.

'I suppose motive doesn't make a case,' he said. 'Perhaps it had better wait until we have some more concrete evidence.'

He left the Duke to his whisky and went out into the hall, where he stood for a few minutes, eyeing the top of the staircase where it branched into two and led off into the East and West Wings respectively. If Dr. Bachmann had not run downstairs at twenty past three, then might somebody else have done it? If so, then who? He turned and saw his grandfather, who was just then coming quietly out of the small salon.

'What are you up to now?' said Freddy.

'Escaping from your mother,' said Nugs. 'My, but she's an exasperating woman! Takes after your grandmother, you know. As a matter of fact I wonder sometimes whether she's anything to do with me. I find it difficult to believe that any real daughter of mine could be quite so irritating as she is.'

'Nugs,' said Freddy. 'You're in the East Wing. Did you see anything last night after you went back to bed? After Ro yelled, I mean.'

'Eh? What's that? What are you talking about?' said Nugs. A guilty look appeared momentarily on his face.

'There's something wrong with the murder,' said Freddy. 'I don't know what it is, but the theory of how he died doesn't seem to fit the facts, and I'm trying to find one that *does* fit. We've been assuming that someone was lying in wait for him in the library, but now I wonder whether it happened quite differently, and that somebody ran downstairs after the disturbance and did it then, either while Goose and I were in Ro's room or while we were chasing the professor through the secret passage. But if you went straight back to bed then you won't have seen anybody.'

'We-ell,' said Nugs, 'If you must know, I didn't go straight back to bed. I went back into my room then came out again.'

'You surprise me,' said Freddy dryly. 'Don't tell me you went and made a nuisance of yourself to Mrs. Dragusha this time.'

'Certainly not!' said Nugs. 'What do you take me for? As a matter of fact, it was all perfectly innocent. I just happened to remember I hadn't finished my glass of whisky when we came up to play the joke on young Uttridge, so I went down to get it.'

'At what time was that, exactly?'

'How should I know? I never notice that sort of thing. A few minutes after the party on the landing, probably.'

'Did you see anybody?'

'Not in the East Wing. I saw you and Goose and Ro from the top of the stairs, though. You were all standing outside her room, jabbering about something. Then you went into her room and I went downstairs. I topped up the whisky, then sat in the study for a bit. I dare say I dozed for a minute or two.'

'Hmm. Then you'd have had to pass the library. Did you see anything?'

'How should I remember?'

'Think! It might be important.'

Nugs blew out his cheeks and thought.

'As far as I can recall the door was ajar and the light was off,' he said at last.

'And you didn't see anybody downstairs?'

'Not a soul.'

'How long did you stay in the study?'

'I don't know. Twenty minutes, perhaps? I started feeling cold after a while, so I went back to bed and missed all the fun after you found the professor.'

Freddy thought. As far as he could tell, Nugs must have come downstairs again at about half past three. The murder had presumably taken place some time around then, so why had Nugs not seen the murderer? Had he been hiding behind something, lying in wait?

'Did you hear anyone wandering around while you were in the study?'

'I don't hear anything these days,' said Nugs. 'Do you mean the murderer? Would he be arriving or leaving?'

'I don't know,' said Freddy.

'Stupid old Codfish, getting himself murdered and ruining everyone's weekend,' said Nugs, with an unrepentant lack of sympathy. 'They're all the same, these ghastly academics. Ridiculously thick-skinned, with no idea how to behave in polite company. What sort of half-wit continues with a theft when he's already been discovered? Didn't he think anybody would notice the pearls were missing after Ro caught him burgling her room?'

Freddy stared. This had not occurred to him, but of course his grandfather was right. Why had the professor not dropped the pearls and made a run for it when Ro woke up and discovered him in her room? Why had he proceeded coolly to take the necklace? For surely he must have known it was inevitable that he would be discovered. Had he intended to steal the pearls after all, rather than just examine them? That reminded Freddy of another question which he had not resolved satisfactorily: why had Coddington had no torch in his hand when he was found? He had been through the secret passage, and his project to take the pearls would have been almost impossible without one. Where was the torch? Who had taken it?

At any rate, Nugs had now accounted for about another ten minutes of the vital time—perhaps from twenty past to half past three. Or had he? Freddy was suddenly struck by a horrible thought as he remembered what his grandfather had said about putting a pillow over Ralph's face.

'Nugs, it wasn't you, was it?' he said half-fearfully. 'You didn't kill him, did you?'

'What?' said Nugs.

'I just wondered whether you'd taken it into your head to play a joke on him and give him a playful tap on the skull then run off, but accidentally hit him harder than you intended. You would mention it, wouldn't you, if that was what had happened? There's no harm in confessing, you know. I mean, let's face it, you'd have no trouble at all in convincing a jury that you're not of sound mind, so there's not the remotest chance they'd hang you. They probably wouldn't even put you in gaol, in fact. They'd send you to a nice, comfortable institution with lots of pretty young nurses to look after you. I expect you'd be very happy there.'

Nugs glared at him.

'Don't think I don't recognize impudence when I hear it,' he said. 'Of course I didn't do it. Where would be the fun in it?'

'One never knows with you,' said Freddy. 'I just thought I'd better ask, that's all. Very well, I suppose I'll take your word for it.'

'Kind of you,' said Nugs, and made to depart. 'By the way,' he said. 'I'd keep an eye on that young woman of yours if I were you.'

'Iris?' said Freddy without thinking.

'Daphne, you ass. Goose is angling to get his hooks on her if I'm not much mistaken. I expect you haven't been paying her enough attention. Women like attention. They're like cats. Stroke 'em and they'll purr, but ignore them and you'll know about it soon enough.'

'Rot. Daphne's not a cat.'

'You think not? Go in there and see her now. They're sitting on the sofa together. He's stroking her just where she likes it and she's purring.'

'I'll thank you to keep your dirty remarks to yourself, you despicable old brute,' said Freddy.

Nugs leered, tapped his nose and sauntered off. Freddy watched him go in annoyance, but after a moment's thought decided that it might be a good idea to return to the salon. Perhaps he had been neglecting Daphne a little.

CHAPTER NINETEEN

O N SUNDAY MORNING Freddy rose late and was forced to breakfast alone, since everybody else had long finished. Afterwards he wandered into the morning-room and found Cynthia and Lavinia Philpott there, sitting facing one another, quite upright and bristling in unspoken deadlock. He beat a hasty retreat, then realized he had left his cigarettes upstairs, and so went to fetch them. As he passed Ro's room he saw that the door was open. Inside, Ro, Mrs. Dragusha and Kitty Fitzsimmons were talking nineteen to the dozen and holding dresses up. Valentina Sangiacomo was standing silently out of the way by the dressing-table, waiting until she was wanted.

'Hallo, what's the to-do?' said Freddy from the doorway. Kitty turned.

'Hallo, Freddy,' she said. 'Isn't it thrilling? I've managed to persuade Mrs. Dragusha to make me a frock while she's here. It's a huge privilege, you know, since she's awfully busy.'

'For you I will make time,' said Mrs. Dragusha. 'When I first saw you I said to myself, "Now, there is a woman I should like to dress." Three, four ideas came into my mind immediately, and I am only pleased that you came to me now, because otherwise I should have had to make you wait. But now I am—how do you say—at a loose end for a day or two, until the police let us go, and I can begin.'

As she spoke she was whisking samples of brightly-coloured silk and satin in front of her new client.

'Yes, that's what Val said,' said Kitty. 'She knew you'd have nothing to do, and so suggested I ask you. You're a clever girl, Val.'

'Thank you, ma'am,' said Valentina respectfully, to Freddy's secret amusement.

'I prefer the pink to the silver,' said Ro critically. 'It flatters your complexion more. I wanted that shade for my birthday frock, but Mrs. Dragusha said it wouldn't look as nice with the pearls, so I chose the blue instead. Not that it matters now,' she added bitterly. Freddy glanced at her questioningly, and she said, 'Oh, the cat's out of the bag, of course. I suppose it was too much to hope for that it could have been kept a secret.'

'You mustn't let what your father said bother you,' said Kitty. 'He was a little grumpy, that's all. I'm sure he doesn't think for one second that you had anything to do with it.'

'Yes he does. You didn't hear him,' said Ro. 'It was as clear as anything what he thought.'

'But is it quite certain they're fake? You were wearing them last night and they looked real enough to me.'

'Father wanted to keep it quiet, so he suggested I wear them and pretend nothing was wrong,' said Ro. 'I should much rather not have, but I didn't want him to be even crosser with me than he already was, so I did it. But I felt sick all the while, and I was sure everybody was looking at me and whispering behind their hands about it. In the end I couldn't stand it any more and came up to bed early.'

'Nobody was whispering about it,' said Kitty. 'I didn't suspect a thing. It was Lavinia Philpott who told me this morning. She'd overheard two of the maids talking about it.'

'I suppose one advantage of everybody knowing is that I shall never have to wear them again,' said Ro. She went across to the dressing-table and picked up the fake pearls with an expression of disgust. 'I wish I'd never set eyes on the stupid things—and I don't even know why we're keeping these ones. They're fit for nothing but the bin.'

With that she dropped the pearls into a waste-paper basket that was standing next to the dressing-table, and plumped herself back onto the bed in a fit of pique.

'Now, darling,' said Kitty. She darted a significant look at Valentina, who fished them out and began picking off bits of fluff and other detritus.

'Oh, well, what's the use in keeping them?' said Ro.

'The police will want them for evidence if Cedric decides to report it,' said Freddy.

Ro was about to reply, but was interrupted by Mrs. Dragusha, who had been draping Kitty in silks and was not attending to the conversation.

'But that is the perfect colour!' she exclaimed, clapping her hands. 'Look, everybody! Is she not the very picture of beauty?'

They all looked upon Kitty Fitzsimmons, who was swathed in a shade of crimson that might have been invented especially for her, so exquisitely did it suit her. The sunlight was shining on her through the window at that moment, and the effect was breathtaking.

'It's rather nice,' said Freddy inadequately, and Kitty burst out laughing.

'Now there's a real compliment!' she said, and turned back to look at herself in the glass. 'I suppose I might be allowed it. I've been a widow too long now for anybody other than the strictest of old ladies to complain about it, and it's certainly a flattering colour on me. Mrs. Dragusha, I believe you are a witch!'

'Not at all,' said Mrs. Dragusha modestly. 'But perhaps I have a little eye for colour.'

The conversation then moved on to technicalities, and Freddy felt his presence was no longer required.

'You'd better lock the necklace back in its box and put it in the safe,' he said to Ro.

She pouted, but swung her legs off the bed and took the pearls from Valentina, who had finished cleaning them off.

'There!' she said, locking them back in the case. 'I'll take them down now, and I hope I'll never have to see them again.'

She went off to deliver the case to her father, and Freddy went to fetch his cigarettes.

As he came out of his room he saw what looked like a mountain of linen with a pair of black-stockinged legs sticking out from under it, wobbling precariously in and out of a cupboard at the end of the corridor. The legs turned out to belong to a tiny housemaid, who was struggling to reach the top shelf.

'You'll get along much better if you do it a few at a time,' said Freddy, stepping forward to help.

'Oh, thank you, sir!' she gasped. 'It's just that I can't fit anything else on the bottom shelves, and I'll be in trouble if I don't put them away quickly.'

She seemed terrified of something. Freddy suspected it was Mrs. Bates, the housekeeper.

'You can't possibly reach up there,' he said. 'Here, give me those last ones and get off with you.'

'Thank you, sir,' she said again, then bobbed and ran off.

He put the sheets on the top shelf, then on second thoughts rearranged them more neatly. He had no idea whether they would meet Mrs. Bates's exacting standards, but he suspected not. This was the same linen cupboard from which they had taken the sheets for the abortive trick on Ralph, and he sighed regretfully at the memory. It was a pity it had all gone badly, although he was really getting too old for silly jokes of that sort. He was reflecting pleasurably on similar triumphs of his earlier youth, when he noticed a pile of sheets that was not lying flat, and reached up absently to pat them down. They refused to allow it, and, puzzled, he lifted up the corner of the pile to see what the impediment was. Something hard was creating an unsightly lump and spoiling the look of things. He poked about, and his eyes widened. A little more effort brought out the object that had been hidden under the sheets. It was long and heavy, and he knew what it was even before he saw it.

'Well, if that doesn't beat all!' he murmured to himself, regarding the sash weight in his hand. He took it out onto the landing to look more closely at it. The light was dim up here, but he thought he could distinguish one or two dark stains.

'What's that?' said a voice at his shoulder. It was Iris. He showed her wordlessly what he had found and she gave a little gasp.

'Is that—is that—' she said, regarding it with distaste.

'I rather think it is,' he replied.

'But how did it get in there?'

'I should very much like to know that myself,' said Freddy. His mind was racing as he considered the possibilities. Had the murderer run up here and hidden his weapon hurriedly in the linen cupboard immediately after killing Professor Coddington, or had he taken it to his room at first then put it here afterwards, worried that the police might find it in his possession? Either way, he had been lucky not to bump into Nugs, who must have been wandering around the house at about the same time.

'Are the police here yet?' he said.

'I don't think so,' said Iris. 'I heard the Duke muttering about it downstairs just now.'

Freddy took a sheet and wrapped the weight carefully in it, then placed it on a shelf so as to avoid any accidental interference with it.

'I need a torch,' he said.

'I have a little one with me. It's in my room,' she said, and ran off before he could object. She was back in a moment with the article in question. 'What are you looking for?'

'I want to see whether our murderer left any traces of himself in the linen cupboard when he came to stow his weapon here,' he said.

He switched on the torch and stepped back into the cupboard. It had shelves to a height of about six feet on each side, all piled with bed-linen, but the back was bare, and panelled to about halfway up the wall. He shone the torch around on the floor, which was slightly dusty, then up and along the shelves.

'Anything?' said Iris.

'Not as far as I can see,' said Freddy, directing the torch back to the floor and then to the walls. There was a piece of loose wood hanging from the edge of one of the panels, and he pushed it back into place, then started in astonishment as the whole section of wall gave way under his hand. For a shocked moment he thought he had accidentally pulled the panelling off, and winced at the thought of confessing to Bea. Then he looked more closely and realized that he had not damaged anything at all.

'I say!' he exclaimed. 'It's another secret passage!'

'What?' said Iris in excitement. 'Goose never mentioned this one.'

'Oh, Belsingham is full of them,' said Freddy. 'The Warehams had a mania for the things. I'm surprised the place hasn't collapsed in on itself given all the excavation that must have gone on.'

'Where does it go?' said Iris.

'I don't know,' said Freddy. The door was about the same size as the one in Ro's room. He bent and shone the torch into the hole, then ducked inside. 'It's just high enough to stand upright,' he said, his voice muffled, and ducked back out. 'What are you doing?' he said in surprise, for Iris had stepped into the cupboard and shut the door behind her.

'This is our discovery,' she said. 'I don't want to share it.'

'You're not coming in.'

'Yes I am.'

'But you'll get filthy.'

'So will you,' she pointed out. 'Anyway, we didn't get filthy the other day. And do you really think I'm going to let you leave me out of an adventure? Now, get on with it.'

There was no use in arguing with her, especially when she was smiling at him in that way, so he gave it up.

'All right, but keep behind me,' he said.

'Of course,' she said demurely.

He ducked inside and she followed. This passage was lower and narrower than the other one, and after about ten feet it narrowed even further. Without the torch the darkness would have been complete, and Iris clutched Freddy's hand tightly as they went. He, meanwhile, was worried about the height of the ceiling and its possible effect on his skull if he misjudged it, and so he kept his head as low as possible.

'This isn't as much fun as the other one,' said Iris after a minute.

'It isn't, is it?' he agreed. 'We can go back if you like.'

'No,' she said. 'I won't be happy until I've seen where it leads.'

It was not long before they found out, for after only a little distance they emerged into another tunnel, and came to a halt in sudden recognition, for they had come out through the low doorway with the cracked wooden beam, and were standing at the end of the passage which led to Ro's bedroom, at the top of the second fork which ended at the head of the spiral staircase.

'So that's where that other passage leads,' said Freddy. 'I thought Goose said it was blocked.'

'He did,' said Iris. 'Are you sure this is the same passage?'

'It looks the same to me. See that split in the lintel there?'

'I think we ought to make quite certain, though. If it really is the same one then the secret door to Ro's bedroom ought to be down here. Come on.'

She set off. Freddy followed, and sure enough they were very soon standing by the door that led behind the tapestry and into Ro's room.

'Is it the right door?' said Iris.

'If it is, then the staircase will be just along here,' said Freddy.

A short investigation resulted in the conclusion that they were indeed in the same passage.

'What shall we do now?' said Iris, as they stood at the head of the spiral staircase, where the passage forked into two. 'I vote we go down to the library and give whoever's in there a shock.'

'No, let's go back through the cupboard,' said Freddy. 'I want to look at something.'

This time they went along the right-hand fork. The torch was beginning to fail and it was becoming difficult to see, and they blundered along half-blindly for a minute or two. Then Freddy stopped.

'Oh,' he said. 'We're outside Ro's room again.'

'How did we do that?' said Iris.

'We must have missed the entrance to the other passage. It's easily done in the dark.'

They returned the way they had come, took the correct turning this time, and at last arrived at the hole in the wall at the back of the linen cupboard. Freddy stuck his head through for a moment, then withdrew and examined the wall of the passage. He seemed to be looking for something.

'Ah!' he said.

'What is it?' said Iris.

'I want to know if it's possible to get into the cupboard this way if the hole is closed,' he said. 'It looks like the mechanism that opens it from the cupboard side works from this side too. Look here, I'm going to shut the passage up, then try and open it again. You go into the cupboard and let me out if I get stuck.'

She ducked through the hole into the cupboard, and he pushed the door shut. It clicked into place, leaving him with only the faint light from the failing torch. He groped for the catch and pulled it, and the door opened again.

'Well, that's clear enough,' he said, as he stepped out into the linen cupboard.

'What's clear enough?'

'Why, it's clear that nothing's clear.'

'Idiot,' she said. 'It's another passage, though.'

'Yes,' said Freddy. He closed the entrance and regarded it with a frown for a moment. 'I wonder why this door opened so easily.'

He turned to see Iris's face gazing dimly up at him in the torchlight. She was standing very close to him, and the cupboard suddenly seemed much smaller than it had before. The torch flickered.

'I think that torch is about to go out,' she said.

As she spoke, it did exactly that, and everything went black. There was a significant pause.

'Why are we standing here in the dark?' said Freddy at last.

'I don't know,' whispered Iris.

'Perhaps we ought to get out.'

'Yes, perhaps we ought.'

'You go first.'

'All right,' she said, but did not move.

She smelt of fresh spring flowers. Dutifully, he tried again.

'I don't think old Ralph would be particularly happy to know you were skulking in a linen cupboard with me,' he said.

'No, he wouldn't, would he? I expect he'd be awfully cross,' she replied. 'You won't tell him, will you?'

'No,' he said.

There was another pause, then she giggled.

Afterwards, when his head had stopped spinning and he was able to think about it clearly, he was almost sure it was she who had started it. But whether she had or not, certain it was that she participated in the kiss with quite as much enthusiasm as he, wrapping her arms tightly about his neck in a manner which left no doubt that she had put Ralph entirely out of her mind for the present. It was undoubtedly disgraceful behaviour on the part of both of them, and how long they would have continued cannot be said; perhaps fortunately, however, circumstances intervened to spare them the necessity of making the decision themselves, for all at once the cupboard door opened, the darkness lifted and there came a loud shriek. Freddy and Iris broke apart instantly, and for a second Freddy had a confused impression of a sea of horrified faces staring at them. Then his brain began distinguishing things properly, and he saw the housekeeper and the maid he had helped earlier, staring at them both in astonishment—and behind them Daphne, who—of all the rotten luck—had evidently been passing the cupboard at that very moment. Freddy's heart sank, but before he could say anything Iris gave an appalled squeak and made a bolt for it. Daphne watched her go, then turned her face back to Freddy with a questioning expression. There was nothing he could say to explain himself, so he said nothing, and after a moment Daphne stuck her nose in the air and stalked off with great dignity.

'I beg your pardon, sir,' said the housekeeper stiffly. 'I had no idea anybody was in here.'

The little housemaid was gazing steadily at the floor, and looked for all the world as though she were trying not to laugh.

'Oh—er—no, quite, what?' he said. The remark was perhaps feeble in the circumstances, but a fuller explanation was obviously impossible, and so he stepped out of the cupboard and prepared to retreat without further ado. Just then he remembered the sash weight and turned back.

'I forgot, I need this,' he said. He took down the sheet with the weight inside it. 'By the way, I should avoid touching that pile of sheets on the top shelf if I were you,' he added. 'The police will probably want to look at them.'

Then he headed towards the stairs, feeling the eyes of the two servants boring into his back as he went.

CHAPTER TWENTY

THE POLICE HAD arrived, which gave Freddy a good excuse to avoid the company of the other guests for a while. Inspector Trubshaw seemed to waver between interest at the story of the second passage and the sash weight, and annoyance at the fact that Freddy had disobeyed his instructions to leave the investigation to the police.

'You ought to have come and found us, sir,' he said. 'We'd have taken care of it all. And you really ought to have left the weight where it was.'

'Yes, I dare say you're right,' said Freddy. 'But I'm afraid I brought it out without thinking. And as for the secret passage, I found that quite accidentally. I was all for coming to tell you, but unfortunately one of the other guests was with me at the time, and she insisted on exploring the passage straightaway.' Having thrown the blame onto Iris without compunction, he went on, 'I don't know whether you've ever tried saying no to a woman, inspector, but if you have you'll know it's not as easy as it sounds.'

'That's all very well,' said Trubshaw, 'but you might have destroyed any evidence that was on the weight by bringing it out.'

'I've been very careful with it,' said Freddy. 'And it was lying under a pile of sheets, so any marks would most likely have rubbed off anyway. But as you can see, there are one or two suggestive stains on it, and I expect you'll find more traces in the linen cupboard.'

'Hmm,' said Trubshaw, peering at the weight. 'Yes, I'd better send one of the men up now before the servants start messing about with everything and destroy the evidence.'

'I don't know where the second passage comes in,' said Freddy, 'but I suppose it does open up other possibilities.'

'Yes,' said Trubshaw. 'We shall have to give them some thought. But next time, if you find any evidence, I'd be obliged if you'd come straight to us with it.'

'Of course,' said Freddy.

He left the study and went into the morning-room, where he found Iris sitting with Ralph and talking gaily as though butter would not melt in her mouth. She barely glanced at Freddy, who decided it would be politic to spend the morning out of doors. He wondered how long it would be before the story was all around the house. Given how quickly the news of the missing pearls had spread, he judged it would not be long. He hoped nobody would tell Ralph about it. Ralph was not exactly the sort to biff a chap on the nose when offended, but he was the sort to make long, injured speeches, which would be both awkward and dull. Still, even if Ralph never found out, there was still Daphne to contend with. Freddy felt a twinge of guilt here. He hoped he had not hurt her feelings too much. There had never been anything serious between them, but there was no denying that it was the height of bad manners to invite a girl on a visit to one's grand relations, only to embarrass her by being caught misbehaving in a cupboard with another girl entirely. He should not have blamed Daphne if she declared she never wanted to see him again. Sooner or later he should have to face her, but he was cowardly enough to wish to avoid her for now.

It was a fine spring day and the weather was warm for the time of year, so Freddy decided to head down towards the lake and sit there for a while. The grass was dry, so he threw himself down in a comfortable spot and lay with his hands behind his head, staring idly up at the sky and thinking about what he had learned that morning. What did the discovery of this second secret passage mean? Did it make Dr. Bachmann's guilt any more likely? Say he had been in the library when the professor had come out of the passage with the pearls. Had he murdered Coddington then taken his torch and come up through the secret passage and out through the cupboard, then shown his face in the West Wing while everybody was still out of their rooms? That would certainly explain why the professor had not been carrying a torch when he was found.

Freddy set himself to think it out carefully, and very shortly came to the conclusion that there were several objections to that theory. First: he had seen no torch in Bachmann's hand—although it was always possible that he had left it somewhere. Second: the timing was all wrong. Ro had screamed at ten past three or thereabouts, whereupon Professor Coddington had escaped into the passage. If one allowed ten minutes for the professor to get from Ro's room to the library (or seven at the very least if he was sprinting, although he had not been an agile man), another couple of minutes for the murder, and another seven to ten minutes for Bachmann to run back through the passage and out into the linen cupboard, that made fifteen minutes at the outside, and more likely twenty. In other words, he could not possibly have arrived back upstairs before twenty-five past three—and yet Freddy had seen him with his own eyes standing with the other guests outside Ro's room at twenty past three and perhaps even earlier, with no sign of being out of breath. Third: how could Bachmann have known that Coddington was planning to steal the pearls and escape through the secret passage? Unless they had been in league together— but no, that was unlikely given their enmity. However Freddy looked at it, none of it made sense.

He sat up. He was looking at the thing all wrong, he was sure of it. He felt in his pocket for a notebook and set himself to writing down all the facts as they were known. Then he read over what he had written. It was rather unsatisfactory.

3.10	Ro sees Prof. C in her room and screams
3.10-3.20	Several guests out of bed. The only people not to come out are Bea and Cynthia P-S
3.25	Corridor quiet again except for FP-S and Goose. Ro comes out and reports pearls missing
3.30-3.40	FP-S and Goose go through secret passage and find Prof. C dead with the pearls in his hand

3.25-3.55   Nugs goes downstairs again. He sees nobody (although in study between 3.35 and 3.55 so might have missed the whole thing)

He frowned. Perhaps he ought to put down the sequence of events leading up to the scream. He added:

2.00   FP-S and Nugs up

2.05   FP-S and Nugs go down to study

2.15   Goose joins party in study

2.35   Joke suggested. FP-S, Nugs and Goose return upstairs

2.35-3.10   Preparation of dummy in FP-S's room

Then as an afterthought:

2.50 (or thereabouts)   Goose runs down to library to fetch torch.

Freddy paused and stared at this last entry for some time as he realized its significance. Why had Goose not seen anybody loitering about when he went down to the library? It must have been very soon after that that the professor had gone into the secret passage, so why had Goose not seen any sign of him when he came downstairs? Freddy made a note to question him more closely about it, for it seemed to him that here was an important clue, although he had no idea what it meant at present.

He looked at his notes again, willing something to leap out at him. He was sure he was missing something. What was it, now? The pearls, perhaps? There was no reason to believe the professor had taken them out of anything other than impertinent curiosity—but there again was the fact that, as Nugs had pointed out, he had gone ahead with the theft even after Ro had raised the alarm. That did not sound like the actions of an innocent man. But in turn the objection to *that* was that the pearls had supposedly been exchanged some weeks or even months earlier—which was the reason for the professor's having taken them in the first place.

Freddy sighed. He was beginning to think he was going mad, and that he ought to leave it all to the police, who surely knew what they were doing and would be able to find out things he could not. It was getting towards lunch-time, so he walked slowly back up the slope towards the garden. Then he stopped as he saw someone standing watching him by the garden gate. It was Daphne. She started forward as he approached, and he drew a deep breath and went to take his punishment. When they met she said nothing, but merely looked at him as though awaiting an explanation.

'I'm sorry, it was all my fault,' he said dutifully. It was the only thing he could say in the circumstances.

'I only hope you're pleased with yourself,' she said. 'You've got what you wanted and she's got what she wanted, so let's not worry about trampling all over anybody else's feelings, shall we? After all, nobody else matters as long as *you're* happy.'

She spoke calmly and with dignity, which only made him feel worse.

'It wasn't like that,' he began, but she went on without listening: 'I suppose I ought to have expected it, since it was perfectly obvious what she was up to. She's been watching you like a hawk since you arrived. I'm only surprised she didn't pounce sooner.'

'I say, don't blame Iris,' he said. 'It was nothing to do with her.'

'Don't be ridiculous. She wasn't exactly fighting you off, was she? In fact, I'll bet she manoeuvred you into it. Look here, it's not as though I didn't know exactly what you're like, so this is hardly unexpected, but you might at least have had the decency not to humiliate me by doing it at Belsingham, of all places. You know half the people here think I'm beneath them, including your mother—oh, don't bother to deny it, she makes it very clear—so I should have thought you might have been gentleman enough to restrain yourself and not make things any worse.'

There were tears in her eyes, and Freddy felt a worm.

'And the servants saw too, so it's not even as though we can keep it quiet,' she said. 'It'll be all over the house by now. I'd like to know what Ralph will say when he finds out.'

'I should imagine Iris will see to it that he doesn't,' said Freddy dryly.

'Perhaps. But if he does then she'll let you take the blame for it all. And you will, too.'

This was true, and he did not bother to deny it.

'Look, I *am* sorry, Daph,' he said. 'You're right, of course. It was beastly of me, and I have no excuse for it.'

'No, you don't. You're being a fool over her, you know. She'll only lead you a merry dance. She's found herself lumbered with a dull stick, and she wants a little fun and excitement before she gets married and has to give it all up. She doesn't really want you—she's just using you.'

Freddy did not want to think about that possibility.

She went on suddenly:

'I only wish the police would let us go away, then I could leave quietly and not have to slink around the house worrying that everybody is pointing at me and saying they knew this sort of thing would happen because I'm a poor tea-merchant's daughter rather than a Lady Somebody.'

'Listen, you're to stop talking in that way,' said Freddy. 'It doesn't matter two hoots what you are or aren't. Nobody cares about titles.'

'You might not, but everybody else does,' said Daphne. 'Lavinia does. She'd be simply thrilled if I married someone with a title, but I'm sick of it all, I tell you. I'm sick of the formality, and the precedence, and worrying whether I ought to say Duchess or your Grace. It's all nonsense. And it's dangerous, too. Do you think Professor Coddington would have been murdered if the Duke had still been plain Mr. Wareham? Of course he wouldn't! None of this would have happened, because there'd have been no fabulously valuable heirlooms to steal. I wish I'd never come here. I'd go back to London now if I could.'

'I'm sorry you feel like that,' said Freddy. 'I expect they'll let us go soon, but they're still collecting evidence.'

'And they've been searching people's rooms, too. All this is bad enough, without having one's things rifled through.'

The luncheon-bell rang just then, slightly to Freddy's relief.

'I'm sorry,' he said again. It was all he could say, for any attempt to excuse himself would have been hollow, and they both knew it.

She gave him one last reproachful look and hurried away, and he followed slowly, reflecting that he had got off lightly, all things considered. But he soon found out that he was wrong in his assumption, for after lunch Bea button-holed him and requested a word in a manner not to be denied.

'What's all this I hear about you and Iris?' she demanded crossly, once they were alone. 'Mrs. Bates came to me in a great state saying she'd found you both doing who knows what in the linen cupboard.'

'*Who knows what?*' said Freddy indignantly. 'We were only kissing. It was all perfectly innocent.'

'Innocent, indeed! In case you've forgotten, she is engaged to Ralph. Now, it's none of my business what anybody gets up to in their own home, but I should like to remind you that you're under our roof at present, and as such you're expected to behave. Mrs. Bates is getting quite tired of bumping into you at awkward moments. She's a nervy sort at the best of times, and I should hate for her to give notice.'

'I'm sorry,' he said, for what felt like the twentieth time that day. 'It wasn't intentional, I assure you. It all happened on the spur of the moment. We found another secret passage, you see, and we wanted to know where it went. That's why we were in the cupboard.'

'Another secret passage?' said Bea. 'Oh, yes, of course. I thought the door of that one had seized up long ago.'

'It seems not,' said Freddy. 'Anyway, we went through it and came back, and then—I don't know. It was a silly thing, really. I know I oughtn't to have done it. I don't know what got into me.'

Bea unbent a little and regarded him with some sympathy.

'If you still like her then why don't you try and win her back?' she said. 'The wedding isn't for six weeks yet.'

'Because it wouldn't work,' he said. 'She wants something I'm not. Ralph's a dry old thing but at least she can rely on him. I—well, you know. I'm not exactly a model of self-control, am I? I can never help getting into scrapes.'

'Scrapes, you call them,' she said, amused. 'Yes, I suppose you could call this morning's adventure a scrape.'

'She'd be unhappy, and I'd have to spend my life abasing myself and begging pardon. She's much better off with Ralph.'

Bea sighed.

'Well, far be it from me to interfere,' she said. 'Just don't do it again, please. And go and apologize to Daphne.'

'I already have,' he said.

'Did she accept it?'

'I'm not sure. She kept her fists to herself, at any rate.'

She laughed.

'That's something. Very well, I've done my duty in giving you a scolding, so now I can go back to thinking about all my other troubles. I don't mind telling you I'm quite sick and tired of all this business with the murder. I dare say you know the police have been searching our rooms this morning? I gather they found something that proves poor Dr. Bachmann might have had a motive to kill the professor.'

'Oh? What is it?'

'Some academic feud or other, I think. They didn't say what. Dr. Bachmann is putting on his most dignified face, but one can tell he's terribly cut up about it.'

'Perhaps you ought to go and lend a sympathetic ear,' said Freddy.

'I don't think he wants to talk to anybody.'

'Nonsense, he'd be overjoyed if you listened to his troubles.'

'Perhaps I shall, then,' she said. 'I do feel I've been neglecting my guests, rather.'

'Hardly surprising, is it? I mean, given what's happened here in the past couple of days.'

'We've had more successful parties, it's true,' she said resignedly, and went off to do her duty to her guests.

CHAPTER TWENTY-ONE

IT SEEMED THE continued presence of the police was making everybody uncomfortable, for all the guests were restless. Everywhere Freddy went he bumped into one or other of them wandering about, looking as though they did not quite know what they were doing. The police had taken over Cedric's study, and he was striding grumpily in and out of the downstairs rooms, snapping at anyone who dared to speak to him. Ro was draped across a chair in the morning-room, replying to all questions as shortly as possible and generally giving the impression of one who hated all mankind. Cynthia was haranguing Nugs about something or other, and he was taking it meekly, while occasionally darting longing glances at a whisky decanter that was just out of reach. Meanwhile, Lavinia was gushing to Goose, while Daphne sat slightly apart from the two of them, doing her best not to seem fed up. There was no sign of either Iris or Ralph, and Freddy imagined she had dragged him off somewhere in a fit of guilt to play the dutiful intended. She was probably hanging on his arm somewhere about the garden, and agreeing with his every word. The thought did not make Freddy feel any better. He looked out through the French windows. Kitty Fitzsimmons was standing on the terrace, gazing across the grounds towards the lake. He went out and joined her. She looked tired, and in the bright sunlight he could see one or two lines around her eyes.

'Hallo,' she said. 'I've had a trying morning and I've come out to lick my wounds in peace. Oh, there's no need to go,' she went on, as he showed signs of leaving. 'I'm just smarting a little, that's all. I expect you are too.'

'Just a little,' admitted Freddy, and she laughed.

'Poor you. And rotten luck for you both—to be caught, I mean. Still, I shouldn't worry. So many things have happened here this weekend that everybody will have forgotten it all by tomorrow.'

'I hope so,' he said. 'Why are you smarting?'

'Because the police dragged up all the old story about Rob,' she said.

'It was a motor-car accident, wasn't it? In the South of France, I seem to recall. He died, but you got out unhurt.'

'Yes. I suppose you remember all the rumours about it at the time. People couldn't understand how I'd got out alive while Rob hadn't. There were some rather unpleasant suggestions that I'd arranged it deliberately.'

'Of course you didn't,' said Freddy, and just managed not to turn it into a question.

'No,' she said. 'I wasn't even there, in fact.'

He looked at her in surprise, and she gave a little laugh, and said:

'The woman in the car with him wasn't me, and she didn't get out at all—she died with him.'

'I had no idea,' said Freddy.

'No, we kept it quite secret. He and I had been living separate lives for some time before then. It was all very amicable, but we kept it quiet because it was no-one's business but our own. But he was an idiot to take the girl with him. She was a nobody—a shop-girl or something—and it could have caused an awful scandal if anybody had found out about it, because of his diplomatic position. He was terribly important to the Government, you know, and it was the sort of job in which one has to be seen to be above reproach, for the good of the country. It would have looked very bad had it come out that he was running around in Nice with a woman who wasn't his wife, so when I heard the news I hurried across to France and pretended I'd been with him, and that I'd got out completely unharmed. The girl's family tried to make trouble, and we had to pay them to keep quiet about it. But rumours have a way of getting out, don't they? And people got hold of the wrong end of the stick and instead of suspecting what really happened, they thought I'd planned the accident deliberately.'

'I'm sorry,' said Freddy, and he meant it, although at the same time he could not help wondering whether his friends and relations would have called Daphne a nobody if the two of *them* had died in a motor accident.

She gave a dismissive gesture.

'No need,' she said. 'I'm quite hardened to it all now. Or at least I thought I was, until the police got hold of me this morning. You see, they telegraphed the French police and got the story from them—the true one, I mean—and gave me an uncomfortable time of it.'

'Why? You didn't do anything strictly illegal, did you?'

'Not as far as I know. Both of them were given a decent burial and I don't think it's against the law to try and stop the papers getting hold of a story. No, it wasn't that. It's just that somebody has told them they saw Professor Coddington pestering me before he died. Apparently I had a guilty look on my face at the time, and whoever it was put two and two together to make—oh, about eleven, I should think—and told the police. Anyway, they wanted to know whether the professor had somehow found out the truth and tried to blackmail me with it.'

'And had he?'

'No!' she said. 'Although it's true he was pestering me. He was terribly superior and dropped some hints that he knew something to my disadvantage, but after about two minutes it became perfectly clear that he was talking about the old rumours that I'd been responsible for Rob's death, so I made some chilling reply or other and escaped as soon as I could.'

'Not such a fine fellow, the professor,' said Freddy. 'I don't wonder someone took a sash weight to him.'

'No,' she agreed. 'But it wasn't me, at any rate.'

'What did the police say about it?'

'Nothing in particular. They were all very non-committal, as you'd expect. One can never get anything out of them. But as a matter of fact, I rather think they're stumped. They asked me whether I got up in the night at all, but I didn't, except for a couple of minutes when everybody else did. They kept asking me what time that was, and of course I hadn't the faintest idea. They seemed a little preoccupied with times, actually.'

'I think they're coming to the conclusion, as I have, that it was impossible for any of the guests to have killed Coddington,' said Freddy. 'I imagine we'll hear shortly that they're causing consternation below stairs by suggesting one of the servants did it.'

'Goodness me,' said Kitty. 'Then perhaps we oughtn't to expect dinner on time, if the servants are in an uproar. You won't tell anybody what I told you, will you? I should hate to see the whole thing chewed over in the papers. I don't like to think of Rob's reputation being ruined—especially not now he's dead. I was terribly fond of him, despite everything.'

'I won't say a word,' he promised, and she smiled gratefully.

'Thank you, you're very kind,' she said. 'I shall trust you, even if you do work for the *Clarion*. But please don't tell your mother.'

'No fear of that. She'd have it in her gossip column before you could say knife.'

'I know it,' she said, then glanced up. 'There's Mrs. Dragusha. She must be ready for me again.'

She waved, and Freddy turned to see the dressmaker standing at the top of the terrace steps, evidently looking for Mrs. Fitzsimmons. Kitty sighed.

'I gather Iris is furious with me for pushing ahead of her in the queue,' she said. 'I had no idea she'd been trying to persuade Mrs. Dragusha to fit her in too. But her waiting list is so long that I simply had to jump in as soon as I had the opportunity. I shall have to try and make peace with Iris as best I can.'

She gave a rueful smile and hurried off, leaving Freddy to think about what she had told him. There seemed to be nothing in Kitty's story that would give her a motive for having killed the professor. It was clear she had made every attempt to prevent the circumstances of her husband's death from reaching the press, but as far as he could tell she had done nothing against the law, exactly. But was she telling the truth about Professor Coddington? She said it was obvious that, despite what he had insinuated, he did not know what had really happened. Had that been a lie? If he had somehow found out the true story and had threatened Kitty with exposure, then would she have been desperate enough to kill him in order to keep it quiet? Freddy considered the possibility for a moment, then remembered Cedric's presence in the West Wing that night. It was almost certain that she had an alibi for the first part of the night, although she would undoubtedly try to avoid using it if it were at all possible. But what about later? He thought back to what had happened. He recalled that Kitty had emerged from her room, had seemed terribly bored by the disturbance, and then had gone back to bed. She might have waited until the coast was clear, then gone downstairs and killed the professor, Freddy supposed—but then, how was it that she had not been seen by Nugs, who had been wandering around the house and had passed the library at just around the time of Coddington's death? Might she have crept out of her room and got into the passage through the linen cupboard? If that were the case, then how had she known about that entrance? Bea had said she thought it had been blocked up long ago.

He went back into the morning-room, and found his mother there, still talking to Nugs, who brightened in visible relief at Freddy's entrance.

'Oh, there you are, darling,' said Cynthia. 'I wanted to talk to you, but you keep running off.'

'If it's about this morning, then I've already had an earful from Daphne and Bea, so you needn't bother,' he said.

'This morning? What happened this morning?' said Cynthia, pricking up her ears. 'What have you been getting up to now?'

'Nothing. Never mind,' he said hurriedly, kicking himself, for it seemed she had heard nothing of it.

'You're not keeping things from me, are you? You may as well tell me now, because I shall find out one way or the other,' she said, although she obviously had other things on her mind, for she immediately went on: 'Now listen, I want to know what you've found out. You must tell me whatever you know, as I have to write my piece. I was a little worried that I might be short of material this week, since we were coming to Belsing-ham for a dull family party—or so I *thought*—but after what's happened there are simply heaps of things I could say if the police would only let me, but they've embargoed almost everything I want to write, so you must give me something I can use. You can keep all the dull news to yourself, but you must let me have the juicy society stuff. What did Kitty say to you just now? Was it something about the murder?'

'It was nothing at all interesting,' said Freddy.

'Nonsense. Whatever it was, you can be sure she told you purposely so you'd pass it on to me. You know how she loves seeing her name in the papers.'

'Oh, very well, if you must know, she was telling me about the frock Mrs. Dragusha is making for her. And don't ask me to repeat what she said, because I was only half-listening.'

'Only that? That's not much. But how did Kitty manage it? I thought one had to wait months for a Dragusha frock. Is Iris getting one too?'

'No, and I hear she isn't too happy about it,' said Freddy.

'Hmm. Now I might be able to work with that,' said Cynthia, considering. 'I expect I can whip it up into a nice little feud.'

'Don't be absurd, there's no feud,' said Freddy, but he could see his mother was not listening, and had already begun to compose the piece in her head.

'I'll just write a few notes down,' she said, and went to sit at a writing-desk at the side of the room. Nugs took the opportunity to escape, and Freddy did likewise. His mother's words had reminded him that he would have to write his own piece for the *Clarion*, and he was just about to go and ask the police how much of the story he might be permitted to publish, when he was accosted by Goose, whose mouth was drawn together in a thin line, and who looked as though he meant business.

'I've come to thump you,' he said without preamble. 'What's this I hear about your playing fast and loose with half the women in the place?'

This was a gross exaggeration, and Freddy opened his mouth to say so, but Goose went on:

'You've upset Daphne, and she says she wants to leave. And I dare say Ralph will want to have a word with you, too.'

'He doesn't know?' said Freddy in some alarm.

'Haven't the foggiest,' said Goose. 'Although if he does he'll probably be telling Iris how disappointed he is in her for the next few hours. That ought to give you plenty of time to escape. No, but seriously, Freddy, how could you do it to Daphne? She's a splendid girl and doesn't deserve that kind of thing.'

'I know she doesn't, and you're about the fifth person to tell me that. I've begged her pardon, but it's nobody's business but ours.'

'It's my business too,' said Goose. 'Or it would be if you'd have the decency to step aside and let me have a shot.'

'I don't know why you're asking my permission *now*,' said Freddy pointedly. 'You've spent the last two days having a shot, as far as I can tell.'

'I most certainly have not! I'm a man of honour, and I'd never steal another chap's girl. I won't deny I've talked to her, but I like her, Freddy. She's a sensible girl and her head isn't at all turned by my title. One doesn't see that very often these days.'

'I rather think your title puts her off, old bean,' said Freddy. 'She finds all this formality a little too much to take.'

'Then she needn't,' said Goose. 'It must be this mausoleum she doesn't like. I mean to say, nobody could possibly find Father and Mother too formal. Why, they're as easy as they come! We none of us were brought up to this. But this place is slightly rattly, I will admit. She wouldn't have to live here all the time. We could have a flat in London if she liked—'

'Oh, you've got that far, have you?' said Freddy in surprise, as Goose stopped and flushed. 'Well, if that's how you feel about her, don't let me stop you. You might have an uphill battle to convince her, though. Still, at least you'll have Lavinia on your side,' he added maliciously.

'Oh, Lord!' said Goose expressively. His usual cheery demeanour had returned, and he had quite forgotten his declared intention to thump Freddy. 'I say, thanks.'

'My pleasure,' said Freddy dryly. 'Now that you've got my girl, is there anything else you'd like?'

'No, that'll do for now, thanks,' said Goose with a grin, and was preparing to depart when Freddy suddenly remembered something.

'Goose, you know the other night when you went downstairs to get the torch from the library?'

'Yes.'

'Was the light on?'

'In the library?' Goose wrinkled his forehead. 'No, it was off. I switched it on and then off again when I came out.'

'And you didn't see anybody?'

'No, nobody. Why?'

'Why, because it was about ten to three when you went down, and Professor Coddington must surely have been up and prowling around by then. If he wasn't in the library he must have been in the secret passage already. Did you look in that direction?'

'No,' said Goose. 'I didn't go into that part of the room at all. I went across to the chest of drawers where the torch was, dug it out and then left.'

'So you didn't see whether the door to the secret passage was open?'

'No. One can't see that part of the room very well, with that beastly great desk in the way and the stairs up to the balcony. But it must have been open, mustn't it? As you say, if he wasn't in the library when I went in then he must have been in the passage already.'

'I wonder why he switched the light off, then,' said Freddy thoughtfully.

'What?'

'Think about it—if you were Coddington and you'd got up and were planning a little midnight jaunt to help yourself to someone's family jewels, what would you do? You'd come into the library and switch on the light, wouldn't you?'

'Not if you didn't want to be seen.'

'But then how did he see to find the book and the catch to open the door?'

'Why, he took a torch with him, of course,' said Goose.

'But that's just it—he didn't,' said Freddy. 'There was no torch in his hand when he was found.'

'But he must have had one if he was wandering around in the passage. One couldn't possibly find one's way up to Ro's room and back down to the library without one. Not quickly, at any rate.'

'No,' said Freddy thoughtfully.

'I expect the murderer took the torch off him after he killed him, then ran off through the passage.'

'But we were in the passage then, so why didn't we bump into him or hear him?'

'Haven't the foggiest,' said Goose, with a shrug. He seemed to have lost interest in the case, and Freddy suspected his mind was on other things now. 'Anyway, I shouldn't worry about it if I were you. That's all for the police to think about—nothing to do with us. I shouldn't be a bit surprised if they decide it was an outside job after all. You just watch—they'll find a broken latch somewhere and some footprints, and they'll have the culprit arrested in no time.'

'Do you think so?'

'I'm sure of it. After all, why should any of us have wanted to kill Coddington? I know he was an ass, but being an ass doesn't generally get you murdered, does it? Why, someone would have taken a heavy object to you long ago if that were the case.'

'Thanks,' said Freddy, and Goose guffawed and went off in search of Daphne.

Chapter Twenty-two

THE POLICE WERE busy examining the linen cupboard and could not speak to him, so Freddy telephoned the *Clarion* and reported the bare facts, then went into the library with some intention of following his mother's example and writing a few notes for a longer piece. As he entered he saw Mr. Wray, who was sitting at a desk, absorbed in some old books. The old man jumped when he saw Freddy.

'Oh, Mr. Pilkington-Soames!' he exclaimed. 'Have you been talking to the police? A fine body of men, and naturally they are only doing their duty, but their presence puts one a little on edge—perhaps because it reminds one continually of the unpleasantness of the past day or two. But that is selfish of me, of course. A man has died, and one must not expect the wheels of justice to turn according to one's own convenience—that is, with as little disturbance as possible. But I feel very much for the Duke and Duchess, who, I imagine, were far from think-ing such a thing could happen here in their house.'

Freddy agreed that the weekend would certainly have been more congenial without the murder.

'Ah, yes, you are a reporter,' said Mr. Wray, spying Freddy's notebook and pencil. 'I had forgotten. Have you come to write? Then I shall not disturb you. No, no—no need to beg pardon, I quite understand.'

And with that he went back to his books. Freddy sat down and scribbled a few notes, but could not get far, for he still did not know how much he would be permitted to publish. He paused and scratched his chin, then saw Mr. Wray looking at him.

'It must be a fascinating job,' said the clergyman, 'to have the power of communicating to many thousands of people, and to know that they will believe whatever you write.'

'Would that that were so,' said Freddy. 'You ought to see all the letters I get telling me I emit only the purest bilge. Only they don't use the word "bilge"—nothing so polite. I think a lot of my readers must be farmers, to judge from their famil-iarity with the digestive systems of various forms of livestock.'

'Dear me!' said Mr. Wray. 'I suppose there are always some who are not easily pleased. But your task is a tremendously important one, and comes with great responsibility, for you must decide what the public may hear.'

'Not I, I'm afraid,' said Freddy. 'It's the editor who decides that. Or the police, in this case. I can't really do much until I've spoken to them. I don't know whether I'm allowed to mention the pearls, for example—I mean the fact that the professor was found with them in his hand.'

'But why should they object?'

'Because it might prejudice any future trial,' said Freddy.

'Then it is customary to withhold information?'

'Oh, we do it all the time,' said Freddy. 'One can't always be exposing people all over the place. Sometimes it's best to let them sin in private. But I expect you disagree.'

'No, not at all,' said Mr. Wray. 'Or, at least, not in every case. There are, of course, times when wrongdoing must be brought to the attention of the public—especially in the case of very grave sins and crimes. But at other times such exposure might do more harm than good. I speak of cases in which nobody is injured, you understand. In such instances I believe it is better that the wrongdoer be given the chance to repent in private and make amends.'

'I don't think Professor Coddington would have agreed with you.'

'No indeed,' said Mr. Wray. 'He made quite a little speech on the subject, in fact. Perhaps you heard it?'

'He got very exercised about the secret passage, I remember. It was the oddest thing. He seemed to think it was a symptom of the irremediable degeneracy of the Wareham family.'

'Perhaps he was a little more vehement than was necessary,' agreed Mr. Wray. 'I see no harm in secret passages myself—on the contrary, I find them fascinating. As a matter of fact, there is something here—' he got up and went across to a shelf of ancient books. 'Hmm—hmm. Now, where was it. Ah!' He took down a weighty tome and brought it to the table. 'The

Duchess was good enough to show me this book a few weeks ago when I expressed an interest in the history of the building. You see, it contains some of the early plans. We must be careful with the paper, for it is very fragile, and I should not wish to destroy such a valuable work of historical interest. But here you see are some plans which show all the secret passages in the house.'

Freddy pored over the book with interest. The page folded out to show a plan of Belsingham, with a legend underneath and handwritten notes in various places around it. The ink had faded to a pale brown and the writing was crabbed, but he could just make out some of the words. The plan itself was clearly drawn, and it was not long before he found the passage from the library. He followed it with a finger, and noted that it showed both exits—the one into Ro's room and the second one into the linen cupboard.

'I say, there's another passage in the hall,' he said at last.

'The Duchess informed me that that one is blocked up,' said Mr. Wray. 'As a matter of fact, most of them are impassable. There is another in the dining-room, you see, but it has a large and heavy dresser against it and so cannot be entered. It is difficult to see from the plan, but I believe it goes out into the grounds. I have read about it in another book, for it was the scene of one of the less honourable escapades of John Wareham, your ancestor. He was the younger brother of the fourth Duke, you will remember, and rather a trial to his family. The story goes that he—shall we say—pressed his attentions upon the wife of one of the Duke's neighbours. Understandably outraged, the neighbour rode to Belsingham with ten armed men and demanded satisfaction, but it seems John Wareham was reluctant to oblige him. He escaped through the secret passage and disappeared for five years, and when he returned he brought with him the Belsingham pearls, which he had obtained in India. By the time of his return the neighbour had died and the wife had remarried, and she was naturally reluctant to have the old story brought up, and so Wareham got off scot-free.'

'Is that so?' said Freddy. 'This John Wareham sounds a most interesting fellow.'

'He was something of a scoundrel, but as is so often the way of things, he survived to a ripe old age, despite doing nothing to deserve it. Fortunately, he was merely a younger son, and so did not inherit the dukedom, which remains in capable hands to this day. No, I may say that, in spite of the occasional black sheep, the Warehams are a most respectable and worthy family, and, I believe, well deserving of the honours that have been heaped upon them over the years.'

Freddy glanced at him thoughtfully, then turned his eyes back to the page, although he was not paying attention, for his mind had begun working. At last he returned the book to its place and settled down to work again, and there was silence for a few minutes until Mr. Wray announced his intention to indulge in an afternoon nap.

'I am afraid my headache has returned,' he said. 'Perhaps a little rest will help.'

Freddy looked up sharply.

'Not the old trouble again, is it?' he said.

The clergyman's brow flickered, and he seemed disconcerted.

'I very much hope not, Mr. Pilkington-Soames,' he said, and with that, hurried out.

Freddy sat for a minute or two in contemplation, then, instead of going back to his work, got up again and went over to where he had found Professor Coddington's body. He looked around, then went to the shelf in the corner, took down the book that hid the catch to the secret passage, and opened it. Then he went across to the doorway into the hall and surveyed the room. A large desk stood between him and the place where the murder had been committed, but if he stared hard he could just see a gap in the shelves where the passage door stood open. It was not immediately obvious when one looked in that direction, so if it had been open when Goose had come in for the torch, it was quite possible that he might not have noticed it.

Freddy wanted to see how long it would take to get to Ro's room without a light, and was about to dive into the passage and try it, when he thought better of it and decided to take a torch for emergencies. Goose's torch had been returned to its place in the drawer, so Freddy slipped it into his pocket then stepped into the passage, taking note of the time as he did so. He set off at a brisk pace, but as soon as the passage turned left a little way along, he was plunged into darkness and had to slow down. He moved carefully onwards, touching the wall and using it as a guide. The floor was rough and he had to take great care so as to be sure not to trip. At last he came to the stone staircase and ascended it with only one or two missteps. From here he knew there was not far to go.

'Ridiculous idea, to do this without a torch,' he said to himself. The remark reminded him of his adventure with Iris that morning, and he was thinking about that when he was suddenly struck by an idea. He hesitated, then instead of setting off along the left-hand fork, which was the shortest route, he groped his way into the right-hand fork instead, and stumbled along it. At the end he knew the passage turned left and went past Ro's room, while ahead was the smaller passage with the lintel above it which led to the linen cupboard. He and Iris had missed their way that morning while making their way back to the cupboard, and had accidentally ended up outside Ro's room—and after flailing around in the dark for a while, he was not entirely surprised to find that he had done exactly the same thing again. He dug out the torch, shone it at his watch, and saw that the journey had taken just over fifteen minutes.

He spent some little time experimenting, then returned to Ro's room, whereupon he realized that since he had been at the back of the procession the other day when they had all come through the passage, he did not know how to open the panel. Perhaps there was a catch like the one in the linen cupboard. He felt around and, sure enough, his hand closed upon a wooden protuberance at about the same height as the other one. He pushed it, then pulled it, and felt something give. The door opened towards him and Freddy stepped cautiously out from behind the tapestry and into Ro's room.

All was quiet up here. He looked at the four-posted bed with its rich hangings, and noted that if the curtains were closed he would not be able to see the dressing-table. Professor Coddington could not have walked to it directly, because the bed was in the way, and he would have had to come some distance away from the passage entrance to see it. Freddy stepped across to the dressing-table. As usual, it was scattered carelessly about with odds and ends, and he was gazing down at it when Ro came in. He whirled around.

'What are you doing?' she demanded.

'Sorry, old thing, I didn't mean to intrude,' he said. 'I was just trying to picture what happened the other night, but I don't quite seem to be able to manage it. I'm finding it particularly difficult to understand what happened in here, but you can help with that. Will you tell me again what you saw?'

She sighed.

'Must we go over it all again?' she said. 'And why are you doing this? Surely it's the police's job.'

'Yes, it is, but I'm incorrigibly curious, and if I can help solve the thing then I'll get the most marvellous story out of it. Old Bickerstaffe will adopt me as his own and I might even get a rise—although perhaps that's too much to hope for. Besides, Trubshaw pooh-poohed the idea when I asked if I might help— seemed to think I didn't have a brain in my head, in fact—and it rather put my back up.'

'You really oughtn't to interfere, you know.'

'I'm not interfering. I shall tell them anything I find out as soon as I find it out. I handed over the sash weight like a good boy, didn't I? So, then, tell me exactly what you saw here the other night.'

'Oh, very well, but it's not much. It took me a while to get to sleep, and when I did I kept waking up because I thought I heard noises.'

'What sort of noises?'

'Doors opening and closing, that sort of thing. I expect it was you lot, tramping around like a herd of cattle, playing your silly joke. I kept thinking it was my door, but now I realize it must have been yours, since it's next to mine.'

'I don't suppose you remember at what time that was?'

'I did squint at the clock at one point, and it was twenty-five past two. But then everything went quiet again and I drifted off, then—I don't know—I must have heard another sound, I think, because I woke with a start. I didn't realize there was anything odd happening at first, so I turned over and was going to settle down again when I saw somebody standing by the tapestry.'

'Somebody?'

'Well, it was too dark to see who it was at first.'

'But it was a man?'

'Of course it was a man,' she said impatiently. 'It was Professor Coddington, wasn't it?'

'Perhaps. If you hadn't been told it was Professor Coddington, then who should you have thought it was?'

She stared in puzzlement.

'Why, I don't know. It might have been anyone, really.'

'Certainly a man, though?'

'Why, yes, I think so.' She stopped and screwed her eyes up, trying to remember. 'I assumed it was a man at the time, although it might have been a woman, I suppose.'

'Tall or short?'

'I'm not sure. It's difficult to tell when one's lying down.'

'Let's say it was a man. What was he doing when you spotted him?'

'Nothing. He was just standing there.'

'Where?'

'There, next to the tapestry. He didn't move at first, but I could hear him breathing—he seemed out of breath. Then he took a step forward and that's when I screamed.'

'And what did he do?'

'He started and looked about him. I thought he was looking for the nearest way out.'

'And then he went back into the passage, yes?'

'I assume so, but I didn't actually see it. I'm ashamed to say I put my head under the bedclothes, so I didn't see where he went. I cowered there for a few seconds, then counted to three to get my courage back, threw myself out of bed and made a dive for the door. That's when I saw you three and assumed it was one of you I'd seen.'

'You didn't see him take the pearls, then?'

'No. I didn't notice the pearls were missing until all the commotion was over and everybody had gone back to bed.'

'Did you see the intruder go near the dressing-table at all?'

'No. I couldn't have, because I only had the bed curtains open on this side. There was a moon that night and it was shining through the gap in the window curtains, so I shut the bed curtain on the window side.'

'Like this, you mean?' said Freddy, pulling the curtain in question across. 'What about the one at the foot of the bed?'

'That one was closed too,' she said.

Freddy pulled the bottom curtain across and sat on the bed. From where he was sitting a large part of the room was blocked from view.

'Isn't it awfully stuffy with the curtains shut?' he said.

'Yes,' she replied. 'But I didn't have them all closed, and I do keep them open as a rule. It was just that the moon was bothering me. The window curtains need rehanging and I keep forgetting to mention it.'

He got up and went across to look at the dressing-table.

'Did you give the fake pearls to your father, by the way?' he said.

'Of course I did. Don't you remember? You saw me take them downstairs this morning.'

'I did see you, yes,' he said, stopping suddenly and staring at her.

'Why are you staring at me like that? What is it?'

'I don't know. Something just came to me, but it's gone now. Something to do with the pearls. What was it, now? I was thinking about the clasp, and then I had an idea, and now I can't remember what it was. You had the clasp mended, didn't you?'

'Yes, you know we did. We took the necklace to London last year and gave it to Keble's, and they fixed it.'

'Was that before or after you met the Farleys?'

'Why, I don't know—after, I think. Yes, it was the day after.'

'And then you got the pearls back and took them straight home without showing them to anyone, and put them in the safe, yes? And there they stayed until Thursday, when you tried them on with your new frock.'

'Yes, that's exactly what happened,' said Ro. 'We've been over it all before. Look here, what's this all about?'

'I'll tell you when I've worked it out myself,' said Freddy. 'I need to think.'

He went out into the West Wing corridor and found that the police must have finished their investigation into the linen cupboard, for everything was silent. He glanced about him. Ro's room was nearest the head of the stairs on this side of the corridor, and from there, if he looked to his right, he could see past the stairs and into the East Wing corridor a little distance away. To his left at the end of the West Wing corridor was a window, and from there the corridor turned left towards some bedrooms which were rarely used. Opposite Ro was Goose's room, with Ralph's next to it, farther away from the stairs. Next to Ralph was Daphne, then Iris and Kitty. Freddy was next door to Ro, followed by Mrs. Dragusha. Some way farther along was the linen cupboard, with Lavinia's room after it, while Mr. Wray's room was tucked away around the corner.

Freddy turned his eyes from one door to another, then stood outside Lavinia's room and looked towards the stairs, screwing up his eyes as he tried to remember the events of that night. At last, he walked slowly to the end of the corridor and gazed out of the window for some time.

'I reckon they're going to arrest Dr. Bachmann,' came a voice at his shoulder, making him jump. It was Valentina Sangiacomo, who had approached so quietly that he had not heard her coming.

'What makes you think that?' he said.

'One of the footmen heard him having a barney in the library with the prof,' she said succinctly.

'Really?' said Freddy. 'Just before the murder, you mean?'

'No, earlier than that. When you were all still up. Seems you were right—that letter was the first he knew that it was your chap who'd reported him. They had a good old set-to—or Bachmann would have liked to, except the prof was all superior and refused to get angry. He just said it was his professional duty to report—what was the word?—copying, anyhow, to the proper authorities.'

'Was it your young man who overheard them? Why didn't he mention it to you before?'

'It wasn't him, it was the other one,' said Valentina. 'Samuel, his name is. He never mentioned it before because he didn't think it was important, but then I happened to tell him what we'd found out about Dr. Bachmann, and he remembered what he'd heard.'

'Don't tell me Samuel overheard Bachmann threatening to kill the professor? That would be too convenient for words.'

'No,' she said. 'But he said he deserved to be punished for what he'd done. Then the prof laughed and said if Bachmann had only behaved himself in the first place this would never have happened.'

'Hmm. Well, we already knew Bachmann had a motive,' said Freddy. 'But what about opportunity? Did anyone see him downstairs at the right time?'

'I don't think so,' said Valentina. 'Wasn't he in this corridor with the rest of you? I thought you all gave each other an alibi.'

'That's what I thought, too, at first. Everyone was here between ten past and twenty past three, when the professor was presumably escaping through the passage, and so they couldn't have done it then. But Lord Holme and I were also in the corridor from twenty past until half past three, and we'd have seen if anybody came out of their room after that. The only people who might have run downstairs and intercepted the professor between twenty past and half past were the Duke, my grandfather and Dr. Bachmann. The Duke says he went to bed, and swears Bachmann did too. He also says that Bachmann couldn't possibly have got up again because his bedroom door squeaks loudly and he would have heard him.'

'What about your grandpa?'

'As a matter of fact, he says he *did* go downstairs afterwards. He also says he didn't brain Coddington, and I suppose I have to believe him. He's an addle-brained old galoot and the scourge of respectable women everywhere, but he's not the sort to go around killing people just because they annoy him. According to him, he went downstairs to the study at about half past three to get some whisky, and passed the library on the way, but he didn't see anybody. Let's say he was shut up in the study by twenty-five to four. Goose and I came out of the secret passage and found Coddington dead at twenty minutes to. Now, it's just possible that someone might have rushed down and killed the professor in those five minutes, but it doesn't seem probable. For a start, even without a torch the professor must have been out of the passage by half past three at the latest—I timed it myself not half an hour ago—so why was he still in the library? He must have known he'd been spotted with the pearls, so why didn't he creep back up to his room at once, instead of waiting to be caught red-handed?'

'Why did he take them at all, for that matter?' said Valentina. 'Once her ladyship screamed he must have known there'd be a hunt for the thief.'

'Yes, that's something else I've been wondering myself,' said Freddy.

'And have you come up with an answer?'

'As a matter of fact, I have,' he said.

'Go on,' she said. 'Don't tell me you've solved the whole thing.'

He glanced at her.

'Not exactly,' he said. 'There are one or two things that are still puzzling me, but there's only one way the murder could have happened that I can see.'

'Tell me,' she said. 'Do you know who did it?'

She seemed eager.

'I'm not sure,' he said. 'Perhaps. But I do know one thing—we've been looking at this all wrong from the start.'

CHAPTER TWENTY-THREE

DOWN IN THE morning-room, Freddy found Dr. Bachmann striding up and down, his hair all up on end, talking to Inspector Trubshaw and Cedric. Bea was there too, listening sympathetically.

'How long must this continue?' he was saying. 'It is not enough that I am hounded out of my university, but now the police continue to torment me with this story and throw it in my face. Yes, it seems I cannot deny that I spoke to this man on the night of his death. It is possible also that I upbraided him for his interference and the part he played in destroying my reputation. But to kill him? Never would I do such a thing! For I am secure in the knowledge that I have friends who believe me, who know my integrity, and they know that the story was false. What need have I to kill when I am secure in myself? When I was shown the paper of Jensen and Lundgren, I saw the similarities myself immediately, and was distraught, for you understand it is galling to see someone else arrive before you. But to suggest that I had copied the idea—why it is unthinkable! We published in two different countries, two months apart, and I knew nothing of their work until afterwards, for they are the sort who like to keep their ideas close to their chests, and publish to great surprise and éclat. It was only when Professor Coddington read of our respective work and decided something underhanded had been going on that there was any suggestion of plagiarism. Before that, my superiors had been sympathetic—but that was not enough for Coddington, who was a—what do you call it?—a busybody of the worst sort, and must needs write letters and make complaints until I was put out of my job. To mourn his death would be impossible and hypocritical, but to say I killed him—no, no, this must not be! I disliked him but I also felt sorry for him, for I had my friends to support me in my misery, and who did he have? Ask anyone in this house. They will all tell you that he was an irritation and an annoyance. Could such a man have had friends? This is what I asked myself when I spoke to him the other night, and I said it to his face, too. But he did not seem to care. He merely smirked and would not admit that he had jumped to a hasty and erroneous conclusion about my work, and in the end I could do nothing but regard him in disdain and question his humanity. Yes, I disliked him—perhaps I even hated him. But did I kill him? Certainly not! I should never have stooped to such a thing.'

He paused for breath, and Cedric said:

'Must you arrest him, inspector? Obviously you want to ask him some questions, but you might as well ask them here, surely? After all, we have several people—including myself—who will swear that Bachmann was upstairs at the time the professor was murdered, and apart from this unfortunate business of the letter and the row, I don't see why you think he was any more likely to have done it than anybody else. Ask him anything you like, but for goodness' sake do it here, rather than in some foul-smelling police cell in Swanage. If you find some actual evidence against him then arrest him by all means, but don't just do it for lack of a better alternative. Nobody will thank you for it, you know.'

Inspector Trubshaw seemed to waver.

'Look here, I'll vouch for him if you like,' went on Cedric. 'You won't make a run for it, will you, Bachmann? You'd better not, or I shall look a dreadful fool.'

Dr. Bachmann drew himself up proudly.

'Of course I shall not, Duke,' he said. 'I should never repay a friend's trust in such a manner. I shall stay here, and if the police find something to my disadvantage then I shall go quietly, as they say. But this will never happen, because I am an innocent man.'

'Very well, then,' said Trubshaw. 'If his Grace is willing to vouch for you, then I suppose there is no need to take you to the station at present. But it is true that I should like to ask you some more questions. Your Grace, may I use your study?'

'By all means,' said Cedric resignedly. 'I'm sure I'll get the place back sooner or later.'

'Inspector, might I have a word?' said Freddy, as Trubshaw and Bachmann prepared to leave the room. 'It's rather important.'

'Not just now, sir, if you don't mind,' said the inspector. 'I'm a little busy at present.'

'But—' began Freddy.

'Oh, let them get it over and done with,' said Cedric. 'It'll wait a while, won't it?' He lowered his voice as the inspector and Bachmann went out. 'Don't interrupt them now—I want my study back!'

Freddy gave it up with a grimace.

'Are you coming to the chapel, Freddy?' said Bea. 'Mr. Wray likes to give a little sermon on Sunday afternoons—just about twenty minutes or so. He says he likes to put the chapel to use, since we always go to church these days and the place is getting rather dilapidated. Do come.'

'All right,' said Freddy. 'I dare say it will do me good to think pure thoughts for a short spell.'

He ran upstairs to fetch a clean handkerchief, and as he came out of his room saw Kitty Fitzsimmons just coming out of Mrs. Dragusha's room next door. He glanced in and saw the dressmaker sitting at a little sewing-machine, examining the seam of a piece of rough white fabric.

'Hallo, Freddy,' said Kitty. 'Mrs. Dragusha is being awfully strict and won't let me try on the toile model yet.'

'No,' said Mrs. Dragusha from within. 'You must not try it yet, or you will think I am a madwoman who has imagined something deliberately to make a laughing-stock of you. I am still developing my ideas, but they must remain a secret until I am ready to show you. I shall take some measurements from you later, but for now you must be patient.'

Kitty laughed.

'I've never been patient in my life, but it seems for you I shall have to learn how, Mrs. Dragusha,' she said.

'That is so,' agreed Mrs. Dragusha. 'But I promise you will not regret it. Everything must be done in the correct order. It would not do to make a mistake at the earliest stage, or I will not be able to put it right.'

'Very well, I shall go and listen to Mr. Wray, and try very hard to think of my sins instead of pretty dresses,' said Kitty.

The chapel was a short distance away, and it was a pleasant walk through the grounds in the late afternoon sunlight. Freddy walked by himself, and sat at the back next to Nugs as Mr. Wray delivered the lesson in his quiet way. Daphne was avoiding him, and was sitting with Lavinia, while Iris sat next to Ralph in a seat across the aisle. Freddy could not help watching her as she sat up straight, listening virtuously to the sermon as though she were absorbing every word. Then she turned her head towards him, and the look she directed at him gave the lie to her demeanour, for it was not virtuous in the least. It was only polite to reciprocate, of course, and the next few minutes were spent most shamefully in silent flirtation. At last Ralph realized that Iris's attention had wandered, and glanced towards her, whereupon she snapped her head immediately back to the front. Freddy felt a nudge in his side, and turned to see his grandfather giving him a knowing leer. He ignored it and did his best to pay attention to the rest of the sermon, reflecting that perhaps this was neither the time nor the place to be making eyes at another man's intended.

On the walk back to the house Freddy sensed that Nugs would make pointed remarks, so he dropped to the back of the little group, well away from Iris and Ralph, and found himself walking next to Mr. Wray. Lavinia Philpott was in front with Dr. Bachmann, who was telling her about his childhood in the Alps, and for once she seemed to be listening rather than talking.

The clergyman replied politely to Freddy's compliments on the sermon, but appeared distracted, for every so often he rubbed at his forehead and winced. Freddy looked at him in concern.

'Is it your headache again?' he said.

'Yes—just a little,' replied Mr. Wray.

'Didn't the nap help at all?'

'I am afraid not. If anything, it has become worse over the course of the afternoon.'

'It's not just a headache, is it?'

'No,' said Mr. Wray, looking worried. 'I am afraid not. I thought that after the unfortunate death the other day the danger had receded, but once again I feel that something bodes ill here at Belsingham. If only I knew what it was then I could do something to prevent it, but once again I have only the haziest sense of what is approaching.'

'Then you have no idea who or what the feeling refers to?' Mr. Wray shook his head.

'There is something,' he said, 'but I cannot quite grasp it.'

'But it has something to do with the professor's death?'

'No—yes—I do not know. I cannot see what else it could be. It is very frustrating, Mr. Pilkington-Soames. If I am to be divinely appointed, then it would be useful to me to know how I am expected to act. There is danger, I feel it, but what am I to do about it? The weight of this headache crushes me until I cannot think!'

'All this is none of your responsibility, you know,' said Freddy.

'Oh, but I feel it is. Somebody is in danger—I know it, and must act. But who is it?'

'I think perhaps it might be you, if you insist on getting involved,' said Freddy gently. 'We've already had one murder, and we don't want another.'

Mr. Wray seemed uncomprehending.

'Look here, old chap,' went on Freddy. 'Go and lie down when you get back to the house, and we'll get Bea to call a doctor. He'll give you something to help with those headaches of yours, and probably something to help you sleep, too.'

'What can a doctor do?' said the clergyman. 'I am not ill, and I must act according to my calling.'

With that, he hurried into the house after Lavinia. When Freddy followed him in he was exasperated to find that the police had left again. But he was determined to speak to Inspector Trubshaw, and so went immediately to the telephone and called him at the police station. The result of the call was unsatisfactory, for Trubshaw was not there, and Freddy was forced to leave a message. He was about to go and look for Cedric, when he was struck by a thought. He picked up the telephone-receiver again and made a call to an old friend of his who lived in Leicestershire. This attempt was much more successful, although the friend had not heard from Freddy in months, and insisted on talking for some time before Freddy could ask the question which was the real purpose of his call. After that, he telephoned Scotland Yard and had a long conversation with his friend, Sergeant Bird, who was most interested to hear what he had to say. When he had hung up, Freddy chewed his lip and wondered what to do next. Over the course of the afternoon many things had become clear to him, and he now thought he knew what had happened on the night of Professor Coddington's death. The only thing now was to prove it, but without more evidence that would be difficult. He was impatient to do something, but it was a job for the police now, and so all he could do was to wait.

CHAPTER TWENTY-FOUR

A T LAST THE dressing-bell rang, and everybody retired to their rooms, some to meditate upon the uplifting message they had just received; others to array themselves in their finery and think of nothing but dinner. Freddy was doing his best to put Iris out of his mind, since it was clear that the thing could not possibly end well. He wanted to make it up with Daphne, for he was fond of her and did not want them to part on bad terms, and so as he dressed he pondered how best to approach her. He came out of his room and as he reached the head of the stairs saw the Duchess coming out from the East Wing, anxiously smoothing down the folds of her dress, an elegant creation in wine-coloured silk which was quite stunning and made her look ten years younger.

'Hallo, Freddy,' she said as she saw him. 'I was just wondering whether this is the right colour. It's a little more vivid than I'm used to.'

'I think it looks jolly nice,' he said approvingly. 'You ought to wear bold colours more often.'

'Do you think so?'

'Why of course! You're our hostess and we've all come to look at you. Where's the sense in trying to fade into the background?'

'I hadn't thought of it like that,' she said, as though struck by a new idea. 'I'm usually too busy thinking about seating arrangements and that sort of thing to worry too much about dress, but this frock is so gorgeous I can't help but feel that perhaps I've been missing something.'

'It's a Dragusha, is it?'

'Yes. I do believe she's a genius. I feel almost radiant this evening.'

'There's no almost about it. Go and show yourself downstairs and you'll see. Take my arm and we'll make an entrance. Dr. Bachmann won't be able to keep his eyes off you.'

'I think Dr. Bachmann has other things to think about at the moment.'

'Then it can't hurt to distract his attention from them and turn his mind to something nicer, can it?' he said, and she laughed.

'You're a good boy, Freddy,' she said. 'You always cheer me up.'

'I'm glad to hear it. Now, let's go and have a drink.'

They went into the small salon, where several people were already gathered. Near the door, Kitty Fitzsimmons was being charming to Dr. Bachmann, who was looking much less agitated than before and was even managing to laugh. They both looked up as Freddy and Bea entered. Dr. Bachmann directed an admiring look at Bea, who flushed slightly, while Kitty gave her one assessing glance and judged it best to retreat. She cast her eyes about for Cedric, but for once he was not paying attention to her; he, too, had just spied Bea, and was staring at her as though he had never seen her before. He came across to stand before his wife, who regarded him uncertainly, waiting to hear his opinion.

'Well—I mean to say—er—you look rather well, what?' he said at last. It was not perhaps the most elegant of compliments, but Bea understood him perfectly. Her face broke into a smile, and she took his proffered arm. Kitty looked briefly taken aback, then recovered herself immediately and fell into conversation with Mrs. Dragusha, who seemed very pleased with the effect her creation had caused upon the room. Conversation, which had stopped, resumed, and Freddy somehow found himself in an awkward tête-à-tête with Ralph, who began to talk determinedly of his and Iris's plans for their wedding tour. Freddy listened until the subject was exhausted and he could politely withdraw, then found himself standing by Ro, who looked across at Ralph and murmured:

'Is the wedding still going ahead?'

'As far as I know,' he replied.

'But has nobody told him—'

'Told him what? There's nothing to tell,' he said. 'And if there *were*, I'm sure you'd keep it to yourself, wouldn't you?'

She regarded him in some impatience.

'You're an idiot,' she said.

'So I understand,' he said dryly.

Just then, Daphne slipped into the salon alone. She was looking very pretty in pale green, and Freddy could not help but feel a twinge of regret at the sight of her. She did not come all the way into the room, but glanced around until she saw him, then indicated by a gesture that she wished to speak to him outside. He followed her out and into the morning-room. It was clear from her face, which wore an expression of displeasure, that she had not yet forgiven him, but still her first words surprised him.

'What have you been saying to Goose?' she snapped. 'He's been hovering around me all afternoon, and he seems to think he has your permission for it.'

'Oh—er—does he?' said Freddy.

'Yes, he does. What do you think you're playing at? Who are you to give anyone permission? I'm not *yours* to give away.'

'Goose is a fathead, if that's what he said,' said Freddy. 'But it wasn't like that at all. He likes you an awful lot—has gone positively gooey about you, as a matter of fact—and all I said was that I shouldn't stand in his way if he wanted to try and win you over. Nobody's trying to give anybody away, I promise you. Of course, if you don't like him, then there's nothing more to be said, but if you don't mind him then why not give him a chance? He's a decent chap—far more so than I am, and a much better prospect, too.'

'Do you really think that's all I'm interested in?' said Daphne heatedly. 'I'm not Lavinia, and I've told you I don't care two straws about marrying a title. And even if I did, you don't really think the Duke would allow it, do you?'

'I don't see why not,' said Freddy. 'He's a crusty old soul, but kind-hearted with it. No doubt he'd prefer something in the aristocratic line, but he won't say no to any young woman his son falls in love with, as long as she's from a respectable family.'

'Well, then, I'm afraid I don't qualify,' said Daphne. She saw his face and gave a humourless laugh. 'What do you think the Duke would say to an embezzler's niece?'

'What do you mean? Who's an embezzler?'

All at once her anger left her and she seemed to sag.

'Morris Philpott,' she said. 'Lavinia's husband. My father was rather high up in the Mahjapara Tea Company, and before he died he got Morris a job there as a favour to my mother. A couple of years ago Morris was killed in an accident, and then it was discovered that he had been defrauding the company for ages. I don't know how he was doing it exactly—something to do with fake shipping bills, they told me—but it turned out he'd made a lot of money out of the scheme. I expect he'd have continued, too, but the accident put a stop to it. It caused a big scandal and was in all the local papers, and we had the police bothering us for months, since they wanted to know whether my father had been in on it too before he died. Of course he hadn't, but I know there was talk, and suspicion followed us around for a good while.'

'Good Lord,' said Freddy. 'Had Lavinia known anything of all this?'

'She says not,' said Daphne. 'She didn't collude in it—that I'm certain of—but you know what she's like. She's the sort who's quite capable of ignoring anything unpleasant and pretending it didn't happen. At any rate, my mother died not long after the story came out, and I was left with Lavinia, and she decided we'd be better off coming back to England.' Her defiance returned and she drew herself up again. 'So now you know everything—and you also know why there's not the slightest use in your trying to pass me off onto Goose, because it will never be allowed.'

'Don't think like that,' said Freddy. 'Every family has its embarrassing relations. Lord knows the Warehams have enough of them.'

'But you know perfectly well you'll never have to apologize for it,' said Daphne bitterly. 'The rules don't apply to your sort, only to mine.'

'I say, I'm sorry,' said Freddy.

She shrugged awkwardly.

'It can't be helped,' she said.

'Professor Coddington knew the story, didn't he?'

She sighed.

'Yes, he did,' she said. 'He was out in India at the time, I gather, and read about it in all the newspapers. He was absolutely beastly about it. He started by dropping a couple of hints, then followed Lavinia around and pinned her into a corner after dinner that first night, and said in that horrid, supercilious way of his that she was lucky to have been invited to Belsingham given that she had a disgraced husband in her past.'

'Did he threaten to tell Cedric?'

'Not as such. He told her not to worry, and that her secret was safe with him, but the way he said it made it obvious that he intended to use it to make her as uncomfortable as possible while she was here. At least, that was the impression she got.'

Freddy said nothing as he tried to digest everything Daphne had told him. Perhaps she misinterpreted his silence, for she said, almost as though she were trying to convince herself:

'Lavinia's a good person, you know. Even if she is clumsy and obvious, she means well, and she's been very kind to me. It was difficult for her to come back to England after so many years, but I believe she felt awful about the damage Morris had done to our reputation, and she wanted to make up for it somehow by taking me to nice places and getting me into good company. I expect I ought to have said no, but—well, I won't deny it was fun, and then I met you, and Goose, and all your smart friends, and I suppose I was enjoying myself too much to put a stop to it. But Lavinia has the kindest heart, she really does. She'll do anything for anyone. Why, she even went to offer Mr. Wray some of her sleeping drops just now because she overheard him saying he had a headache.'

'What?' said Freddy suddenly. 'When was this?'

'A few minutes ago,' said Daphne, surprised at his sudden change of manner. 'She said not to wait for her, as she was going to see whether he was in his room—what are you doing?' she said, as Freddy opened the door.

'Sorry, but I've just remembered I left something upstairs,' said Freddy, and headed out of the room. She followed him into the hall.

'What is it?' she said. 'There's something wrong, isn't there?'

Goose was just coming out of the small salon as they hurried towards the stairs.

'Hi, where are you going?' he said. 'It's nearly time for dinner.'

'Is Mrs. Philpott down yet?' said Freddy.

'No,' replied Goose.

'Then you'd better come with us,' said Freddy, and took the stairs two at a time. They hurried after him as he headed along to the end of the West Wing corridor and around the corner. He did not bother to knock, but opened Mr. Wray's door without ceremony. They all paused for a second on the threshold, and Daphne cried out in astonishment at the unexpected sight of Lavinia Philpott in deadly struggle with Mr. Wray, whose usually pale face was suffused with blood as he tried desperately to unclench her strong hands from around his neck.

'Lavinia!' cried Daphne.

They all rushed forward, and Lavinia started and let go of the unfortunate clergyman, who fell back, panting.

'Oh!' she said, but got no further before Goose took her arms firmly and dragged her away.

'Thank you,' said Mr. Wray faintly.

'Are you all right?' said Goose. 'Perhaps we ought to fetch a doctor.'

'And the police, too,' said Freddy. 'Tell them we've found the murderer of Professor Coddington.'

'What?' exclaimed Goose.

'But Lavinia didn't kill him!' said Daphne, horrified.

'Not Lavinia,' said Freddy. 'Mr. Wray.'

CHAPTER TWENTY-FIVE

'IT COULDN'T REALLY have been anyone else,' said Freddy, as they all sat in the small salon after dinner. Lavinia was making the most of her invalid status, and was sitting in a comfortable armchair, sipping sherry delicately and allowing Daphne to attend to her. Mr. Wray had at last agreed to take some of Lavinia's sleeping drops, and had been persuaded by Bea to go to bed. He would be safe there until the police arrived, although they had taken the precaution of locking his door and removing all heavy objects from his room. 'However I looked at it, I couldn't see any possible way in which the professor could have died at the time we thought he did. There were simply too many people wandering around the house between ten past three and twenty to four, when we found his body. The murderer would have to have been extraordinarily lucky not to have been spotted by somebody. Nugs and I were both up just after two, but I didn't think the professor could have died before that, for various reasons—first, one would have expected the police doctor to have spotted that he'd been dead much longer than we thought, and second, there was all this business with the man in Ro's room. Our biggest mistake, you see, was to assume the intruder was Coddington, come to steal the pearls, whereas in fact it was Mr. Wray, who had merely got lost in the passage as he tried to escape. He was trying to get to the linen cupboard, but he went in without a torch, missed his way and ended up at the entrance to Ro's room. It's easily done—I did it myself twice today, in fact.'

'I don't think I follow,' said Cedric. 'If Coddington didn't take the pearls, then why was he found with them in his hand?'

'He did take them,' said Freddy. 'He went into Ro's room through the door quite openly at twenty-five past two and took them from her dressing-table. She heard him, but decided later that it must have been Goose, Nugs and I banging about in the corridor. But at twenty-five past two we were all still in the study, drinking, so it couldn't have been us. It must have been Coddington. I'd always wondered why he didn't have a torch with him when he was found, but of course he never went into the secret passage at all, and so had no need of one. I can't be sure, but what I *think* happened is that Mr. Wray was up, saw the professor coming out of Ro's room and followed him down into the library, where he found him preparing to examine the pearls. There was an altercation of some kind, and Professor Coddington came off worst. It's easy enough to see how it might have happened—Lord knows, any one of us might have done it if we'd happened to have a sash weight handy just as the professor made one of his pointed remarks. At any rate,

Mr. Wray found himself suddenly and distressingly responsible for the existence of a fresh corpse, and I expect was hoping to sneak back to his room and pretend it had never happened, when unfortunately for him Goose came downstairs looking for a torch. I think Mr. Wray was just coming out of the library when he spotted Goose coming down the stairs, went into a panic and decided to escape through the secret passage instead. He ran back in and opened the door, then at the last minute remembered to run back and switch off the light. He was just in time to disappear into the passage when Goose came in. You, of course, didn't spot the professor or the open passage door,' he went on to Goose. 'And why should you have? He was lying behind that big desk and you went to quite a different part of the room.'

'I say,' said Goose, disconcerted. 'I had no idea. Do you mean to say I nearly tripped over a dead body and didn't notice?'

'It seems so,' said Freddy. 'So, then, at ten to three or thereabouts Mr. Wray, still holding the sash weight, went into the passage without a torch, got lost, as we know, and accidentally stumbled into Ro's room. She yelled, and he immediately realized his mistake and made his escape. A few minutes later he came through the door into the linen cupboard, hid the weight and came out—only to find, much to his horror, that Ro's scream had woken the rest of the household, and they were all holding merry session out there in the corridor. He was about to withdraw hurriedly when he saw that Mrs. Philpott had spotted him, and decided to brazen it out, since she seemed unsuspicious—which she was, as she'd taken her sleeping-draught that night and was only half-awake, so didn't understand at the time what she'd seen. She assumed the door he'd come out of was the one to his room, and it wasn't until the next day that she realized it wasn't his room at all.'

'Yes, indeed,' said Lavinia, nodding. 'I remembered the next day that poor Mr. Wray's bedroom was around the corner from mine, so I went and peeped in through the door I'd seen him come out of, and found out sure enough that it was a cupboard. I was *most* puzzled, but in the end I thought Mr. Wray must have been searching for the—er—small room, and had taken a wrong turning. I didn't draw attention to it, because one doesn't like to embarrass people by pointing out their mistakes, does one? But today I overheard him talking to Freddy and he sounded terribly unwell, and it struck me that perhaps I might be of assistance, so I knocked on his door and offered him some of my drops. I take them to help me sleep, but they are also very efficacious in soothing a sore head—and safe, too, quite safe. He seemed puzzled, so I confided my fears about his health, and said I was sure he couldn't have slept much recently—not with such bad headaches—and I expected that was why he was confused and had made the mistake about the cupboard. When I said that he went positively white in the face, and attacked me quite without provocation, to my great surprise. Fortunately, I'm not the sort of woman to take that kind of thing lying down, and I fought back as hard as I could, but I'm very glad that Freddy and Lord Holme turned up when they did, or I don't know that my strength would have held out.'

'Yes, we arrived just in time,' said Goose. 'But how did you know what he was going to do, Freddy?'

'I didn't—not for certain. It was just a suspicion, since I knew he was feeling ill again, and it occurred to me that he was probably a little unbalanced when he was having these attacks. Mrs. Philpott meant to be kind by trying to help him with his headache, but I knew she'd seen him coming out of the cupboard, and was worried she'd mention it to him and unwittingly put herself in danger. And so she did.'

'I'm afraid I got hold of the wrong end of the stick, and thought you were attacking him,' said Goose. 'I do beg your pardon, Mrs. Philpott.'

She accepted the apology graciously, and took another sip of sherry. Freddy went on:

'Once I'd realized that Mr. Wray had come out of the cupboard and not his bedroom it was easy enough to work out the rest. Everyone thought the passage door into the linen cupboard had seized up years ago, but it opened quite easily when I accidentally stumbled upon it, so it was obvious that somebody had been through it recently, and Mr. Wray was the only guest who had been here long enough to have explored all the secret passages and got the door working again. He showed me a plan of the house himself, and was obviously very familiar with the place, so I knew he was almost certainly the culprit, but I hesitated to speak at first because he didn't seem to have a motive. He told me that first evening that he felt the house was threatened by a great evil, and he later said he sensed it had something to do with the professor. I assumed he believed he'd foreseen the professor's death, but now I rather think what he actually meant was that he felt the professor himself to be evil. I don't suppose he said anything when you put him to bed, Bea?'

'Yes, he did,' replied Bea. 'And you're quite right. The poor thing saw the professor with the pearls and thought he'd come to ruin the family. The professor actually confessed as much—said he believed the pearls were fake, and the fact ought to be exposed.'

'But that's not reason enough to kill, surely?' said Freddy. 'Why should he care about what happened to you?'

'Family pride, I expect,' said Bea. 'Mr. Wray is a Wareham, you know. As a matter of fact, he's the grandson of John Wareham, who brought the Belsingham pearls to England.'

'Really?' said Freddy. 'But wasn't that about a hundred and twenty years ago? Mr. Wray can't be that old, can he?'

'John married twice, the second time very late in life to a woman much younger than he. She bore him a daughter, Maria, who was Mr. Wray's mother. Mr. Wray became a little heated on the subject upstairs just now, but I gather Professor Coddington taunted him about it. You know, of course, that John Wareham spent some years trying to prove that his elder brother had forfeited all right to the dukedom, and that he himself was the rightful heir. It's all nonsense, but Professor Coddington told Mr. Wray he'd found some evidence that the story was true, and that it was a pity Mr. Wray was descended from John through the female rather than the male line, because then he might conceivably have had a claim to the dukedom himself. Apparently Mr. Wray became very dignified and said that, unlike his grandfather, he would never dream of behaving so badly as to try and claim something to which he was not entitled, upon which the professor said something that goaded him past all endurance, and in his fury he picked up the weight and—well, you know, of course. I don't know what that final taunt was, though, as Mr. Wray refused to say.'

'I expect it was something about his birth,' said Cedric. 'There's a story that Maria Wareham was thrown out of the house and married Mr. Wray senior in rather a hurry, from which I suppose we must draw our own conclusions. It was in a long, rambling letter Coddington sent me before he arrived. I didn't pay too much attention to it at the time, but I read through it carefully after he died, in case there were any clues. It was certainly the sort of sneaking thing he'd do—make impudent remarks about a fellow's parentage. I shouldn't be surprised if he threatened to put it all in his book, in fact.'

'Mr. Wray would have hated that,' said Bea. 'He was very confused, poor thing. He's terribly proud to be a Wareham, but hates the fact that he's descended from one of the less worthy ones. And to have everybody knowing that his mother wasn't exactly what she ought to have been either would have tortured him, I imagine. I don't know why Professor Coddington thought he had to mention it. If he'd had the sense to leave well alone then he might still be alive.'

'I doubt it. If not Mr. Wray then someone else was bound to have landed him one on the noggin,' said Goose cheerfully. 'Sorry, Mother,' he added, as he saw Bea's face.

'Mr. Wray is very ashamed of what he did,' said Bea severely. 'With any luck the police will let him sleep for a while when they get here. I have the feeling he hasn't slept in days.'

'I'm sure I shan't sleep a wink myself tonight, after all the excitement!' said Lavinia. 'Thank you, Daphne. Perhaps I shall have just another *little* glass.'

She looked up in surprise to see Cynthia approaching her, pen and notebook in hand.

'Now darling,' said Cynthia briskly, 'I know you won't mind, but I simply *must* put you in my column this week, given everything that's happened. All London will be simply dying to know about the events here at Belsingham once the story gets into the papers. Of course my readers are more interested in the human side of things, so we'll start with that delightful frock of yours. Now, would you describe it as fuchsia or cerise?'

'Oh!' said Lavinia, gratified.

Chapter Twenty-six

'COME INTO THE study and have a drink,' said Cedric, once Freddy had finished telling his tale and the guests were all eagerly talking over the events of the evening. 'Good show all round,' he said, once they were seated. 'The police will be here shortly, and they'll take him away, and I can have my house back. I don't suppose they'll hang him, since he's quite patently off his rocker, although I dare say Bea will want me to bring Jephson in—his firm has represented the Warehams for centuries, you know—but that can wait until tomorrow after the old fellow's had a good night's sleep. Still, order has been restored, more or less, and all I have to do now is decide whether to report the theft of these damned pearls. The whole house knows about it now, so the news is bound to get out sooner or later. Perhaps I'll bite on the bullet and tell the police when they arrive. The publicity will be ghastly, but at least there's a chance they might be found.'

'Ah, yes, the pearls,' said Freddy. 'As a matter of fact, I have an idea about that.'

'What's that?' said Cedric.

'It's just an inkling. I may be wrong, but if I'm not then there may be no need to report it at all.'

'Well, then, out with it, dash it!'

'Are the fake ones still in the safe? Might I see them? And I'll need an eye-glass, if you have one.'

'There's one in the safe with the jewels,' said Cedric. He took his key and fetched the enamelled box containing the fake pearls from the safe. Freddy turned on a desk lamp and examined the necklace carefully through the glass. Then he straightened up and handed the pearls to Cedric.

'Have a look at the clasp,' he said. 'Can you see any sign that it's been mended?'

'No,' said Cedric after a minute, and handed them back. 'None at all. But if this is a fake, then there wouldn't be a sign, would there? Because it never was mended—only the real pearls were.'

'Exactly,' said Freddy with satisfaction.

'I don't understand,' said Cedric.

'You will in a minute,' said Freddy. He dropped the pearls and the glass into his pocket, then went out and came back. 'Everyone's still in the salon. Let's go and have a look around upstairs before the police arrive. Be quiet, though. We don't want anyone to see us.'

They went upstairs and into the West Wing, Cedric still mystified. Freddy stopped outside a bedroom door, glanced about, then entered. Inside, a sewing-machine stood on a table, while hanging from the door of the wardrobe was an unfinished toile model of an evening-dress, studded with pins and covered in mysterious chalk markings. Freddy ran his hands over the fabric, as though feeling for something.

'Well, well,' he said. He picked up a pair of scissors from the sewing-table and applied them carefully to the dress, where a wide fabric belt attached the bodice to the skirt.

'Mrs. Dragusha will flay you alive if she sees you doing that,' began Cedric, then his eyes widened as he saw Freddy draw something out from inside the band of toile. 'Good heavens, the pearls!' he exclaimed, as Freddy held up the necklace in triumph.

'We'll compare them to the ones in my pocket in a moment, but I think you'll find these are the real ones,' said Freddy.

'What do you want?' said the Duke suddenly, and Freddy turned to see Valentina Sangiacomo standing in the doorway, staring at the pearls in astonishment.

'You'd better not say a word, Val,' warned Freddy.

She did not reply, but continued to gaze at the pearls as though hypnotized.

'Don't tell me Kitty had anything to do with this,' said Cedric, 'because I won't believe it.'

'No,' said Freddy. 'This frock was merely a convenient place to hide the pearls while they were being smuggled out of the house. Nobody was searching for them, but the police were buzzing around, and if you'd decided to report them missing, then things might have got a bit awkward.'

'So Mrs. Dragusha took them? But how?' said Cedric.

'It was easy,' said Freddy. 'A simple case of misdirection, and very effective with it. She arrived on Thursday and immediately began to lay the ground-work for her plan by hinting to everybody that she believed the pearls were fake, although they weren't at all—not at that point. I expect she was very careful not to go anywhere near them, so that nobody could possibly accuse her of having swapped them before her accomplice arrived. That was Mr. Laurentius, of course. I don't suppose he came down from London at all—in fact, I imagine a little investigation will show that he was staying somewhere in the area, waiting for Mrs. Dragusha to summon him. He came at your request, too—that was another smart move of hers, intended to make you think it was your idea, and that everything was above the board. He arrived, the very picture of a respectable jewel-dealer, announced that the pearls were fake, and was very careful to hand them back. He even insisted you get a second opinion from Keble's, because he knew that by the time you spoke to them the real pearls would be long gone and Keble's would merely confirm his verdict. Once he'd convinced us all that they weren't real, Mrs. Dragusha was free to exchange the real ones for the false ones at her leisure, in the knowledge that Ro was likely to be particularly careless with them if she believed them to be worthless.'

He glanced up. Valentina was still standing in the doorway, listening attentively.

'We ought to have realized at once, because Mr. Laurentius made a mistake by mentioning that the clasp had been mended. But only the real pearls had a mended clasp, while any copy would have been flawless, since whoever made the forgery didn't have the real ones to work from, but presumably only photographs. And then there was Mrs. Dragusha's supposed discretion. If she was so concerned with keeping the thing quiet, then how is it that the whole house knew? Because, of course, the success of her plan depended on everybody's believing that the pearls had been exchanged months ago, so that no suspicion could fall on her. It was very important that people should know of her pretended doubts, and so she took care to tell several people of them.'

'Including Professor Coddington, I dare say,' said Cedric.

'Yes, and that's where I have to admire her audacity. I expect she never imagined for a second that her story would prompt Coddington to go and steal the pearls. She must have been horrified when he got himself killed for them. A lesser woman would have backed out of the plan there and then, but she was brazen enough to carry it through—partly, I think, because she knew the police would probably not be consulted about the pearls, since you'd be unwilling to report the theft if you thought Ro had had something to do with it.'

'But I thought the woman was a respectable dressmaker. What's she doing stealing our jewellery?'

'Oh, it's quite a little side-line of hers, I gather. You might remember that she mentioned similar thefts in other great houses. I remembered it myself this afternoon, and called an old friend of mine, who happens to be the son of the Earl of Ashfield, and whose stepmother is another of Mrs. Dragusha's clients. He told me in confidence that the Countess claimed to have lost some jewellery a while ago. Interestingly, Mrs. Dragusha was staying in the house at the time, and had hinted delicately that she believed the diamond bracelet was a copy. A cousin of hers was called in to confirm it, which he duly did.'

'Good gracious!' exclaimed the Duke.

'At any rate, the family didn't make too much of it publicly as the Countess is known to have something of an addiction to the horses, so they thought it was just the usual trouble—although she denied it absolutely—but doesn't it sound familiar? After that I telephoned Scotland Yard, who, it turns out, have had their eye on Mr. Laurentius for some time now, although they have nothing specific on Mrs. Dragusha. She seems to have developed her reputation as a dressmaker in a very short time, however. Does anybody know where she sprang from?'

Cedric was about to reply, when he was interrupted by a little gasp from Valentina, and they looked up to see Mrs. Dragusha herself standing in the doorway. Centuries of good breeding immediately rose to the fore in the Duke's mind, and he straightened up and reddened with all the embarrassment of a respectable gentleman who has just been caught in the act of entering a lady's bedroom without invitation.

'Ah, Mrs. Dragusha, now, the thing is—' he began.

But Mrs. Dragusha was not interested in his apologies. She pushed Valentina into the room before her, then came in and closed the door, and they now saw that she was holding a little pistol in her hand.

'Ah,' said the Duke again, somewhat inadequately in the circumstances.

'It seems I have been careless,' said Mrs. Dragusha. 'Or rather, Philip has. He told me of the mistake he had made, but he said he believed no-one had noticed it. It appears he was wrong.

Now, let us not waste time in useless conversation. Since I imagine I am no longer a welcome guest in your house, your Grace, you will please to give me the pearls at once, and I will bid you farewell.'

Freddy looked down at the pearls in his hand and hesitated. Mrs. Dragusha's face hardened.

'You will find that I am not to be trifled with,' she said. She took a step forward and raised the pistol. Valentina's eyes widened, and she moved close to Freddy and clutched his arm as though to protect him.

'Don't shoot him!' she said, then turned to him. 'For goodness' sake give her the pearls, you idiot. Don't you know when you've lost the game? Here, give them to me. At least one of us has some sense.'

Before he could object, she grabbed the pearls from his hand and gave them to Mrs. Dragusha, who put them into her pocket with some satisfaction.

'There,' said Valentina. 'Now you'd better run for it.'

'Thank you, your Grace,' said Mrs. Dragusha with mock politeness, then turned and left the room without another word.

'Quick! After her!' said Cedric. 'I'll get my shotgun. We can't let her escape with the pearls! Quick, man, what are you waiting for?' he said, as he saw Freddy make no move.

'I'm not sure she did get the pearls,' said Freddy, glancing at Valentina, who shrugged.

'What?' said Cedric.

Freddy brought the other necklace out of his pocket.

'You did, didn't you?' he said to Valentina.

'You'd better make sure,' she said.

He dug the eye-glass out and examined the clasp of the necklace.

'You must teach me how to do that one day,' he said. 'That was as fast as lightning.'

'What the devil are you talking about?' said Cedric.

'These are the real ones,' said Freddy. 'Val took the fake ones out of my pocket just now and gave them to Mrs. Dragusha.'

'Good Lord! Are you quite certain?' said Cedric with dawning hope. He took the necklace and the eye-glass and examined them himself. 'Well, of all the—I say, well done, young lady! That's very quick thinking on your part. I shall tell Mrs. Fitz-simmons what a good girl you are.'

'Thank you, your Grace,' said Valentina respectfully, although Freddy sensed a slight air of complacency.

'Still, we must catch Mrs. Dragusha at once,' said Cedric. 'She can't have got very far. I'll send the men out with the dogs just as soon as I've put these back in the safe. We don't want anybody else trying to get his hands on them. We'll have Keble's down here and have them pronounce on the matter once and for all, but I should say there's no doubt we've got them back. Excellent, excellent!'

He departed, and Freddy was left alone with Valentina. There was a brief silence.

'Why did you give them back?' he said at last.

'What do you mean?'

'I saw you take them this morning,' he said. 'When Ro dropped them in the waste-paper basket you picked them out and swapped them for the fake ones then, didn't you? That was how Mrs. Dragusha got hold of them to put them in the dress. She was watching out for an opportunity, and created a diversion just at the right moment to allow you to make the exchange. I saw you do it, but didn't realize what I'd seen until later. But why did you decide to swap them back?'

She chewed her lip, as though wondering how much to tell him.

'It's all up with her now,' she said at last. 'The game's over, and if she gets caught then she'll be better off without a crime this big to her name. Silly woman ought to have left these ones alone. I told her to go for something less obvious, but she would have her own way. A diamond bracelet here and there, now—that's one thing. But something like the Belsingham pearls—why, everybody knows about them! Oh, I know his Grace made noises about not telling the police so as to protect his daughter from scandal, but he'd have thought better of it sooner or later, and then the hue and cry would have started, and we'd all have been in danger—including me, now everybody knows what she is.'

'But where do you come in? Why did you help her?'

'Don't you do ever do things for your ma that you'd rather not?'

This was a revelation.

'She's your *mother*?' he said.

'So she says. I've never known any other, at any rate.'

'Good Lord!' he said, eyeing her in astonishment.

'I can't help it any more than you can help yours,' she said with a touch of defiance. 'And if you're wondering whether I do this for her all the time, well I don't. I make my own way, thank you very much, but sometimes if she wants something doing I might step in, that's all.'

'You were worried she might have killed the professor,' he said suddenly, remembering one or two cryptic remarks she had made.

'She's got a bit of a hot temper,' she said, without bothering to deny it. 'I didn't see how she could have done it, but I wanted to be sure. I didn't want to get involved in a murder.'

'But you'll be in trouble now, won't you?'

'With who?' she said coolly. 'The police? Try proving I did anything. On your side all you can say for definite is that you saw me pick the necklace out of the basket to give back to her ladyship. No more than that. But I can prove I risked my own skin to get the real pearls back and give them to the Duke. Why, they ought to give me a medal!'

'I wouldn't quite go that far. But as a matter of fact I was talking about your mother. Won't she be angry when she finds out what you've done?'

'Probably, but I can always talk her round. She's excitable, but she always calms down after a bit.'

'I expect they'll be hunting high and low for her now,' said Freddy.

'Let them try. They'll never find her,' she said. 'She'll be off abroad, most likely.'

'And what shall you do now?'

She glanced at the clock and put a hand to her mouth in dismay.

'Oh, Lord!' she said, and hurried to the door. 'Mrs. Fitz-simmons will be wanting me any minute, and I haven't got anything done!'

'Goodness me, I do believe you've gone native!' he said maliciously.

'Don't be stupid,' she retorted. He had the satisfaction of seeing that she looked slightly disconcerted, but before he could press the point she was gone.

Chapter Twenty-seven

THE POLICE CAME, and were persuaded, with all the force of the Duke's personality and many mentions of the Chief Constable's name, not to arrest Mr. Wray until he had had a good night's sleep. Inspector Trubshaw was reluctant, but eventually agreed on condition that Cedric hand over the key to Mr. Wray's room. Meanwhile, Bea called a doctor to come and examine the old clergyman.

'He can't possibly be right in the head,' she said the next morning to her husband, once the party consisting of the police, Mr. Wray, and Mr. Jephson the solicitor had departed. It was early, and they were the first ones up. 'I'm quite sure they'll end up putting him in a hospital somewhere. Do you know, I've been thinking—I wonder whether it was the lightning bolt to his house that made him ill. They say electricity can do strange things to one. Do you think it might have affected his brain?'

'I've no idea,' said the Duke. 'But I was right when I said it was a hint, wasn't I?'

'Not *exactly*,' said Bea. 'Still, I'm glad we could give the police something to do last night, since we wouldn't let them arrest Mr. Wray. Do you think they'll find Mrs. Dragusha?'

'Freddy seems to think not,' said Cedric. 'I should have said he was talking his usual rot, but he did solve the murder and find the pearls, so perhaps he's not quite the pure idiot we've always supposed.'

'Oh, no, certainly not a *pure* idiot,' said Bea. 'In fact, I should say he had a lot of sense underneath it all, if he were only prepared to use it.'

'Rather an eventful evening, wasn't it? I must say you looked jolly nice in that frock of yours.'

'Thank you. Mrs. Dragusha did a marvellous job. It's only a pity I won't be able to get her to make me anything else now she's run off.'

'Pfft! Plenty of other dressmakers,' said Cedric. 'You've got the raw material, old girl, and you really ought to make more of it.'

Bea, correctly interpreting this as a compliment, flushed slightly. Cedric went on:

'Look here, why don't we go away for a few days? It's been a while since we went abroad, or did any of those fun things we used to do. What do you say to Deauville? Or we could even go to Paris, if you like.'

'Paris!' said the Duchess wistfully. 'It's years since we've been to Paris. Why, I don't think we've been since you inherited Belsingham!'

'Then it's high time we went back,' said Cedric. 'Let's go next week.'

'I should love to,' said Bea in surprise.

'Well, then, that's settled,' said Cedric, and went away before he could talk himself out of it.

It was late morning before Freddy came downstairs, and he found the house in a bustle as everybody prepared to leave a day later than expected.

'There you are,' said Bea, when he rolled into the morning-room, yawning and rubbing his head. 'I thought you'd never get up. Your mother has been looking for you since half past eight.'

'Which is precisely why I didn't get up,' said Freddy. 'I don't suppose they've caught Mrs. Dragusha?'

'No,' said Bea. 'There's been no sighting of her anywhere. They think she must have had a motor-car waiting, in case she had to make a quick escape.'

'Pity,' said Freddy. 'Still, at least she didn't get the pearls.'

'No, but it seems she's got the jewels of half the county women in England. Cynthia's been telephoning everyone she knows, and they all seem to have some story of valuables that were discovered to be fake on Mrs. Dragusha's say-so. They all kept it quiet because they suspected each other and didn't want scandal, but it's quite extraordinary how she managed to trick so many people in such a short time.'

'Well, she was bound to be found out sooner or later,' said Freddy.

'She was certainly very clever. She seems to have chosen people she knew either needed money or had a reputation for having been careless with their things in the past.'

'I expect that's my mother's fault,' said Freddy. 'She puts all this sort of nonsense in her column, so anybody can find out about it.'

'I must read it one day,' said Bea. 'We don't take the lower London papers as a rule.'

'The *Clarion* is a great and venerable organ of righteousness,' he said with dignity.

'Of course it is. And Lavinia is very excited at the prospect of appearing in it this week.'

'In that case, let's hope Mother writes something flattering about her, because it's an even chance that she won't. By the way, that reminds me, I have a question for you: do you like Daphne?'

'Daphne?' she said. 'Yes, I believe I do. She's much nicer than I expected. I should say she had both feet on the ground, which one can't always say about young women—just look at Ro, for example. Why do you ask?'

'Because Goose is in love with her.'

'Is he?' she said, staring.

'Do you disapprove? Her people aren't at all the thing, you know. The Warehams aren't the only family to have one or two scandals in their past, but she's a decent girl and suitably embarrassed by it. And anyway, it happened in India, so it can easily be forgotten.'

'Oh,' she said hesitantly after a moment. 'Why, no, I don't disapprove, exactly. She's behaved perfectly charmingly and properly while she's been here. Mrs. Philpott might leave a little to be desired, but Daphne can't help that. I suppose she's not exactly what we'd hoped for, but I have nothing against her if Goose really likes her.'

'Then go and speak to her. She's feeling awkward and unwelcome, and you might put her at her ease. She's furious with me at the moment because of Iris, and she's taking her anger out on Goose. But she's going today, and you might make all the difference if you take some notice of her. She has no parents and only Lavinia for company most of the time. Go and make her feel welcome, at least for her last few hours here.'

'Oh, the poor thing!' said Bea. 'I had no idea she was feeling so down. You're right, of course. I've rather left everybody to their own devices this weekend, but what with one thing and another it simply couldn't be helped. I shall speak to her as you suggest. I should hate her to go away thinking we were all horrid. Where is she now?'

'In the small salon, talking to Dr. Bachmann—or she was a few minutes ago, at any rate.'

'He'll be telling her all about his telegram, I dare say,' said Bea. 'Apparently his friends at his old university have been trying to put together a case to exonerate him from the charge of plagiarism, and one of them thinks he's found something that will do it, so Dr. Bachmann is feeling rather cheerful this morning. He was always an optimistic soul. I'll go and talk to them both now.'

She went off, and shortly afterwards Kitty Fitzsimmons came in.

'Hallo, Freddy,' she said. 'I'm feeling mournful today, because I won't get my beautiful Dragusha dress after all.' He commiserated with her, and she went on cheerfully, 'How selfish that makes me sound! As though that were the worst of it.'

'Isn't it the worst of it?'

The dimple appeared.

'No!' she said. 'The worst of it is that my maid gave notice quite unexpectedly this morning, and has left the house already without so much as a by-your-leave. It's an urgent case of an aged cousin who needs nursing, apparently, but it's most inconvenient for me.'

'Poor you,' he said. 'I can't do anything about your maid, but perhaps you might take the model Mrs. Dragusha left and have it made up by someone else. Although I shouldn't have thought anybody would want to wear a Dragusha now that they know what she really was.'

'My dear boy, it's clear you know nothing of fashion,' said Kitty loftily. 'Why, a Dragusha dress will carry more cachet than ever now! I shall take the model and see if I can't have something done with it, although I doubt the finished dress will have quite the same shine.'

She spoke lightly, but she was looking out through the French window and seemed to be thinking of something else. Freddy followed her gaze and saw Ralph strolling through the garden with his hands behind his back, looking about him in evident enjoyment of the weather and the surroundings.

'I believe I shall take a walk,' Kitty murmured, not entirely to Freddy's surprise, and went out into the garden, leaving the French window open. A minute or two later Freddy wandered out onto the terrace and surveyed the grounds. The view was all very fine, although he thanked his stars that he was not responsible for maintaining it. A little farther along the terrace, outside the doors to the small salon, he could see Bea, Daphne and Goose. Their voices drifted along to him. They seemed to be talking about horses.

'—had no idea you liked to ride,' Goose was saying. 'Why, if you'd only said so then we might have gone out. I should never be off a horse myself if I had any choice in the matter—'

Freddy smiled to himself and went back into the morning-room, where he found Iris, seemingly looking for someone.

'Have you seen Ralph?' she said. 'He's meant to be taking me back to town, only I can't find him anywhere.'

'He's in the garden,' said Freddy. She went across to the French window and gazed out. By the fountain, Kitty was standing with Ralph, smilingly holding up a flower to her hair, and from the looks of it asking him what he thought. His reply could not be heard, but he was staring fixedly at the dimple in her cheek as though mesmerized.

'Hmph,' said Iris, not in the least discomposed. 'She's dreadfully obvious, isn't she?'

'Don't you mind?' said Freddy.

'Not especially,' she said. 'It's me he likes, not Kitty. She's all take and no give, but he's smart enough to know that I'm the one who'll make something of him.'

'Does he want anything made of him? I rather thought he was doing well enough alone.'

She made an expressive gesture.

'Well *enough*, yes. But men never have direction, do they?'

'Don't they?'

'Do you?'

'Why—er—I've never thought about it.'

'Exactly,' she said, as though he had proved her point. 'I could never have done anything with you.'

'But I don't want anything done with me. I'm happy as I am.'

'I know,' she said sadly. She tore her eyes away from Ralph and Kitty and looked at him, then came closer and put a hand to his cheek. 'I shouldn't have minded it, you know—all the silliness with other girls, I mean. I know it wouldn't have meant anything. But you're far too much your own man. You don't need my help—or me, even, so what would there be for me to do? I need a purpose, and Ralph needs *me*. I'll see to it that he becomes far more successful with me as his wife than he ever could on his own.'

'Do you love him?' said Freddy before he could stop himself.

'Well enough,' she said.

It was an unsatisfactory reply, and Freddy's thoughts turned back to the kiss in the cupboard. He was almost sure it had not been a deliberate or calculated move on her part, but had sprung from pure impulse. Still, she had made her choice, and he could not even say it was the wrong one, for he knew his faults as well as anybody.

'You'll have to behave yourself once you're married, you know,' he said. 'No more running around in secret passages or hiding in linen cupboards.'

'Hardly. Just because I'm getting married doesn't mean I can't have fun,' she said.

'Fun? What kind of fun?'

'Why, the respectable kind, of course. It wouldn't do to be naughty, would it?'

'Oh, no,' he said.

The look she was giving him at that moment was not unlike the one she had directed at him in the chapel the day before, and it would have been so easy to kiss her again that very minute, but, perhaps fortunately, Cedric came in just then, looking for Goose. The two of them moved apart hurriedly, then Iris decided she had better go and rescue Ralph from Kitty and went outside, leaving Freddy to struggle with mixed feelings for a few minutes. True to his nature, however, he brightened up soon enough, and went back upstairs, whistling, to throw his things into his suitcase before his mother found him and started talking at him.

They stayed for lunch, then there was a great commotion as the guests prepared to depart. Freddy paid his respects to the Duke and Duchess, who seemed far less tired of him than they generally were at this stage of his visits, and far less keen to see him off the premises. Ro, too, was in a good mood for once, and thanked him for finding the pearls.

'I should never have dreamed of suspecting Mrs. Dragusha,' she said. 'I only hope they find her soon. I hear she's been stealing from half her clients. It's only a pity she had to ruin everything—her dresses really are gorgeous.'

'Yes, they are,' said Freddy. 'Still, she ought to have contented herself with taking the money for them instead of helping herself to everybody's family heirlooms.'

'I really am awfully pleased she didn't get away with the pearls,' said Ro. 'Although Mother thinks she might have taken some of the silver instead, to make up for it. There are several knives and spoons missing, as well as a milk-jug.'

'Are there?' said Freddy. 'Odd—that doesn't sound like her sort of thing. Perhaps she didn't want her trip to be completely wasted.'

But his mind had jumped involuntarily to Valentina Sangiacomo, who had left in a hurry that morning. She was not the sort to let slip any opportunity that might present itself, and he wondered whether she had taken her pick of the breakfast-things before she left.

'You are going to wear the pearls to this bun-fight of yours next week, aren't you?' he said. 'After my desperate struggle with an armed criminal to wrest them from her grasp I shall be most offended if you don't.'

'Of course I am,' said Ro. 'I shouldn't dream of wearing anything else.'

'I'll take that to mean what you presumably intended it to mean, and not what it sounded like,' he said, and she slapped him on the arm.

'Ass,' she said amiably. 'Go home and reflect on your sins. And make sure you dress up nicely for the ball. I have lots of pretty friends who will want to dance with you, so you'd better be on your best behaviour.'

'I'll see what I can do,' he promised.

'There you are, darling,' said Cynthia, breezing out. 'Now, you have got everything, haven't you? Let's not delay—I have a rather important dinner to attend tonight, and the sooner we set off the better. If we leave it too late your grandfather will fall asleep in the car and you know how his snoring drowns out the conversation. Where is he, anyway?' She looked around.

'Bidding a sentimental farewell to Lavinia Philpott, I imagine,' said Freddy.

Nugs was indeed found exercising all his notions of old-fashioned courtesy towards Mrs. Philpott, who was only too delighted to receive such flattering attentions. Daphne was standing a little way off, and Freddy went to make his own goodbyes to her.

'You don't hate me, do you?' he said.

'I should say the feeling's closer to exasperation,' she said, but there was half a smile on her face and her manner was not wholly unfriendly. Freddy looked across to where Goose was hovering. 'He's taking me to the ball next week,' she said, before he could ask the question. 'I don't suppose it can do any harm.'

'None at all,' he said. 'He's a decent chap, and jolly good company.'

'Yes, he is,' she agreed.

'I won't listen out for wedding-bells just yet, though.'

'Better not,' she said, then sighed. 'I expect Lavinia's going to be unbearable about it.'

'If you think Lavinia's unbearable then you ought to try sitting in a car with my mother for three hours,' said Freddy with feeling.

She laughed, then was serious again.

'You're not going to whisk Iris from under Ralph's nose and marry her, are you? I shouldn't like that.'

'No,' he said. 'You needn't worry—I'm not exactly the marrying sort.'

'Not now, but you will be one day,' she said. 'Just you watch. It'll creep up on you when you least expect it, and before you know it you'll be spending your evenings in an armchair with your pipe and slippers, with children running round you and a pretty wife sitting in the other armchair, darning your socks.'

'Good Lord, I hope not,' said Freddy, horrified, and she laughed at his face.

'You'd better go,' she said. 'I think your mother's getting impatient.'

'Goodness me, is that the time?' said Lavinia. 'We must go, Daphne. Goodbye, Lord Lucian, it's been a pleasure.'

'The pleasure is all mine,' said Nugs, gallantly. He attempted a flowery bow and had to be assisted back into an upright position, then he and Freddy went to where the Wolseley and Cynthia were waiting. Freddy handed his mother into the car.

'You took long enough to say goodbye,' said Cynthia to Nugs. 'Goodness knows what you found to say to the silly woman.'

'Silly, do you call her?' said Nugs, as he was established in possession of the back seat and the car drew away. 'I rather like her. She's very kind, and patient with it. Just the sort of woman to appeal to a man of my age, and with a nice, piercing voice, too, so one doesn't have to keep asking her to repeat herself. I believe I shall invite her out to dinner when we get back to London. It's about time I married again, don't you think?'

'*What?*' said Cynthia, horrified. She turned around to see Nugs leering at her wickedly.

'Caught you,' he said with great satisfaction.

She glared at him, then turned back to face the front, her lips pursed in disapproval.

Freddy glanced round at his grandfather, who gave him a wink.

NEW RELEASES

If you'd like to receive news of further releases by Clara Benson, you can sign up to my mailing list here.

CLARABENSON.COM/NEWSLETTER

Or follow me on Facebook.

FACEBOOK.COM/CLARABENSONBOOKS

New to Freddy? Read more about him in the Angela Marchmont mysteries.

CLARABENSON.COM/BOOKS

BOOKS IN THIS SERIES

- A Case of Blackmail in Belgravia
- A Case of Murder in Mayfair
- A Case of Conspiracy in Clerkenwell
- A Case of Duplicity in Dorset
- A Case of Suicide in St. James's

ALSO BY CLARA BENSON:
The Angela Marchmont Mysteries

Made in the USA
Columbia, SC
31 March 2021